Cherokee Warriors

The Lover

GENELL DELLIN

Cherokee Warriors

The Lover

AVON BOOKS
An Imprint of HarperCollins*Publishers*

AVON BOOKS
An Imprint of HarperCollins*Publishers*
10 East 53rd Street
New York, New York 10022-5299

ISBN: 0-7394-2876-4

Printed in the U.S.A.

Chapter 1

Salado, Texas
Spring, 1870

Eagle Jack Sixkiller woke up in jail.

There was no getting around that fact. Although his eyes wouldn't open more than a slit and he could barely lift his head beneath the weight of the pain, he glimpsed iron bars on the door—and a sign, too, in case he had any lingering doubts as to his location. SALADO JAIL was written across the front window of the sheriff's office in big letters (backwards of course, from this direction).

The war drum pounding in his head felled him flat onto the bunk again.

Never, ever, had he had such a hangover. He must've really heard the owl hoot last night.

Scraps of memories flashed across his pain-wrenched eyelids. No. It wasn't liquor that'd left him in this shape.

The fight. He hadn't been drinking; he'd been in a fight.

Yes. And he'd just been getting into the spirit of the fray when he'd glanced around to see a two-by-four hovering over him, already on its way to come crashing down on his head, wielded by one of the owners of the sleek gray Thoroughbred stallion that Eagle Jack's spunky, scruffy mare, Molly, had left in the dust.

He grinned.

That made his head hurt even more and roused a raw pain on the skin of his cheek, but he grinned even more widely.

Sweet victory. Those shysters learned a thing or two about running their pretty gray Thoroughbred against an ugly little Indian pony.

Maybe they wouldn't be so quick to judge a horse by its looks next time.

Carefully, disturbing no more muscles than he had to move to lift his hands, Eagle Jack forced his eyes open enough to see them. His knuckles looked as raw as a fresh hide. At least he'd gotten a few good licks in.

Matter of fact, it would've been a downright enjoyable fight with its challenge of two against one, and he would've found his rhythm and come out on top if they had played fair. Crooked bastards.

The truth hit him then: those sons of bitches stole his racehorse!

Damn! And just before he started up the trail.

He sat straight up, his head screaming with new pain. Grabbing it with both hands to try to steady himself, he swung his feet to the floor, scrambling to get out of there.

Of course. That's why they'd laid him out cold with a board—they wanted Molly, the fastest pony on the Brazos. Maybe the fastest pony alive.

He managed to get his bootheels planted on solid wood and his legs propped against the edge of the bunk so he could thrust his battered hands into the front pockets of his jeans. They came up empty. The lowlifes got his money, too.

Well, money was only money, but Molly was a whole different deal. There'd never been another mare like Molly, and it wasn't just her speed and her deceptive looks he loved. It was her personality. What a girl!

He'd trail those horse thieves to the end of the world. He'd get that mare back in his possession if he singlehandedly had to hang both of that fast-talking pair of Kentucky gentlemen (to hear them tell it) who were traveling through Texas and the South campaigning the greatest running Thoroughbred of all time.

He'd make them rue the day they ever crossed the Texas line. He'd scalp them before he hanged them.

"Hey!" he yelled. "Sheriff! Let me outta here."

Nausea surged in his stomach. He clamped his

lips tight and waited, reaching for the bars with one hand so he could stay upright.

Nobody answered him, but he could hear voices out there in the sheriff's office somewhere. Eagle Jack gathered his forces and hollered again.

"I can make bail," he said. "All I have to do is go to the bank."

The sheriff or somebody with a deep voice let out a guffaw and yelled back at him, "Sure, and I own the King Ranch. Sleep it off back there, and shut up."

Somebody laughed from inside the cell, and Eagle Jack looked behind him. The gesture made his head swim and his vision blur, but he could see three other inmates, one grinning, two solemn, looking at him from bleary eyes and another sleeping fast on a bunk in the back. He'd been hurting so bad he hadn't even noticed he had company.

"Set back down there, Injun," said the grinning one, "or they's liable to cut yer hair off."

Eagle Jack ignored him and concentrated on turning his head very, very carefully, to look through the bars again.

The voices out front were still talking. A heartbeat later, though, while he was trying to think what to say that would get the sheriff to come open the cell, they stopped. The bell sounded and the front door swung open, then slammed closed again. Eagle Jack moved nearer to the bars to try to get a better view.

"Ma'am?" the deep voice said. "Can we help you?"

"Yes," a woman's angry—hot and righteous—voice said. "I need to bail a man out."

In spite of his hurts and his worries, Eagle Jack grinned again. Now *there* was something to be thankful for on this pain-filled morning—another little example of why he was glad he'd never stuck his head in the marriage noose. Somebody's wife was mad as an old wet hen. She'd clean that old boy's clock for sure and probably make him sleep on the floor for a month.

A chair scraped back and feet hit the floor.

"Who might that man be, Mrs. . . . ?"

"Copeland."

"Mrs. Copeland." The sheriff repeated her name respectfully, but she was already sweeping around the corner into the hallway like a high wind.

Eagle Jack's pain lessened at the sight of her.

Now here was nothing short of a passionate woman. She had pretty cheeks burning pink with anger and sparks of purpose flying from her blue eyes. Her dress was a well-worn divided skirt with a man's blue shirt tucked in and a leather, flat-brimmed hat that was also made for a man. She wasn't stylish and she wasn't well-off, but here was a woman to be reckoned with.

Just the kind he liked. Too bad she was a Mrs.

The sheriff trotted right behind her, his voice

deferential as he repeated his question. Clearly, despite her eccentric clothes, she was the kind of woman a man deferred to at any time, but especially when, as now, she was in high dudgeon.

"Who is it that you're bailing out, Mrs. Copeland?" he said.

"I don't know yet," she said, and came to a stop on the other side of the bars from Eagle Jack.

Total silence fell, both in the cell and out.

Her scent drifted to him, all fresh and faintly like sunshine—a great contrast to the stale sweat and sour whiskey odors in the air, which he hadn't noticed until that moment. She glanced at Eagle Jack, lingered only an instant, then swept the whole cell with her gaze. Her eyebrows lifted, her jaw tightened, and her lips set into a straight line.

Which was a crying shame. Left to their own devices, her lips were as lush and full as he'd ever seen, bar none. Buxom, yet long-legged, she was. One of his favorite shapes of woman.

The sheriff moved around to her side and cleared his throat.

"I thought perhaps your husband . . ." he said.

"A stranger will do," she said.

"Why would you pay bail for a stranger?"

But Mrs. Copeland had had enough of the sheriff. She spoke to the men in the cell instead, with another glance spared for Eagle Jack.

"My name is Susanna Copeland and I need a

man to pretend to be my husband," she said. "That man will hire me a crew and help me take nine hundred head of longhorns up the trail."

So. She was a freethinking woman, too.

The stunned silence broke into a chorus of guffaws and catcalls.

"Here I am, honey."

"Whereabouts you goin'?"

"Pick me, sweetheart, I've been up the trail a time or two."

More laughter.

It didn't faze her in the least. She waited for it to die down, her blue eyes snapping all the while.

"Which one I choose will depend on what y'all say now," she said. "Answer me some questions."

"What's the pay?" asked the grinning nosy Nellie who'd called Eagle Jack Injun.

"Of course. The pay," Susanna Copeland said. "At the end of the trail, I'll pay you the going wage for a trail boss—forty-five dollars a month. Also, I will bail you out of this jail right now, with money that you need not pay back."

A murmur ran through the cell. A couple of the men exchanged thoughtful looks, as if they were beginning to consider the offer.

"But first let me say that there'll be no liquor in my outfit," she said. "It appears that every man of you is one who likes his whiskey. If you can't live without indulging in strong drink, say so right away and save us all some time."

The inmate who'd appeared to be asleep, his eyes still closed, raised his hand.

"Very well," she said. "I won't bother you."

The hand fell back down onto the bunk.

Then she fixed on the bleary-eyed man who'd asked about the pay and started firing questions at him. Had he ever been in jail before and for what? Had he ever been a boss of other men and how many? How well could he ride and rope? Did he know cattle?

She listened to the answers, then moved on to another man who answered those same questions. Both of them clearly had brains still addled by drink. Eagle Jack watched Mrs. Copeland—Susanna—with growing amusement. She was serious about this wild plan of hers. Plenty serious.

The next man shook his head to stop her when she came to him.

"I reckon there's no way I could work for a wo—a lady," he said. "I ain't never done it and I don't never aim to."

That brought all the snap back into Mrs. Copeland's big blue eyes and deepened the color in her cheeks. Well, hey. This must be the bee that had been in her bonnet when she came in the door.

She stiffened her spine and glared at every one of them in turn.

"Why, in the name of everything sane, are men so set on not working for a woman?" she asked.

Even the man who'd made that remark didn't answer. The sheriff started to speak, but then he bit the words back.

Susanna turned to Eagle Jack.

Here was his chance to get out of this jail right now. Not to mention a chance to have some fun while getting out of this town.

"I'm sure I can't help you with that question, ma'am," he said, using his most charming smile, although it nearly ripped the rest of the skin off his face. "I myself have no such misgivings."

That surprised her. "You don't?"

He reached to touch the brim of his hat before he realized he wasn't wearing it.

"Eagle Jack Sixkiller at your service, ma'am. I'm always happy to be in the company of a lady."

Even if it hadn't been true—which it was—he would've said it. He would say anything to get out of here this minute and start tracking Molly. The thieves might still be in Salado.

"I'm talking about a woman *hiring* you," she said.

That was twice now that she'd called herself a woman instead of a lady. Fine by him. Maybe she wasn't a lady.

He stood very straight and tried to ignore the pounding in his head.

"I have no quarrel with working for a woman if she knows her business," he said.

"No need for that," she said. "The man I hire

will be the trail boss. He'll be free to use his own judgment."

Of course. Naturally, she didn't know the trail driving business. How could she? Women never, ever, went up the trail.

"I've been up the Chisholm Trail to Abilene," he said, "and the Shawnee Trail to Kansas City."

"Abilene is my destination," she said. "I've decided the Chisholm is the easier route."

He nodded agreement, although the brief movement nearly tore off his head. Let her think he'd take her to Kansas, let her think he'd hire her a crew. If push came to shove, he'd take her cattle north and *that* was what she was after.

What *he* was after was release from the Salado Jail.

"I'm a riding, roping fool," he said, with a grin. "And a peerless leader of men."

He held her attention for a long heartbeat. Those blue eyes of hers were so deep a man could fall right into them and drown. He thought he saw a flash of amusement in them in response to his sally, but he couldn't be sure.

She'd be a challenge and a half, would Susanna Copeland—enough to entertain a man on the trail, all right.

No way, though, would he take a woman into such danger or deal with the burden of responsibility that she would be on a thousand miles of trail with a dozen other men in the outfit.

What was he thinking? His goal was to get out of jail.

He kept the grin and used his most persuasive tone of voice. "You won't go wrong with me, ma'am."

"I certainly won't," she said, prim as a schoolmarm. "Or with any other man."

So. She had caught the double meaning in his words. She, too, had felt the pulse of attraction between them.

But then she only looked at him, biting her luscious lower lip thoughtfully.

What if she'd decided he would try to take advantage of her? Maybe she was thinking that would be too much trouble to deal with if she hired him as her foreman.

Yet the main thing he saw in her was not caution but determination.

"If you intend to do what you came in here for, Mrs. Copeland," he said, "you'll have to take me. My cellmates can't walk out of here under their own steam, much less drive a herd to Kansas."

The dizziness hit him again and he swayed just a little, back onto his heels. He took a tighter grip on the bar he was holding, and that steadied him.

She tilted her head and looked him over some more.

"Looks to me like the pot calling the kettle black," she said.

Eagle Jack used his best smile one more time.

"You'll need men and horses," he said. "I can judge both at a glance."

"You wouldn't be just a little bit stuck on yourself, would you, Mr. Sixkiller?"

"No, Mrs. Copeland, I would not. That's a fault."

She tried to keep her stern expression—he knew because he watched her beautiful lips—but try as she would not to, she smiled back at him. Susanna Copeland was beyond beautiful when she smiled.

And it didn't take her all day to make up her mind. That was another trait he liked in a woman.

"You're hired," she said, and reached in through the bars to shake on it.

Her grip was strong for a hand so small that it fit in the palm of his. Her soft glove was made of good quality leather but it had holes in two places.

He would pay her right back for the bail.

Susanna had to slow her pace for a second time before they even made it past the broad window that said SALADO JAIL. Eagle Jack Sixkiller was barely steady enough to keep his feet under him and now he'd come to a complete stop at the edge of the sidewalk—standing there looking up and down the street at the vehicles going past as if he intended to flag down a ride.

She set her jaw. He could forget that. Drunk or

not, he was all the man she had and he wasn't going to quit her, no matter what.

Absolutely, she was not going to lose the only home she'd ever owned because some footloose, liquor-loving joker couldn't settle down to work instead of play. Selling those cattle at a profit was the only way for her to keep her beloved Brushy Creek Ranch, and if she had to make a trail boss out of a worthless drunk to take them north, then she would do that very thing.

She went to him and nudged his elbow.

"You agreed to hire me an outfit," she said, "and you can't do it lollygagging around out here. Come on. Drink some coffee and sober up."

"Go on," he said. "I'll meet you at the café."

A chill hand of fear touched her spine.

"I'm not letting you out of my sight," she said. "I didn't pay the last hard money I had in this world to get you out of jail for nothing."

His dark brown eyes flicked to her and she glimpsed a trace of his quick grin.

"Don't you trust me?"

She should've thought about that grin before she laid down her money. He'd taken her lightly from the very first, right there in the jail.

"About as much as I trust a rattlesnake."

That only made his grin widen.

"Always like to know where I stand," he said.

He turned and started down the street, walking much faster than he had before.

Susanna stayed right beside him. They passed the barbershop and came to the saloon, where he stopped.

"Wait here," he said. "I'll only be a minute."

She stepped between him and the half doors, her heart beating like a hammer in her chest.

"You heard me back there in the jail," she said. "You have to learn to do without liquor and you have to start now."

"I don't intend to drink a drop."

There was that little twitch of his lips again.

Her anger bubbled over. She set her fists on her hips.

"Why in the *world* do men have to be such dense creatures?" she cried. "Look at you. Anyone can see you have a problem with drink. You're a fine figure of a man, Mr. Sixkiller. Don't let your natural bent for whiskey ruin you."

His grin vanished.

"In other words, you're calling me a drunken Indian. Isn't that right, Mrs. Copeland?"

Colder fear grabbed her by the heart. Would he take so much offense that he'd quit her for sure?

She gathered all her strength.

"Some of your people—"

"I was the only sober man in that jail cell," he interrupted. "And obviously the only Indian. Yes, ma'am. I'm Cherokee and proud of it."

He took off his hat and bent his head, turning so that she could see the spot where he held back his long hair, which was tied with a leather thong. A huge pump knot swelled behind his ear.

Susanna gasped before she got hold of herself. Showing him sympathy wouldn't help either of them. It would defeat her purpose.

"That should've taught you a lesson, right there," she said. "When liquor's in control of you, you can't control anything around you."

He straightened up and replaced his hat, all the while giving her a hurt look.

"They hit me with a two-by-four," he said. "There were two of them. They could've killed me."

"That's exactly what I'm telling you. Drunks get into lots of fights and bad situations. You'd better stay sober."

"I'm not so sure about that," he said, the corners of his mouth twitching as if he wanted to grin. "I was stone-cold sober when I got into *this* bad situation."

A cold hand clutched her stomach. He wasn't going to back out now. She would *not* let him.

"At the end of the trail you'll thank me," she said. "You'll be amazed how much better you'll feel after weeks of good, hard work in the open air and a true victory over demon rum."

He looked at her for a long minute with that piercing gleam of humor coming back into his dark brown eyes.

"It'll be very good for you to go up the trail at

the head of my outfit," she said. "The responsibility will be good for you, too."

Of course, she'd have to be the *real* head of the outfit. There was no telling when he'd try to find a saloon again. Or when he'd take some happening lightly and laugh about it when it should be taken seriously, instead.

"You're a hard girl, Susanna," he said. "Any other woman would have sympathy and a natural urge to take care of a hurt man."

She was not going to give in to him. If she were not so perfectly desperate to get her hands on any man, she'd tell him to forget it this very minute. She should've known better than to get a man out of a *jail*!

"So would I," she said, "if that man hadn't helped himself get hurt."

He reached for her arm, turned her around, and marched her right through the swinging doors of the saloon. He walked her toward the bar, which was sparsely populated in the middle of the afternoon.

The bartender stopped what he was doing to come to meet them.

"Jonas," Eagle Jack said, "have you seen those Kentucky fakers since yesterday?"

"Not a glimpse," the man replied. "Heard they left town after they won your mare."

"They stole her," Eagle Jack said. "Any word which way they went?"

"Nope."

"Much obliged."

He dragged Susanna back out to the street as unceremoniously as he'd taken her in there. Back on the sidewalk, she pulled loose from his grip.

"Don't touch me again," she told him.

He was walking much faster than she'd thought possible.

"Don't stand in my way again," he said.

"Look," she said, "you're my trail boss, not *my* boss. Nobody drags me anywhere, much less into a saloon."

"What difference does it make? You've already been in the jail today. That's no place for a lady, either."

"Social dictates don't tell me where to go. Neither does any one person. Especially not a man."

He threw her the briefest glance.

"*Never,*" she said.

"Hey," he said, with a trace of that irritating grin of his, "get the burr out from under your saddle. *You're* the one who said you aren't leaving my side."

"What I said was that I'm not letting you out of my sight."

He shrugged.

"Same thing."

"I could've kept my eye on you over the barroom door."

"Aw, come on," he drawled. "You'd argue with a fence post, Susanna."

"Mrs. Copeland to you."

"I thought we were friends," he said, with a teasing, sideways glance. "You can call me Eagle Jack."

He absolutely did have the most aggravating way about him.

Then she remembered.

"As a matter of fact," she said. "You do need to call me either Susanna or Mrs. Sixkiller."

"*What?*"

He stared at her as he stepped down off the sidewalk and held out his hand to steady her as she did the same. His brown eyes showed such surprise that she wanted to laugh.

"On the trail we'll have to pretend to be married," she said. "It's the only way the men will respect my presence. I said that at the jail before you took the job."

He shrugged. "No problem. I'll get your cattle to Kansas."

He looked down the side street they'd just turned into. "If by some miracle I have reason to reach for my gun," he said, "get away from me."

"Look," she said, "you're working for me now. You can't be going off somewhere tracking horse thieves . . ."

His hard glance stopped her tongue.

"I'm not leaving Salado until I know for sure they've hightailed it."

"Ever since we turned into this street, I've known you were coming to get your horse and start out on their trail," she said. "I cannot allow it. My business is urgent and now, as my foreman, it's your business, too."

That made him get serious at last.

"Don't *worry* about it," he said.

Now he, too, was irritated.

"I told you I'd get your cattle to Kansas, and I will."

This time she heard him.

"Our agreement is less than an hour old and already you're going back on it," she said, in her most formidable manner. "Don't even try that with me, Eagle Jack."

"I'm not. I just *said* I'd do it."

"And I will help you do it. I'm not letting my *cattle* out of my sight, either."

He gave her a frustrated look.

"Take a deep breath, Mrs. Copeland. I'll trail your cattle to Kansas. You have my word."

The way he spoke and the way he set his jaw then made her know that it would do no good and quite a bit of harm if she said another word about it. He could be quite formidable himself, could Eagle Jack Sixkiller.

Walking steadily, he strode up to the wide

opening of the livery stable where a boy was sweeping the hard dirt of the entrance.

"Howdy, Mr. Sixkiller," he said.

"Nathan. You seen those Kentuckians with the gray running horse today?"

Nathan seized that excuse to lean on his broom.

"They lit out," he said.

"They say where they're headed?"

"All I heard was that short one—you know that short, fat one?"

He wouldn't go on until Eagle Jack had nodded.

"Well," Nathan said, basking in such close attention from not one, but two adults, "that 'un was sayin' that lots of outfits goin' up the trail are braggin' they got a whole remuda full o' fast horses."

Eagle Jack thought about that.

"Any mention of one trail in particular?"

"No sir. Not that I know of."

Eagle Jack nodded.

"Let me see your horses for sale," he said. "I need to get on the road."

Susanna walked around to the pen in the back with them and watched Eagle Jack Sixkiller pick a horse from the dozen or so that Nathan drove into a trot and then a lope along the fence. Her trail boss was as good as his word in that respect, at least.

He didn't give them more than a glance apiece at each gait until he made his choice.

"Get that tall bright sorrel ready," he said, to the boy, "I'll be right back."

Then he looked at Susanna.

"You have thirty minutes to take care of any unfinished business, get your horse, and be ready to leave town," he said. "I'm going to the bank, the saddle shop, and back to the livery here. In that order."

"Then so am I," she said.

His jaw hardened and the skin tightened across his high cheekbones.

His brown eyes looked almost black as they bored into hers.

He wanted to tell her to get lost. She knew that as certainly as if he'd blurted it out.

She waited. This was where she'd find out if he really was a man of his word.

"At the bank I'll get money to pay you back for the bail," he said.

"I won't take it," she said. "You can't buy your way out of our deal."

For some reason that brought the glint of humor back into his eyes, even if he did shake his head in despair.

"I wouldn't even think of trying," he said.

Chapter 2

Eagle Jack cudgeled his brain as they walked the two blocks to the bank. He had to think of something. He had to *think.*

By damn, it was going to be harder to escape from Susanna Copeland than from the Salado Jail. He would have to take her cattle north, yes, because he had said he would and never would he let it be said that Eagle Jack Sixkiller went back on his word.

But that didn't mean he had to have this bossy woman as his constant shadow.

He decided to try his famous charm again. After all, he had never met a woman he couldn't melt right down into her shoes if he put his mind to it. He was known as a ladies' man all over Texas, wasn't he?

"Sorry if I'm walking too fast for you, Susanna," he said, slowing his pace and flashing his smile at her. "If you want to go and get your horse, you can meet me—"

She interrupted.

"I'm not falling behind, am I?"

It was true. Her long legs had kept up with his every step since they'd left the livery.

"And my horse is tied near the saddle shop. I'll get him when we're done there."

Her blue eyes met Eagle Jack's with an annoyed glance.

Unfortunately, his charm might not work *every* time. At least, not on her.

Which made her a very unusual woman, indeed.

And it made her a challenge. He was not going to let her ruin his perfect record, especially not when she was one of the most beautiful women he'd come across in all his adventures.

"You needn't be in such a hurry," she said. "I bailed you out of that stinking jail to hire me a crew and I intend to see that you do it before we leave Salado."

Quick anger seared his nerves. She was a challenge, all right. His headache flared, its pounding worst right between his eyes.

"I'll *get* you a crew," he said, through clenched teeth, "in my own good time."

"We'll need them tonight," she said. "My cattle should be at Brushy Creek when we get there."

He stopped in front of the saddle shop and stared at her.

"How many cattle?"

"I'm guessing close to nine hundred, but it'll depend on how many more the brushpoppers can catch. My guess was around seven hundred head already gathered when I left home this morning."

More than he'd imagined, from the looks of her clothes. Way more. Throwing them in with his would make one of the biggest herds on the trail. He would need four more men, at least.

But it did explain one thing.

"Is that why your husband sent you to hire the crew?"

"My husband has long since gone on to his great reward," she said, with a bitter irony in her tone, "whatever that might be."

Well. A widow. So she wasn't married, after all.

But why did he care? She'd be just as much trouble romantically as she was in every other way.

And just as surprising, probably. He'd like that.

"Did you kill him?" he said.

She gave a little burst of laughter.

"No. But I'm glad to see I've got my bluff in on you."

He grinned.

"I didn't really take you for a killer," he said, "but you don't sound too sad about him being six feet under."

"I'm not. He was a bully and a brutal man in many ways. I wish I'd thought twice before I married him."

Eagle Jack's headache couldn't keep his curiosity down. He always wanted to know why a woman did what she did. Women were fascinating creatures because all of them were different from one another—except for the fact that they didn't think one bit like men.

"Why did you?"

For the first time, she hesitated.

"I was a foolish young girl," she said. "Too young to know better."

"Did he beat you?"

It was a personal question that would have offended many women but she seemed to recognize the spirit in which he'd asked it.

"At the very first, he would have," she said, seeming to think it through as she spoke, "but even though I was very young, I wouldn't stand for it."

"What did you do?"

"When he raised his hand to me, I told him if he hit me he'd better never go to sleep drunk again."

"Why?"

"Because I would sew him up in the bedsheet and beat him senseless with the broom."

Eagle Jack threw back his head and laughed, in spite of his pain.

"I'm surprised he'd put up with that."

"We were on the move by then," she said. "It was too much trouble for him to stop and find somebody else to be his servant."

She glanced up at him sideways. A matter-of-fact glance.

"Everett was a lazy cuss," she said. "He liked his food and drink and he liked his sleep."

He shook his head, grinning in spite of his pain. She was spunky, he had to hand her that.

But he had to stop this line of thinking. He'd fallen into a whole more with her than a dalliance—he'd fallen into a whole lot of work in a short amount of time. He'd better get his mind on the task ahead.

"We've got a lot to get done today," he said. "What kind of help do you have?"

"An older couple, May and Jimbo—they live in my cabin."

"They can't—," he said.

"—hold a herd," she interrupted. "I know. I asked the men who gathered the cattle not to leave them until we get there."

"Are you telling me that you've been running around all over town trying to hire men that you have to have *tonight?*"

"Pretty much. Tucker, the brushpopper who's running my roundup, promised to stay there with his men until I get home with some help."

The look in her eyes was earnest.

"I'm paying them by the head and I know there's a couple of dozen more cow and calf pairs in the mesquite out there."

Eagle Jack felt trapped and weary already.

"So we also have to *count* cattle tonight."

Susanna looked exasperated.

"Or *today*, if we get there before dark," she said, "which might happen if we don't stand around here jawing all afternoon."

Three young men came out of the saddle shop, pushing both doors open, talking quietly among themselves about the saddle one of them carried.

"Excuse me," Susanna said, as they started past. "Do any of you happen to need a job? Would you like to go up the trail?"

Shocked that a strange lady had spoken to them on the street, they stopped and turned. Too shy to meet Susanna's gaze, they looked at Eagle Jack.

"I—" he began. He didn't quite know what he was going to say and Susanna didn't let him find out.

"This is my husband," she said, "Mr. Sixkiller. We're looking for drovers to go up the Chisholm Trail."

It was all he could do not to grab her and shake some sense into her. It was all he could do not to turn on his heel and walk away. She had no business butting into the job she'd hired him to do.

But these did look like fairly steady men. And he did have to have some help. No way did he intend to ride around a herd all night long by himself. Not to mention who would hold the cattle while he rode all over the countryside tomorrow trying to hire the oldest son of every war widow hanging on by the skin of her teeth or some hired hand who didn't know he was too old and broken-down to stand up to life on the trail. He couldn't wait for his own men to come with his herd from home because he had to get after Molly as soon as he could.

So he did what he'd done a thousand times in his adventurous life and grabbed the situation to make the best of it. If these men turned out to be lazy or trouble, he could replace them when he got to Waco.

My husband, she'd said, so fast he couldn't even form a sentence on his tongue. It made him grit his teeth.

It made his headache blossom into its original glory.

But, knowing what he knew of her from this short acquaintance, if he wanted to accomplish anything here, he'd better go along with the charade. But only for the moment. Later, when he could get her alone, he'd tell her in no uncertain terms that it wouldn't be necessary to pretend that they were married because she wouldn't be going up the trail at all.

"Right," he said, "we're putting together an outfit. Are you men available?"

It took a couple of minutes for one of them to get his tongue working. It was the taller one with the saddle. None of them looked to be more than twenty years old, if that much.

"To tell you the truth," the boy finally said. "We're on our way right now to see a man about a drive."

Eagle Jack opened his mouth but he never had a chance to get a word out. She was way too quick for him.

"We'll pay more than that man will," Susanna said. "Is he offering you the going rate?"

Eagle Jack wanted to slap his hand across her mouth and hold it there. He set his jaw. They had an understanding to reach and they were going to reach it very, very soon or he would be gone.

With this kind of aggravation, it didn't seem so important that no one could ever say that he broke his word. His reputation be damned if he had to put up with this for another minute, much less a thousand miles.

"How much more?" the young cowboy said.

Eagle Jack gave Susanna a look that, to his surprise, actually stilled her tongue. He spoke before she could recover.

"Two dollars a month more," he said.

The cowboy looked at his companions.

Without a word passed among them, he turned back to Eagle Jack.

"Done," he said. "Marvin Dwyer's my name."

He held out his hand to shake. Eagle Jack shook with all of them and introduced himself as they spoke their names.

Shyly, they tipped their hats in Susanna's direction, but Eagle Jack couldn't bring himself to introduce her as his wife. They had that impression already. And it wouldn't be necessary, anyhow. By this time tomorrow she'd be settled on her own ranch again, and he and these boys would be pushing her cattle north.

"Where should we meet you at, Mr. Sixkiller? And when?" Marvin asked.

He shifted his saddle to his other hand and waited.

"At Brushy Creek Ranch," Eagle Jack said, "as soon as you can."

He smiled. He had actually beat Susanna to the punch for once.

Then his triumph vanished. He didn't know how to direct them to get there, not even whether the ranch was east or north or south or west of town.

Great. There was nothing like a trail boss who didn't know where he was going.

"I'll let Miss Susanna tell y'all what road to take," he said. "I have some business to see to and we all need to get out there right away."

He turned on his heel and left her standing there with the crew she'd hired. Great jumping Jehoshaphat, he'd never known a woman to talk so much—or interrupt so much—and he'd known a lot of women. He couldn't wait to get her back to her ranch and get away from her for a while.

He couldn't wait to be alone. Some peace and quiet might do wonders for his head.

Yet he hadn't been in the shop long enough for anything but to greet the proprietor, scan the used saddles, and decide that his stolen one wasn't there when Susanna followed him in.

"Mr. Sixkiller," she said, "the new hands asked me to tell you that they'll start for the ranch in an hour. Maybe less. I asked them to go ahead and take delivery of the herd if we aren't there yet."

He froze.

Then he crossed the shop to her with a whole new fire in his belly. She was the most aggravating woman on God's green earth but that didn't mean she had to be the dumbest. If he was going to put up with this nonsense, he was going to accomplish something. Left alone, she didn't even have a pair of decent gloves and pretty soon she wouldn't have anything at all.

"When the *hell* will you ever learn to let me do what you hired me to do?" he said. He kept his voice low so the saddlemaker wouldn't hear and that took all the strength he had. He wanted to yell at her at the top of his lungs. "How'll you like it if they drive that herd off onto somebody else's place and sell them? Or just start up the trail with your cattle all by themselves? Are they trail branded?"

She looked up at him, her eyes wide and full of startlement.

He was standing closer to her than he'd realized. Her scent was fresher and crisper than he'd realized. And her eyes were bluer.

But he couldn't think about that.

"Your busy little tongue is going to create a disaster if you don't learn to control it," he said. "*Damn* it, Susanna. I can't do the job you hired me to do. I can't even get a word in edgewise."

"You walked off and left us," she said. "You weren't trying to talk right then."

But he couldn't pursue the subject for listening to the echo of the last question he'd asked her. He had to know.

"Are your cattle trail branded, Susanna?"

"No," she said, "they're not trail branded, but it's all right. Those boys didn't look—"

His headache and his weariness grew heavier. Great. He also had to brand the herd, besides holding and counting it.

"They may be rustlers by profession for all you know," he said. "Have you ever seen a rustler?"

"We-ell, no, but . . ."

"Then you don't know what one looks like," he said. "Now—right now—we have an agreement to make, and if you can't live up to it, I'm gone."

Her eyes narrowed dangerously.

"If you're gone, I'm on your trail," she said. "I invested my last money in you, Eagle Jack Sixkiller, and you gave me your word."

"And you gave me yours," he said. "You promised me and all those other poor old down-and-out boys in the jail that whoever you hired as trail boss would be free to use his own judgment."

"So?"

"So you stay out of my business, Mrs. Copeland, or bust somebody else out of some other jail to take your cattle up the trail. Understand me?"

That was a yes or no question, as far as he could see, but Susanna, naturally, had to argue with it.

"When I said that, what I meant was that you're to use your own judgment in decisions having to do with the *trail.* Where to cross rivers, where to camp, when to stop for the night, what tolls to pay and about outlaws and wolves and cattle rustlers and—"

"You'd be telling me what to do about every one of those things, Susanna."

She whirled on her heel and marched away with her spine straight as a board.

Now he had really made her mad. Maybe she'd fire him.

He sincerely hoped that she would.

He caught up with her. "And I would not be hearing you," he said, close into her ear. "I have free rein or I'm gone."

She didn't answer.

"Thank God, I'm not going to take you up the trail," he said. "I first thought your company would be amusing but I was wrong. I swear a thousand miles of this and I'd either gag and tie you and throw you in the back of the wagon or I'd shoot myself."

The stricken look on her face when she whirled around made him wish he could take back the words.

But not for long. The shock that paled her skin turned to flaming fury.

"Don't even think it," she said. "I'm going."

"Women don't go up the trail," he said.

"This woman does."

She set her jaw and looked at him with even more hot determination in her eyes. It was a pure, unwavering force.

So. Laying down the law to her—which she constantly inspired him to do—was not the way to get her cooperation.

He would have to think of another way.

His head throbbing, he turned and walked away from her. All the way across the room to the saddle racks, he encouraged himself.

You're not a stupid man, Sixkiller. You've wrapped a hundred women, maybe more, around your little finger. You can get any woman to do anything you want if you have a little time with her.

If he could just be strong enough to survive a little more time with Miss Susanna.

He tried to rest his mind while he picked out a saddle and a set of saddlebags, plus a leather-covered canteen, and went to the counter to pay, yet he barely knew what he was buying because his thoughts were swarming around her so busily.

Now he wouldn't be able to talk to her or charm her or try to convince her to stay home because he'd blurted out such a clumsy ultimatum about the trail. Not a smart move.

That was another thing she did to him. She roused his temper as fast as another man would and made him forget all about treating her like a woman.

Yet he was still thinking about the fact that she was a widow. How could he even care? He could never consider even a passing dalliance with her for fear of losing his mind entirely.

When he took his money out of his pocket, his eye fell on a stack of ladies' riding gloves. He glanced over his shoulder.

Susanna was busy looking at the sets of harness and lines, her straight, stubborn—but shapely—back firmly turned to him.

He picked up a pair of the gloves and added them to the saddle.

"Wrap 'em up and put 'em in the saddle bag," he said to the proprietor.

Now there was an idea. Gifts usually melted a lady's heart. He would save this one until a crucial moment.

But it wouldn't be enough. Susanna Copeland was the kind who had to make her own decisions. Or think that she was.

He'd have to have another tactic, too. Then, when he went up the trail with her cattle and left her at home, he could give her the gloves as a farewell gesture to prove there were no hard feelings between them.

That plan made him feel some better. He was about to get a handle on this deal now. He had to. If he didn't succeed in taking only her herd north and leaving her behind, it would be about the same as sitting on the hurricane deck of a bronc for three months.

Although, if he did succeed in that, he and she would, no doubt, have a devil of a time even coming to an agreeable accounting in the fall. Envisioning that scene made him grin a little. He would bring her a pretty gift from Abilene, too, and that would make her smile that gorgeous smile again.

Suddenly his natural optimism came surging to the fore. Why was he worried, anyhow? With any luck, they'd not even be able to agree on the count of the cattle or the branding and she'd lose her temper and fire him and he'd be free as soon as tonight. That would definitely be for the best.

Definitely. He usually got what he wanted. He could make that happen.

Passionate or not, beautiful or not, he already knew Susanna Copeland was far more trouble than she was worth.

As soon as they were horseback and riding out of town, Eagle Jack started his campaign.

"On the trail, you'll have to have much better equipment," he said. "That bridle you're using isn't safe."

He hated to say something like that to her when he knew she had no money to buy another one, but this was war.

And it was for a good cause. He was trying to make her stay home for her own good, not just to preserve his sanity.

Susanna glanced at her bridle with its double-tied knot holding the broken headstall together, then she looked at him.

"I'll be driving the wagon," she said. Then she added, "I haven't hired a cook."

He felt a leap of elation.

"Hmm. In that case, I'd say you'd best reconsider this whole deal, Susanna," he said.

His voice came out in such a thoughtful tone he felt he really should stroke his beard, if he had one. This was the way to do it. Hold his head and his temper and talk her into seeing things his way.

She tilted her flat-brimmed hat so she could see him better and looked at him some more.

"Oh?"

"It's too late now to get anybody who could cook a meal fit to eat," he said. "There must be a half million head of cattle going up the trail this year and even though it's early in the season yet, the decent cooks have been spoken for since last year."

"So," she said, "it's too late to hire someone?"

Her calm, conversational tone heartened him. She was going to come around to his way of thinking. Women always did, didn't they? He shouldn't have worried so much. He shouldn't have doubted his own powers.

He shook his head sorrowfully.

"I'm afraid so, Susanna," he said.

"Are you thinking that I'll have to give up the idea of the drive because of it?"

This was a dangerous question. The wrong response could put her right back into her stubborn, not-to-be-reasoned-with mood. He was doing so well, he mustn't let that happen.

He shrugged. "Well, that's your decision, of course, but you're a shrewd businesswoman . . ."

She pulled back and raised her eyebrows at him in a silent question.

". . . or you wouldn't have picked me there at the jail," he said. "And you know as well as I do that the one reason a cowboy can honorably quit a herd on the trail is bad food."

They looked at each other.

The horses trotted side-by-side.

"I know," Susanna said, with a little chuckle in her tone, "don't let it bring you to tears, Eagle Jack."

He sent her a sharp glance. Was she not buying his act after all?

"You're pretty shrewd, yourself," she said.

He tried to read her face but couldn't.

"Why do you say that?" he asked.

"Oh, just a general impression. You know that those young men might steal my cattle. You know that drovers have to have good food or they'll leave a herd." She shrugged and then gave him a full-blown grin full of mischief. "So you're bound to know that you were the only man in that jail with sense enough to come in out of the rain. Really, Eagle Jack, just as you remarked to me once before, I had no choice."

He didn't quite know how to take that.

"So what's the point you're making here, Susanna?"

"That my choosing you is no proof of anything but my desperation. I may not be half as shrewd as you seem to think."

"But, then again, you may be even shrewder," he said.

They looked at each other, taking each other's measure.

"That is always a distinct possibility," she said.

He grinned back at her. Riding with her might turn out to be quite an amusement, after all.

And she certainly was easy to look at.

Scary thoughts, both of them. Firmly, he put them away and tried to regroup.

"Susanna, are you planning to do the cooking yourself?"

Her blue eyes still twinkled at him.

"Yes. Unless you want to do it?"

His anger stirred again, despite his bemusement. She was making fun of him, that was all there was to it, and doing it to avoid the truth. He was going to make her face it.

"Have you ever cooked for eight or ten men three times a day? On the ground? With cattle chips instead of wood?"

"No," she said, holding her gaze steady. "But that doesn't mean I can't do it."

He sighed.

"Susanna, you're living in a dream world."

"I'm going to be famous as a trail cook," she said. "All the other herds will hear about our food and make up excuses to drop by our camp."

"What makes you so sure?"

"I'm taking lots of dried fruit to make pies and when I can, I'm going to have an oven in the ground and, above ground or not, I can make biscuits and bread and bear sign. I already have my sourdough working."

Eagle Jack got a sinking feeling deep in his stomach. This was not going to be easy. She had her mind and her heart set.

He clenched his jaw and then unclenched it, willed his voice to be calm.

"What the men need isn't so much sweets as good, solid meals to stick to their ribs. Beef cooked where it's not tough and . . ."

"And vegetables and fruit," she said. "I can recognize every edible plant on the trail. We'll have poke salad and wild onions and I'll look for wild plums and blackberries."

She gave him a quick look that seemed completely sincere.

"I'll help you look for your stolen horse, too, Eagle Jack," she said. "When I drive my wagon on ahead of the herd so I can have more time to prepare the food."

Eagle Jack wanted to put his head in his hands.

Dear Lord, preserve him.

That was all he needed: to worry about protecting her while she was out alone, racing ahead to dig an oven in the ground to make a pie.

Why, *why* hadn't he simply harangued the sheriff until he let him out? Barring that, why hadn't he just served his time?

Chapter 3

During the entire ride out to the ranch, Susanna alternated between trying to read Eagle Jack's mind to gauge her success and silently berating herself for even caring whether she had begun to change his attitude about her going up the trail. She didn't have to persuade him, she didn't have to talk him into being happy about it.

He *had* to take her to Abilene. That was the deal they had made.

But it had been fun, teasing with him that way. It seemed a long, long time since anything had been fun—at least anything involving another person of approximately her own age, not to mention a handsome man.

She'd had fun, very exciting, scary fun, trying to ride through the brush without getting knocked off her horse and rope the mavericks that had drifted onto her ranch. Including the cattle that had belonged to her and Everett but had gone completely wild in the five years he'd been dead.

Only Maynell's taciturn husband, old Jimbo, had been with her for that fun, though, and they hadn't exactly traded witticisms and grins and twinklings of the eye as she'd done with Eagle Jack. Their conversation had been more like grunts of surprise when they finally caught some wild-as-a-buck cow and sighs of relief when the time came to go to the house.

And after all of that sweat and blood and agony, they had gathered only a couple dozen head of cattle and put them in the one small pasture that still had its fences standing. Then came that beautiful, rainy day when she'd found the money Everett had hidden under the hearthstone before he went off to the war.

He had hidden it from her. That was the thought that sent a cold shiver through her when she'd noticed the edge of the stone was raised a little and realized something was beneath it, holding it up. He hadn't cared if she starved to death or if the livestock did, too, while five gold coins lay in hiding within her reach, waiting for his return.

That was customary behavior for Everett. Well, it served him right that she'd found it. She had never dreamed they had that much cash money.

Not enough to make up for the last two years of

bad luck with both the orchard and the corn, which had meant no cash crops. Not enough to pay off the mortgage he'd left along with the ranch. Not enough to hire the many men she needed to clear away the brush that was fast choking the grass out of her pastures and taking her crop land.

But enough—she knew it by the thought that God dropped into her head as the money dropped into her hand—to put together an outfit to go up the trail. Enough to pay a few men to gather the wily cattle hiding in the brush all over her ranch so she could drive them north.

That was all people talked about in town. How much more those cattle would bring in Kansas than in Texas. How much of a profit could be made.

And the drovers didn't have to be paid until the drive was done. Perfect!

Since Everett had been gone, she had sold off everything of value that she owned to keep the banker from foreclosing on her land. She could've used the found money to replace the good bull and the spare plow horses and the decent harness she used to have. She could've used part of it to pay the mortgage for this year.

Then she could've hunkered down and prayed for rain, holding on piecemeal for as long as she could.

Instead, she had decided to gamble, and it was too late to back out now.

Now she'd hired a trail boss who was trying to leave her at home. He must be pondering on that again, because he hadn't said a word for at least two miles.

"Brushy Creek is the next ranch," she said to him. "We're almost there."

She didn't leave home very often, usually only once a month or so to get supplies, but every time she did, she felt the same thrill at returning. This bend in the road that they were taking curved so sweetly around the grove of big live oak trees and, up ahead of that, her own lane came meandering down to meet the road where an old sweetgum tree stood sentinel at her gate. That sight lifted her heart every time. Brushy Creek Ranch. Her own place.

But the thought brought those cold, familiar fingers of fear to clutch her stomach. She took in a long, deep breath to try to loosen their grip.

No. She could not lose Brushy Creek. She would not. The drive north would make all the profit that it promised, she would pay off the whole mortgage against her ranch, and she would have enough money left over to make all the improvements it needed.

She would pay off the whole mortgage! Then, even if she couldn't sell any cash crops, her home would be secure. Never again would she have to worry about having no home of her own.

She looked at Eagle Jack, who still hadn't answered her. His mind seemed a million miles away.

"See that lane up there that branches off from the road?" she said. "That's the entrance to my ranch."

That woke him up.

"Good," he said. "We'll have all afternoon to start the branding. We might get half done today. Do you think we could hire the men who did the gathering to stay and help?"

She stared at him.

"How can you be my trail boss if you don't listen to me any better than that?"

He stared back. "What I heard you say was that that's your place right up there."

Somehow his saying the words "your place" sent that shard of fear through her heart again. He believed it. The neighbors believed it. The mortgage banker believed it. It wasn't just a dream that she owned a ranch. It really *was* her place to keep or lose.

Susanna said the quick prayer she always said when she thought about the money she'd borrowed.

Lord, don't let me lose it. Please help me keep my home.

"Earlier," she told him, "in town, I told you that I spent my last money on you. I can't hire any more help that has to be paid before the drive."

He looked her up and down as if he thought she'd lost her mind.

"You also said you were going to pay Tucker or whatever his name is and his brushpoppin' buddies for the gathering when you got home."

He said it flatly, as if calling her a liar.

It flew all over her, after the years and years with Everett and his hateful ways of talking and behaving.

"I am." She held his gaze without wavering and spoke just as flatly. Her financial situation was none of his business. She didn't need to tell him anything more. "You're my trail boss, Eagle Jack. Not my husband."

"Thank God," he said.

"Yes," she said, "thank God. And I'll never have another one."

"Right," he said. "Marriage never looked too good to me, either."

The sudden agreement took the wind out of the argument's sails for a heartbeat. They exchanged a startled look.

But she knew him already. He wasn't going to give up. Sure enough, he began to push again.

"You want to get on the trail as soon as possible, don't you, Susanna? The sooner we get 'em branded, the sooner we hit the trail. The sooner we head 'em out, the sooner we load 'em on the rail cars in Kansas."

"I know all that," she said. "I tell you, I can't pay for help to do it all *sooner*."

"Don't worry about the money. It's my decision, as trail boss."

"We're not *on* the trail. Yet."

"My point, exactly."

Her temper snapped. "You are, without doubt, the stubbornest man who ever lived," she said. "Listen to me. I have exactly enough money to pay Tucker what he asked for the gathering and he'll pay the other men. That's it. That's all. I saved that much back."

"*You* listen to *me*," he said. "I'm hiring help if there's help to be had, and I'll pay for it. I'm not going to lay over here for a week counting and branding this herd and packing a chuck wagon so you can make a pie while the best horse that ever ate grass is God knows where and having to put up with God knows what kind of treatment."

That stirred all the old rage Susanna carried deep inside.

"I've had five years of independence now," she said, "and never again will I abide a man's domination. I can tell you that, right now, Eagle Jack."

He stared at her as if he couldn't believe his ears.

"Domination?" he said. "That's puttin' it a little strong, isn't it? All I'm doing is my job."

"I don't care what you think," she said. "All my life my aunts and my cousins and my uncles and their dogs told me what to do and I had to obey because I was living under their roofs and eating their food. Then it was the same with Everett."

Tears threatened and she swallowed them back. "Even though I thought was getting a home of my own when I married him."

Eagle Jack slowed his horse and waited, not saying a word.

"You're not about to put me into your debt," she said, finally. "No. I will not owe you money. Then I'd owe you obedience, too, and I'd have no authority over my cattle or anything else."

"That's not true," he said.

She ignored that. "I'm the owner and I'm the one who pays the help. I have no more money and I can't trade work, since I'll soon be gone for months. Besides, how could I help a neighbor with the branding, since I've never branded so much as a goat?"

Eagle Jack smiled at that.

"Well, you're fixing to learn," he said. "I'll put you at the fire handling the irons."

That made her fear flare again.

"If you do, that'll be the last time you try to put me anywhere," she said.

The look in his eyes was hard to read but he was watching her face steadily.

"I was only teasing you, Susanna," he said gently. "Trying to lighten things up."

His voice soothed her, almost like a hand patting her shoulder.

But he didn't understand. He still hadn't backed down.

"I've had some years of hard experience," she said, "with a hard teacher. No man will ever give me orders again."

They reached the end of her lane and she turned into it. Eagle Jack followed for a minute or two.

Then he rode his horse up beside hers again.

"Ol' Everett," he said, seeming to muse to himself as the horses slow-trotted side by side. "Reckon it's possible that his soul didn't fly upward when he died?"

" 'Probable' might be a better choice of words," she said wryly.

Eagle Jack nodded sagely.

"Sorta what I was thinkin'," he said, "based on what you've told me about him so far. But I'm too polite just to come right out say so out loud."

Susanna shook her head. In spite of her worries, he was lightening her heart a little bit. But it was only to get what he wanted. She had to remember that.

"You are not," she said. "Eagle Jack, there's not a polite bone in your body except when you think it'll help you get your way."

He raised his brows in mock surprise.

"Susanna! I know we just met but still I can't believe you don't know me any better than that."

"I know you well enough," she said. "You are totally still determined to go against my wishes and hire help with your own money."

That truth tied her stomach into a knot.

What if he quit? Maybe she could do without him, now that she had a three-man crew.

No, she couldn't. Three men couldn't handle the herd, and from the looks of him, that boy Marvin she'd hired right off the street didn't know any more about how to take a herd to Kansas than she did.

But she could not lose control of her cattle, either.

"Distracting me isn't the same as convincing me to change my mind," she said. She looked him straight in the eye. "I'm not going to give permission for you to hire more help now, Eagle Jack," she said. "Keep your money and we'll just be a day or two later getting on the trail. It won't matter."

He didn't answer right away and in the silence, the terrible seriousness of it all came over her again. The ancient longing that had been with her since her very first memory turned to a blind fear that seized and shook her like a giant's hand.

"My whole ranch—my whole *life*—is at stake,"

she blurted. "I can't bear to be homeless, ever again."

Her voice shook with a growing urgency. She couldn't look at him. She couldn't choke back the flood of fearful words, either.

"I'm way too far in debt already," she said. "So far in I may never get out. It was hopeless before I ever bought the chuck wagon and the supplies and everything's riding on what happens now."

Susanna managed to take in a deep breath, but it didn't calm her enough to stop the panic pouring out of her.

"I've stepped off a cliff here," she said, "and invested everything in this trail drive. I just can't bear another debt hanging over my head. I worry about money all the time as it is."

She bit her tongue and held it. This was making her look ridiculous and he had to respect her if she was going to be able to boss him at all.

Finally, thank goodness, her mind took over from her emotions. She was telling him too much. She was letting her fear control her.

And for nothing, probably. Where had she found this man, anyhow?

She took another long, deep breath and tried to compose herself. Then she looked at him straight.

"Eagle Jack, thank you for the offer," she said, "but I can't let you pay for anything. I'm the owner, I'm supposed to pay. Besides, if you couldn't get yourself out of jail, how can you pay for any hired hands?"

"In jail, I couldn't get to my money," he said.

He looked at her for a minute as they rode along, then he added, "I have a little saved up."

"Keep it," she said. "I'll never rest easy, all the way up the trail, if you don't."

"How about this?" he said. "I hire the help we need and you pay me back at the end of the trail."

She thought about that.

"Out of your profits," he said.

"I don't know. I already have the mortgage on my place, and I'll owe Mr. Adams for the use of his horses and mules. I have to pay you and the drovers. I don't want to owe all that."

"It won't be all that much more that you'd owe me," he said. "Only a couple of days' work for your brushpopper Tucker and his men."

"No, I—"

"*Think,* Susanna," he interrupted her. "If we can get on the trail even one day earlier, it might determine whether you *have* profits or not. There's a record number of herds going north this year and if too many of them are ahead of us, we won't have enough grass."

Shock ran through her with the force of a blow. It must've showed on her face. She slowed her horse to a walk.

Somehow, she had always assumed there

would be plenty of everything, except she did know that there were one or two places on the Chisholm that they had to go a day without watering the cattle.

"Same with water," he said, as if he could read her mind.

Desperation stabbed her.

"But I'll have *some* profits," she said. "If steers are eleven dollars a head here and they bring twenty in Kansas . . ."

"Things change," he insisted. "It'll be three months till we get there. Plus the cattle can't be skin and bones and still bring twenty."

Susanna drew in a hard-won breath. Her throat had closed up and so had her lungs.

Now she had visions of cattle skulls and skeletons, long, dry drives with no water, cattle bawling from hunger and thirst.

Here was another gamble. Here was where she was going to prove that she could be the boss and still bend. With the suddenness of a bolt of lightning she knew that there'd be many, many more times before those cattle got to Kansas that she'd have to either bend or break.

She had wrapped her destiny and that of her herd up in this brown-eyed man who was sitting his horse so quietly, just waiting for her decision. He *was* letting her make *this* decision.

But he knew what her answer had to be. And if

it was different, he could just turn and ride away. He really could. Even if he had given his word to her at the jail.

He was a stranger to her and she didn't trust even the people she knew—except for Maynell and Jimbo—but she had to trust him.

"If you pay Tucker the extra money and then trust me to pay you that much more when we sell the cattle, will that be enough? Will you not try to take over all my authority?"

He folded his arms across his saddle horn and gave a sigh, removed his hat, and resettled it at another angle. Then he cocked his head so he could look right into her eyes again.

"There'll be times when you'll think I'm taking over, Susanna. And there'll be other times when I truly am. Times when I *will* gag and tie you and throw you in the wagon, if I have to."

He waited a minute so she could think about that.

"But I promise you now, those will be times of life and death, times of great danger, if you are advocating the wrong course. The rest of the time, we can make decisions together. We can talk them over just as we've talked about this one today."

His eyes were deep, dark brown and full of truth.

"All right," she said. "Once again, I have no choice. Hire Tucker and his men to stay for as long as you can afford and let's get started making a profit. Such a big profit that I can pay you back and have money left over."

Then she smooched to her horse and loped away toward home, trying to leave Eagle Jack Sixkiller behind.

He confused her, he infuriated her, he scared her to death, and if he wanted to, he could seduce her when he looked at her with that smile in his dark brown eyes. But it was more than that. What really drew her to him with the power of the sun and moon and stars was the kindness in him.

She'd never really known a kind man before.

All she knew for certain was that she'd better get a good handle on her feelings before they started up the trail.

Eagle Jack tried to get a grip on his plan as he followed Susanna.

Maybe the problem was that he needed a new plan. Or had he ever had a plan, in the first place?

It's too late for plans, Sixkiller, you dolt. What you need is a new brain. Blabbermouth.

He took off his hat and slapped it back on again.

Man, he hated worrying! He hated responsibility, too.

And he'd taken on a wagonload of both when he'd let his tongue get away from him. How could he have possibly told her she could go up the trail?

He took his hat off again and ran his fingers through his hair.

He was helpless. It was a hopeless mess.

His gaze already stuck to her like glue, though, as if he'd accepted that it was his job to watch out for her.

Well, it wasn't bad to just *watch* her. Her pert little bottom sat unmoving in her saddle and her perfect rhythm with her mount promised that she could spend all day horseback. She was a good rider.

Which didn't really matter that much. She would be on a wagon seat all day, off by herself on the trackless prairie looking for poke salad and berries, or else she'd be trying to drive along with him while he scouted ahead.

A new pain began to throb in the back of his head.

It must be this devilish headache that had scrambled his mind so much. There he'd been, riding along minding his own trail boss business and trying get them on the *trail*, for goodness sake, when he was blindsided by pity.

She wasn't able to trust anybody, and that was sad. She was scared to death of losing her ranch, and that was sad, too.

But, damn it, her ranch was where she belonged, where she'd be safest and do herself the most good. She had no business on the trail and he didn't need her. He would have Cookie from the Sixkiller home ranch, the Sixes and Sevens, to do the cooking, and he would have his own men for drovers. All he wanted was to get her cattle ready to go, let the boys they'd hired in front of the saddle shop help him drive them north, and his men could meet them on the Chisholm Trail.

Cookie would kill him if he brought another cook along.

Susanna would probably kill him if he tried to leave here without her.

Why couldn't he get her to do whatever he wanted, when he wanted?

All the other women did. Hundreds of women did. At least for as long as he *cared* what they did.

He watched her trotting on ahead, picking up now, to a lope.

Orders wouldn't do it. Charm wouldn't do it. Logic wouldn't do it.

But discomfort might. Reality. A good dose of what it would be like on the trail—but now, not when it was too late to turn back.

She'd seemed the most horrified when he'd told her she had to handle the fire and heat the branding irons. He probably wouldn't try to make her do that. But he could insist that she cook dinner for them all outside instead of on her stove, couldn't he? For practice?

That'd be a logical thing that she couldn't refuse to do and it would surely take the excitement out of doing it three times a day for months on end. Because, God help him, he had to do something. He could not take her with him.

It'd be hard for her to refuse to help, especially in front of the men.

He would even ask, especially, for pie. Probably, digging one pit to use as an oven would be plenty to make her think again. He would explain that she'd have to do that herself every day on the trail because he'd not be able to spare a man for it.

After they ate, they'd work until dark and he'd ask her to help with the cattle if that plug she was riding had any cow sense. Or he'd put her on a different one. She was certainly a fine little rider.

He should've been riding back here all along, watching her great natural seat on the horse. The tall, gangly horse's gait looked so rough, she'd be bouncing all over the place if she weren't pretty darn good.

Almost, he put his heels into his horse to ride up there beside her and tease her about watching her neat little seat in the saddle, but he stopped himself in time. He was not going to joke around with her anymore. He was not going to flirt with her.

All right, he had a plan and he would concentrate on it. He would make her start the hateful work she'd have to do on the trail. He would insist she keep it up through the next couple of days and by then she'd be changing her mind and starting to make noises about staying home after all.

Only then would he tell her that he already had

a cook and that that would be just fine. Well, he'd just as well get started. He might as well get this whole drive organized and find out what else needed to be done.

A remuda, for one thing. They would only need it until they joined up with the herd from the Sixes and Sevens, but that'd be a couple of hundred miles. Everything, including their lives, depended on the horses.

A scrap of their conversation floated through his head. What was it she had said about using somebody's horses and mules? What kind of a deal was that—borrowed horses on a trail drive?

Especially for a woman who was hysterically afraid of being beholden to anyone?

He smooched to his new mount, who was turning out to be a fairly comfortable one, and rode up beside her.

"What was it you said about paying somebody for the use of their horses and mules?" he said. "Do you mean for the drive?"

She glanced at him, and for a moment he thought she wouldn't answer.

"I have to know about this, Susanna. It's vital for the trail." Another hesitation, and he knew for sure she didn't want to talk about it. "If I'm going to talk things over with you then you must do the same with me," he said.

"This is different," she argued. "This decision has already been made."

He reminded himself that demanding an answer would not work with her.

"I only need to know the quality of horses," he said. "You know our lives will depend on our horses."

"They seem good quality to me," she said. "I think they'll be fine."

Something was wrong. She'd just blurted out something as personal as her financial troubles to him, but this was like pulling teeth.

He leaned on his patience, which could be considerable when that was the only way to get to his goal.

"Do you have delivery yet?"

"No. They'll probably bring them over this afternoon. Tucker was going to send word when the gather is done."

"Send word where?"

"To Mr. Adams."

Eagle Jack waited. He wanted to shake more words out of her but he stayed quiet.

"My neighbor," she said. "To the east over there." She gestured vaguely.

"Does Mr. Adams run a livery?"

"No, he's just doing me a favor and making a little money on his extra animals at the same time."

"Are y'all good friends?"

"No, we're acquaintances. He let me ride one of

his horses back from town one day when mine went lame."

"Pretty good horse?" he asked.

"I thought so."

"Good," he said. "I'll be anxious to see what he's got."

And he let the conversation drop.

A few yards on down the road, Susanna picked it up again.

"Eagle Jack?" she said. "Don't forget that Marvin and his friends think we're married."

He looked at her sharply, but her face told him nothing.

Chapter 4

The dust cloud up ahead grew darker and the noise of bawling cattle carried to them on the wind.

"That's in my south pasture," Susanna said. "Maybe Tucker and his boys have about got them all out of the mesquite."

Now whatever had been worrying her seemed to be gone. He could hear only excitement in her voice, and that was a relief.

It was true that he was curious about everyone and she was interesting, but he'd felt such a jolt of sympathy at her dire straits that it had unsettled him. Next thing he knew, he'd be feeling even more responsibility for her than he already did.

"I'm banking on that," he said, forcing a light tone into his voice and hoping it'd be contagious.

"I'd sure rather count and brand them than to chase them out of the brush."

"I'm praying they got them all," she said. "I can't wait to see how many there are." She turned and flashed that rare smile of hers. "I just look at them and think: 'each one is twenty dollars on the hoof'."

"If we can get them enough grass on the way north," he said.

Her smile faded.

He felt bad that he had burst her bubble and added to her worries, but all he'd told her was the truth. Anybody going up the trail had best be ready for all the dangers.

Hey, Sixkiller, get a grip. Go soft with her now and you'll have to worry with her all the way to Abilene.

Eagle Jack looked at the dust cloud and took himself to task. He *could* not, he *would* not start feeling sorry for her now. He'd never live through three months and a thousand miles of nursemaiding Susanna.

You've got a plan, boy, and you'd best stick to it.

Whoever heard of a woman on the trail! What he was fighting for, here, was his own survival, so he had to stay tough.

And he would. In the next two days, he was going to put her through as much of what she'd face on her way north with a herd of cattle as he possibly could. He would be merciless.

They rode up to the herd from the south side and a brushpopper he assumed was Tucker came loping out to meet them.

"Them three boys over there say you've done hired 'em for the trail, Miss Susanna," he said, briefly taking off his hat to her. "I put 'em to work holding the herd."

"That's right, Tucker," she said. "How many head do you guess y'all have gathered?"

He wiped the dust from his face while he thought about that.

"I'd say near eight hundred but I can't guarantee it."

"Are you done?" she asked.

"As close to done as we're gonna get," he said. "That one bald-faced brindle bull we never did bring in. We choused him around a time or two and got a rope on him once but we never could get him out of that little ravine he likes so much."

She nodded. "Leave him. You've done the best you could and it's time to get on the trail." She turned to Eagle Jack. "This is Tucker Banyon," she said. "Tucker, this is my husband, Eagle Jack Sixkiller."

The title of husband sent another shock through him, as it had done the first time. It seemed unnecessary, but then maybe not, since she had already started this charade in Salado with Marvin and his gang and now they were here.

Tucker leaned from his saddle to shake hands and so did Eagle Jack.

It certainly didn't matter. He'd never see this man again, anyhow.

Eagle Jack grinned to himself. It was a good thing he wasn't taking her with him any farther than this. If word of his "marriage" got back to the Sixes and Sevens it would cause a riot.

As he sat back and half listened to Susanna talking to Tucker about her cattle, he had a flashing vision of his family's reaction to such news. His mother would be beside herself with happiness that he was settling down at last. In fact, even if he told her it was all a pretense, she would refuse to believe that and would try to convince him to make it real and give her some grandchildren. His father and brothers and all the hands would hoorah him unmercifully and Grandfather Bushyhead would insist on doing a medicine ceremony over him and Susanna.

Yes, if he ever got married, it would cause a great stir, since he was known far and wide as a ladies' man who never stayed long with just one. All the young girls whose mamas were angling for them to marry into one of the richest families with one of the biggest ranches in Central Texas, Indian or not, would be crushed. Or at least their mamas would be.

And all the girls who chased after him because

he was Indian and therefore dangerous and forbidden by their mamas would be mad at him. He'd surely hate to disappoint them like that. Why, if he ever got married, everything would change in his life and even he wouldn't be able to recognize himself.

"Somebody comin'," Tucker said.

Eagle Jack turned to look. "Must be your horses, Susanna," he said.

Tucker went back to the herd and Eagle Jack and Susanna turned to go meet the arriving remuda. She rode ahead of him, one slender arm high in the air to signal the incoming riders to follow her. Then she lifted her awkward mount into a lope and headed for the house, an unpainted cabin on a low knoll to the north.

She was first to reach the large corral on the flat below the house. Leaning from her saddle, she opened its gate and Eagle Jack caught it and fastened it back.

He eyed the horses as they loped through the opening, picking and choosing. They wouldn't need all of these, even if they were taking only Susanna's cattle and not joining up with the Sixes and Sevens herd. Mr. Adams must be giving Susanna a lot of choices in horseflesh. Maybe he was a very generous man.

Or a very greedy one. If she used them all to herd her cattle on her way north, when she brought them back this fall Adams would collect rent on each one—plus compensation, no doubt, for any that got killed or lamed.

Three young cowboys and one older man stayed behind as the last horse went through the gate and Eagle Jack closed it. The older man, who must be Adams, started toward him and Susanna.

"Well, there you are, missy," he called to her. "Now you've got what will be the best remuda on the Chisholm Trail."

It didn't look so hot to Eagle Jack. The two mule teams looked strong and sturdy but some of the horses looked as if they were on their last legs, like the dregs of an auction barn.

The old coot might be setting things up so that Susanna would, without fail, have to pay some compensation when fall rolled around.

As he got closer, Eagle Jack saw that his saddle was old and worn, as were his ancient-looking clothes.

"He looks like a pauper," Susanna muttered, "but he owns half the county and the town, too." She raised her voice.

"Thank you for the use of your animals, Mr. Adams," she said.

She sounded tense and her whole body had stiffened.

"My pleasure, my dear," the man said and then he was close enough for Eagle Jack to see his pale face.

His small eyes, a washed-out hazel color, were fixed on Susanna. He behaved as if Eagle Jack were a post in the fence.

"However, I think you'll need to take some of them back home with you, Mr. Adams," she said. "We agreed on two teams of mules but I wasn't expecting you to bring this many horses."

Eagle Jack looked at her with new respect. She wasn't quite as much a tenderfoot as he'd thought.

Adams waved her words away. "I got my hands on a few extra horses the other day, and want you to take them," he said.

"But I can't afford too many . . ." she said.

"Now, don't you worry about anything like that," Mr. Adams interrupted. "If you don't make as big a profit as you're expecting, and you can't pay me in hard cash, then I'll understand." He rode up to them and stopped on the opposite side of Susanna, holding his horse right beside hers, head to tail.

Eagle Jack didn't like the gleam in the old man's eye.

And neither did she. He knew her well enough by now to tell.

"Remember what I told you," Adams said, adding some oil to his scratchy voice, "we'll work out some other way for you to compensate me."

He spoke very low, but Eagle Jack heard every word.

And everything he didn't say. There was absolutely no doubt what Adams meant by 'some other way', since the old lecher was openly leering at Susanna. There was no other word for it.

Eagle Jack felt a surge of anger like he hadn't known for years. If he only knew it, the old reprobate was about to get his teeth shoved down his throat.

"I'll pay you in hard cash, Mr. Adams," Susanna said. "That was our agreement."

Her tone was sure, almost hard. But her hands convulsed and clasped each other more tightly above her saddle horn.

Eagle Jack watched closely. So this was what had been bothering her earlier and causing her to be so evasive when he'd asked about the remuda.

"No, no, beautiful Miss Susanna, I don't want you upset in your mind all the way to Abilene about paying for the use of my horses," Adams said. He frowned as if that would upset his mind terribly, too. Then he swept off his hat, laid it over his heart, and pasted an ugly smile onto his equally ugly face. "Of course, I *would* like to think that from time to time your thoughts might roam back to me, my dear." He widened his fawning smile. "That would be the desire of my heart."

Susanna sat very straight in her saddle and looked at Adams with a wry, cool smile.

"I'm sure I'll think of you each time I look at

your horses," she said. "And I'll do my very best to bring them back to you in good condition."

Adams kept his smile and his stare on her for another long heartbeat, then he replaced his hat on his head with a sweeping gesture evidently meant to be a graceful flourish.

Eagle Jack had to restrain himself from leaping across Susanna's horse's neck and knocking the dirty old man out of the saddle and onto the ground. Adams had no right whatsoever to look at her like that.

But he couldn't mix in her business without getting deeper into this mess, could he? He could not tell the old bastard to take his horses out of there and never set foot on Brushy Creek again or he'd be setting himself up as Susanna's protector and meddling in her personal life.

Her personal life was what he was trying to stay out of.

All he was going to do was be a sort of business partner until her cattle were sold. That was it. That was all.

And even as far as business was concerned, she had been right, back there on the road. This was a decision she'd already made before he'd come on the scene. He had to let it be.

"My only concern is that you bring your own beautiful self back from Kansas in the same condition that you left Texas . . ." Adams said.

Eagle Jack's thin patience snapped. "Sorry to interrupt," he said.

The apology came out of his mouth in a slow, dangerous drawl that contradicted the words themselves.

Adams lifted his beady eyes from Susanna's face and looked at Eagle Jack for the first time. He sneered.

"We're burning daylight here," Eagle Jack said. "We've got branding to do."

"Who are you to speak for the lady? She's accustomed to conducting business for herself."

"Not with rattlesnakes, she isn't," Eagle Jack said. "A lady accustomed to dealing with decent people is at a disadvantage dealing with scum."

Adams stared at him.

Susanna, too, was staring at him—he knew because he could feel her eyes on him but he didn't even glance at her. He couldn't take his eyes off Adams and he couldn't think of anything but how much he wished the man would go for his gun.

But Adams was probably too much of a coward to carry one. No doubt one of the men with him was his gun hand. Eagle Jack didn't even deign to glance in that direction.

He motioned low at his side for Susanna to move her horse back and silently thanked God when she obeyed.

Adams had two spots of color in his cheeks

now. He had not moved a muscle. "Who are you?" he asked, his voice slipping a notch higher.

"I'm Susanna's husband. Eagle Jack Sixkiller is my name."

Adams's narrow eyes widened. He looked at Susanna. "Husband? Why didn't you tell me you were married?"

"You didn't ask," she said.

Eagle Jack looked toward Adams's men. They were slumped in their saddles, quietly talking and smoking.

He opened his mouth to tell Adams to take his men and his horses and hit the road but he shut it again. Even with Tucker and his men helping, the crew couldn't brand several hundred cattle in two days and then drive them up the trail far enough to meet the Sixes and Sevens herd without fresh horses.

And it had to be done in two days. Molly was getting farther and farther away from him, running her heart out in the horse thieves' clutches.

"I'll buy your horses," he said to Adams, who was actually turning paler, although that would've seemed impossible since he was so pasty-faced to start with. "I'll give you two hundred dollars for the lot of them."

They were worth no more than three hundred at the most, including the mules.

Adams stared at him. "Susanna," he said, without turning his head to look at her, "is it true that this man is your husband?"

"Yes," she said firmly, "he is. And he's going up the trail with me as trail boss for my cattle."

Eagle Jack stared at Adams some more. "You won't be talking to my wife again," he said. "So take the money or take your horses and get off her land."

"Four hundred," Adams said.

"Two and a half," Eagle Jack said. "Last offer."

"Hard cash," Adams said.

Without looking away from him, Eagle Jack reached into his shirt pocket for the money he'd gotten at the bank in Salado. He opened the small pouch and shook out double eagles into the palm of his other hand until he had enough.

"I don't have time or paper for a bill of sale," he said, "so you need to know this. If you call these horses stolen and set the law on me, I'll come back here and kill you."

Adams didn't flinch. "I wouldn't bother," he said.

He held out his hand, took the money Eagle Jack gave him, signaled his men, and rode away without a backward glance.

Eagle Jack put his pouch back in his pocket.

"So it begins," Susanna said, in a voice he'd never heard before.

Startled, he looked at her.

Immediately he realized that, although he'd

thought he'd seen her angry before, he never had. Her eyes blazed.

"You're determined to take over and run this drive, aren't you?" she said. "Now it's out in the open. You never meant to talk things over, did you?"

It made him mad all the way to the bone. "Don't bother to thank me, Susanna," he said. "All I did was pay way too much for a bunch of broomtails so we could get your cattle branded."

"All you did was overturn a decision I had already made—without so much as a glance at me for my opinion—so that you can get on the trail of your stolen horse. Forget thanks from me."

She sat frozen in her saddle, glaring at him with eyes big as saucers, looking shocked as if he'd slapped her face.

He didn't know a woman could be this unreasonable. He didn't know he could get as furious as he was this minute.

"All I did was rescue you from the clutches of a nasty old man."

"All you did was make me a dangerous enemy," she retorted. "He'll still be here when I come back to Brushy Creek without you."

A small shard of concern stabbed through his fury.

He rode his horse closer.

"You should've had more sense than to have any dealings with him at all. He's a snake."

"I can handle him," she said.

"Then why're you worried about coming back here without me?"

"I'm not."

Her voice was full of bravado and it didn't tremble but her lips did. They were full and luscious and inviting and he ought to kiss them.

To shut her up. Only that.

"This is going nowhere with you starting to contradict yourself," he said. "What you need to be doing, Susanna, is building a fire and digging an oven in the ground. That bunch out there working your cattle will be hungry in just a little while."

He turned his back on her and galloped away, sending his horse toward the herd.

To get started counting the cattle. Only that.

There'd never been any danger that he might kiss her.

Because now things were different. In Salado, he'd thought a short dalliance might be entertaining but he would never consider it now. It would only confuse an already tangled situation.

He still couldn't believe that the words "my wife" had actually come out of his mouth and he couldn't believe that he'd actually meddled in her affairs to the tune of two hundred and fifty dollars, just to try to protect her when she came home in the fall. All that got him more tied up in thinking about her, and meeting Mr. Adams made it harder to try to talk her into staying home.

Damn it all! He'd gotten in far too deep here in the last few minutes to ever let himself kiss her. And that was good.

Because kissing her once would never be enough.

Susanna was in such a state by the time she got into the house that, at first sight of her, Maynell threw up her hands and dropped her potato-peeling knife clattering onto the table.

"What happened?" the woman asked. "Oh! Did one of them boys out there get gored?"

That thought helped jolt Susanna back to herself. "No," she said, forcing the words out past the knot of fury in her throat, "and thanks for reminding me that it could all be worse."

Maynell could never control her curiosity for a minute. "Then what is it that's next-to-worse?"

"I hired my pretend-husband and trail boss, that's all. And now he's made me so mad I could cheerfully stuff him in a sack and throw him in the river."

Maynell tilted her head in her birdlike way and looked at Susanna closely. "Well, I—" she began.

"If you say 'I told you so', Maynell, I'll swear I'll—"

Maynell put on her very best hurt look. "I'd

never say such a thing as that." She pushed back her chair to get up.

"Oh, yes, you would," Susanna said. "Don't lie to me, May. I've had enough. My new 'husband' has been lying to me all day."

Maynell shook her head wisely and padded off to the work table. "Not a good sign," she said. "A lyin' man is trouble."

Susanna jerked a chair out from under the table and dropped into it. "As soon as I can breathe again, I think I'll go out there and run him off," she said. "I know as well as I'm sitting here that he's going to try to ride off with my herd and leave me home. He doesn't think a woman should go up the trail."

Maynell poured a dipperful of water from the wooden bucket into a bowl, wet a cloth, and came back to the table with it. "Here, wash your face and calm down," she said. "You're pale as a sheet except your cheeks are flaming like you've got the scarlet fever."

Maynell sat and took up her work again. Susanna obeyed, thankfully holding the cool cloth against her hot cheeks.

"Thanks, May. This does feel good."

But Maynell was done with sympathy. "If you couldn't find no good man you could trust, if you settled fer just breath and britches, then what kind of crew do you think he'll get for you?"

Susanna gritted her teeth. That was the hardest

thing about Maynell and Jimbo living as a hired couple in the other end of the dog-trot cabin—Maynell's scoldings and preachings. But who else would work for her for no money, for only a place to live and food to eat?

"Maynell—"

"They're liable to gang up and steal your cattle and leave you lost and alone out there on the prairie somewhere . . . if they don't kill you first."

To her surprise, Susanna rushed to Eagle Jack's defense.

"He's not *that* kind of liar, Maynell."

Maynell gave the potato in her hand a vicious swipe with the knife. "I wasn't aware there was more than one kind," she said.

"Well, he's more the kind that . . . I guess you'd say he changes his mind about what he said before."

"Like what?"

"Like agreeing to my deal, then an hour later trying to back out on taking me up the trail with my cattle."

Maynell's tight mouth turned up at the corners. "Well, he might be forgiven for that," she said wryly, "depending on what all you did and said in that hour."

"Thanks a lot, May."

But Susanna smiled, too, in spite of herself.

Maynell was irritating beyond belief, but she did have a way of putting things into perspective.

Eagle Jack probably had expected to go to the bank, get his money, pay her back for his bail, and talk her into letting him out of the agreement they'd made.

Well, she had fooled him, hadn't she?

"I picked the crew," Susanna said, "at least part of it. We hired three men."

"I seen 'em ride in," May said. "Tucker put 'em right to work. And Jimbo, too—he's buildin' a fire for the brandin'."

"Well, that's good," Susanna said. "We're wanting to head out day after tomorrow at the latest."

Maynell got up again and brought Susanna a cup of cool water. "Now," she said, "tell me about that big Indian."

Susanna stopped in mid-swallow and stared at her.

"I'm old but I ain't blind yet," May said. "I seen that long black hair and that handsome profile from the porch." She smiled and looked off out the open door as if she could still see him. "Rides like a Comanche, too," she said, musing to herself. "Always did like a handsome man who could ride."

It was true. Eagle Jack was a handsome man. Horseback or not, any woman would turn her head to look at him twice. Or three times.

"He's a Cherokee," Susanna said. "His name is Eagle Jack Sixkiller."

"Pretty name," Maynell murmured. "Always did like a handsome man with a handsome name." Then she fixed her steely gaze on Susanna and picked up her knife to get to work again. "Where'd you find him?"

Susanna told her the story from the minute she'd walked into the Salado Jail to the moment Eagle Jack had ridden away and left her down at the corral. In detail. Maynell, who hardly ever went anywhere, demanded detail in her stories because stories were few and far between. Brushy Creek had few visitors.

But in this story Maynell especially wanted detail because she—judging him completely on looks, of course—was so taken with Eagle Jack.

But the main reason Susanna didn't mind telling every detail was that it gave her a chance to try to figure him out.

"You see, May, in the jail I instinctively thought that I could trust him, that he was an honorable man. But it wasn't an hour later that he was saying he *wouldn't* take me up the trail and he's been back and forth on everything ever since."

Maynell gave her that narrow-eyed, suspicious look of hers.

"What d'you mean by 'everything'?"

"Then he said he *will* take me up the trail and that we'll talk over all the decisions except when it's life or death—at which point, he'll gag and tie me and throw me in the wagon—"

Maynell chuckled heartily. Susanna refused to dignify that with an acknowledgment.

"—yet *he* decides we need extra help with the branding so we can get on the trail fast, and then he scares me half to death to make me agree to it. He's paying for it, now I'm in his debt."

"Hmm," Maynell said. "Sounds like a sensible man."

Susanna set her glass down, hard, and frowned at her.

"Whose side are you on here, anyhow, Maynell?"

"Does he have brown eyes?" Maynell asked.

"What difference does that make?"

"I always did like a brown-eyed handsome man."

"You're acting like a silly schoolgirl, Maynell." Then Susanna smiled. "He has a grin that could melt an iceberg," she confessed.

"Well, thank the Lord," Maynell said. "Up till now, I was thinking you'd plumb lost all your senses."

"He's a charmer," Susanna said. "He's used to getting his way with women. And so he doesn't know what to do with me."

Maynell gave a low chuckle.

"Oh, I'd bet he does, honey. All you have to do is give him a chance."

Susanna was horrified.

"Maynell! *You've* lost *your* senses."

"Well, I know I told you hiring a stranger to pretend to be your husband was foolishness, but now I'm thinking you've made a right fine choice."

"Good Lord, Maynell! You're only saying that because he's brown-eyed and handsome."

"Always did like a brown-eyed handsome man who'd speak right up and tell you how it's gonna be," Maynell said. She fixed Susanna with that look again. "He's one in a million, girl. You oughtta nab onto him."

Sometimes Susanna wondered why she'd ever let Maynell and Jimbo live in the other end of her cabin. This was one of those times.

"Listen to me, Maynell. My 'right fine choice,' Mr. Brown-Eyed Handsome One-in-a-Million, has just gotten me in a whole lot of trouble. He insulted Mr. Adams and insisted on buying that whole remuda and now I'm in even more debt to him. Big debt."

Maynell listened, wide-eyed.

"Mr. Adams has an interest in the bank. He can probably make them foreclose on this place if I don't come back from Abilene with enough money."

"Why did he insult old Adams?"

"Adams was implying that he'd rather take his pay in another way than money."

"Always did like a handsome man that'd step up and take a handle on any situation," Maynell said.

"Maynell! Listen. Worse than putting me two hundred and fifty dollars in his debt is that he did not consult me. He took over, don't you understand that? He overturned a decision that I had already made."

Maynell just looked at her and kept on peeling potatoes.

"I can't let him take over my herd and my life," Susanna said, the urgency rising in her again. "What if he takes over and doesn't consult me on any decision and I'm just the cook all the way up the trail and when we get to Abilene he takes over the sale of the cattle and everything?"

"You jist said he ain't the kind of liar to steal your cattle."

"Well, he's not. Actually, he isn't really a liar . . . in a way. He just keeps changing his mind about—"

"About what to do with you," Maynell said. "Well, you can't blame him for that. It's a big question, missy, because you are a handful, if I do say so myself."

"Thank you so much."

Susanna's tone was sarcastic but she really didn't take offense. Maynell, whom she'd never met until two years ago, was the closest thing to a mother that she'd ever had. Maynell loved her. She knew that.

Maynell was the only person who had ever truly loved her because Susanna's mother had died birthing her.

"You're looking at the debt he put you in,"

Maynell said. "And him making the decisions and all that. But that ain't why he insulted old Adams and it ain't the important thing, neither."

Susanna stared at her.

"He done it protecting your womanhood, Suzy," Maynell said. "He could've got hisself shot. You best be grateful for a man like that."

Chapter 5

Somebody came galloping up to the porch before Susanna could think of an answer to Maynell's proclamation. Thank goodness.

Much more of this drivel from Maynell and she'd be giving her whole world over to Eagle Jack and thinking about what he really meant by what he said and did and obeying his every command like a puppy dog. It was already turning her mind to mush and filling her with a bunch of confusing feelings.

She got up and went to the open door. It was Jimbo, bareback on Buster, the one mule that she had not yet been forced to sell. Jimbo rode in a circle in the yard, as if he didn't have time to stop and talk. She stepped out onto the porch.

"Susanna!" he called. "Boss wants you to come

down to the herd. Big pow-wow about what the trail brand's gonna be."

He rode away, hunched over the neck of the big mule like a jockey, looking about as big as a fly. The normally solemn Jimbo was surely in his sixties, but now he was as excited as a boy.

Susanna watched him race back to the herd. Well, well. Another staunch supporter for Eagle Jack?

Surely *Jimbo* wasn't taken with him because he was a brown-eyed handsome man.

When she came back from Abilene, she must see to it that Jimbo and Maynell got out more. They needed to go to town, see other people. She'd send them for supplies instead of going herself.

"Maynell," she called, as she strode back into the house, "I've been summoned by the boss."

"I heard," Maynell said. "That's good. See there, he ain't makin' all the decisions. He's askin' your opinion on the brand."

"Which is the least he could do, considering they are my cattle," Susanna pointed out.

She went into her bedroom to get a fresh bandana, glancing at herself in the mirror as she passed the dresser.

It wouldn't hurt to have a fresh shirt, too. She was covered with dust from the road and the corral, plus she needed to feel her most confident in this confrontation, which it certainly would be.

When had she and Eagle Jack ever had a conversation that wasn't a confrontation?

The way she looked would affect how much her authority would be accepted by the men. She went to the armoire and rifled through her meager pieces of clothing.

"Not the tan," she muttered to herself. "Surely my other blue shirt isn't dirty."

She found it. It was made of a slightly heavier cloth than the one she had on but if she got too hot, she could change back later. She would change, anyhow, when she came back to the house to help Maynell cook supper for the men.

Thank goodness, she had washed the dust off her face.

She unbuckled her belt, started pulling out the tail of her dirty shirt and unbuttoning it. At least the other one fit her—it was a real woman's blouse and not one of Everett's old shirts like this one was.

Once changed, she took her time tucking in the blouse and buckling her belt a notch tighter than before. She did think her waist was getting smaller. Maybe she was losing weight, as Maynell had been saying. She stepped closer to the mirror.

Only to get the bandana out of the dresser drawer.

But she did look into the mirror, too. Yes. This shirt was exactly the same blue as her eyes.

She smoothed back her hair, then took it loose

from the scrap of braided ribbon that bound it at the nape of her neck. Funny. She and Eagle Jack wore their hair the very same way but he had his tied with a leather thong.

His hair was so black it had blue lights in it. It was beautifully thick.

But she wasn't interested in his hair or his brown eyes or his handsome profile. She'd better remember her goal.

She combed out her hair, then gathered it up in one hand and picked up the ribbon with the other. The real boss of this outfit was Susanna Copeland, and the men needed to know it. Neatness would help her establish that.

Turning away from the mirror, she went back into the main room to get her hat.

"Well, sakes alive," Maynell said, from the stove where she was putting the potatoes on to boil, "you're looking mighty clean and fresh. They's some vanilla over there in the pie safe, in case you want to dab some on behind your ears."

That just flew all over Susanna. "I'm only trying to wear an air of authority," she said. "The men won't be getting close enough to smell me, May."

"Most of 'em won't," Maynell responded, her little eyes twinkling.

Susanna slapped her hat onto her head and stalked out the door without another word.

Maynell loved to get her goat. Well, she wasn't going to succeed.

Fred was still ground-tied where she'd left him, and as she gathered the reins and swung up into the saddle, she tried to concentrate on the details of the drive. Tonight and tomorrow wouldn't be much time to finish stocking the wagon and thinking about what all she'd need, in the way of equipment and staples. She just had to be careful that she left enough for Maynell and Jimbo to survive on.

At least that was one area where Eagle Jack wouldn't be meddling—the chuck wagon.

Jimbo, Eagle Jack, Tucker, and Marvin were sitting their horses, talking, while the other men rode around the herd. They all touched their hat brims when she arrived, and Eagle Jack and Marvin opened the circle to let her in between them.

"We're talking about a trail brand, Susanna," Eagle Jack said. "We need something easy to do with a running iron."

"Of course," she said. "I'm going to use an 'S.' For Susanna."

To her complete shock, Eagle Jack nodded agreeably.

"That'll work," he said.

She was so taken aback that she stared at him for a minute.

Wasn't he going to find some objection, some

way to argue with her and undermine her authority?

Well, whatever he did, this was a battle for the respect of the men. A struggle to decide, before the drive ever started, whether she'd be only the cook or the owner first and the cook second and the way to do that was to prove she wasn't a greenhorn.

"The 'S' is easy and fast," she said, "only one stroke. And it has no corners to burn too deep."

Eagle Jack nodded again. "Good thinking," he said.

Yes, he was agreeing with her, but she did consider his tone a bit condescending. And the remark, too, come to think of it.

"I've been ranching on my own ever since my hus—my first husband . . . died," she said. "I learned about branding then."

"Main thing we couldn't do was catch 'em," Jimbo volunteered.

Susanna turned and stared at him, hoping the look would shut him up.

But he shook his head ruefully and rambled on.

"Danged if'n' we didn't come right near gittin' ourselves killed," he said. "Ain't no good at brushpoppin', me and Miz Suzy here."

Great. Jimbo hadn't said that many words all strung together since he'd been at Brushy Creek. Now, at this moment, he had to get a flapping jaw and make her look like a tenderfoot when she'd just made a little bit of progress toward being the boss. You'd think Eagle Jack was paying him.

"Now, Jimbo," she said. "You have to admit we did catch quite a few," she said.

She looked at Marvin and Tucker, mostly Marvin because he'd be on the trail.

"You'll find some cattle that are already branded," she said. "That'll show you the way I want the brand to look—slanted to the left."

The men, including Eagle Jack, were looking at her solemnly. They nodded. Were they humoring her?

"We'll get it done," Eagle Jack said. He lifted his reins as if to turn his horse back toward the herd, then he stopped in midmotion. "Susanna, dear," he said, giving her that charming grin of his, "you'll make us some pie for supper, won't you? I was telling the men that we'll have pie on the trail."

"Yes, ma'am," Tucker said. "If'n' I wasn't so scared of water and crossin' rivers, I'd sign on right now to go with you all. Won't be no other camp with pie, 'least not too often."

Well. What *was* it about being around Eagle Jack? Tucker normally didn't talk any more than Jimbo did, and here he was, making a speech.

Susanna fought her flaring temper and stared at Eagle Jack.

"Maynell has already started supper," she said.

"I'll have to see what she's got planned."

"I'm thinking you're the boss," Eagle Jack said. He said it flatly, as if that settled the matter.

So now if there was no pie for supper, all the men would know it was her fault. She wanted to strangle him for that, not to mention for the fact of the hollow words themselves. He didn't intend for her to be the boss of anything.

"And, since we haven't been married long enough for me to try your pie," he said clearly, "I'm looking forward to it as much as Tucker is."

"So'm I, ma'am," blurted the apparently shy and reticent Marvin. He blushed at his own boldness and tugged at his hat. "Thank ye very much, ma'am," he said, even more softly.

Susanna bit her tongue and grabbed her saddle horn to keep from attacking Eagle Jack, both verbally and physically. She longed to reach out and slap him with the ends of her reins, right across his thigh, that hard thigh bulging with saddle muscles beneath his tight, faded jeans.

"I have to pack the chuck wagon," she said. "If we're leaving day after tomorrow, I need to make sure it has everything."

"Right you are," Eagle Jack agreed, turning his horse to get back to the work. "Build you a fire and cook outside tonight for a dry run. Only way to ever know what all you really need."

They started turning their horses to get to the work, but Eagle Jack had a final shot to make.

"You know, darling," he said, "we ought to sleep outside tonight. Let's put up your tent and try it out, too."

He spoke just low enough for that to appear to be the private communication it should have been, but loud enough for all three of the men to hear. In fact, the one of Marvin's friends who was riding past on that side of the herd looked over at them. He had heard, too.

Susanna had to answer. They were all looking at her from the corners of their eyes. Listening, too.

"I'll see what I can do," she said in her sweetest voice.

Then she choked, so she turned her horse and headed for the house. She was going to horsewhip him. She had no choice.

Maynell helped her set up boards across the two barrels to make a table out in the yard and she helped her carry the supper to it just before sundown, but Maynell was not happy about the extra work. However, the main thing Maynell was not happy about was that Eagle Jack had asked for pie and he wasn't getting any.

Susanna set her jaw. "May, I cannot jump every time he says 'frog,'" she said. "If I did, I couldn't live with myself."

Maynell scowled as only she could do. "You'd best be thinking about living with *him*. After all, he is your husband."

"He is *not*. You're losing your mind. Pretending that it's true doesn't make it so."

"For the next three months he might as *well* be your husband."

"What do you mean by that?" Susanna asked.

But Maynell wouldn't say anything more.

Susanna rolled her eyes as she rang the dinner triangle. "You don't get out enough," she said. "You've got to start going into town once in a while."

"Hmpf," said Maynell.

Susanna shifted the basket of hot bear sign to the other end of the table and gathered the tin cups for the coffee. Sweets were scarce, and the yeasty doughnutlike fried treats called bear sign were scarcer still in the cow camps. The men would appreciate the dessert and Eagle Jack *wouldn't* get his way.

She should never have told May what Eagle Jack said about the two of them sleeping outside tonight in her tent.

But if she argued with her too much, May would go to her end of the cabin in a huff and quit helping entirely.

No, she wouldn't. She wanted to see Eagle Jack up close.

"Maynell, you need to be helping me think what I can do with him tonight."

"Already did," Maynell said, with a dreamy smile.

"You know what I mean," Susanna said sternly.

"Yes, ma'am, I surely do."

Susanna laughed reluctantly. "All right, get your mind on the supper," she said. "Here they come."

Actually, she did feel remarkably light-hearted at the moment, despite May's grumbling. She had refused to let Eagle Jack dictate to her, yet, by bringing the food outside and serving some kind of dessert, even if it wasn't pie, she was putting on a show of cooperation with his orders that would satisfy the men of the reality—and happiness—of their marriage. At least, it should.

Two men stayed with the herd and the rest washed up quickly at the pan she'd set up beneath the big sycamore tree. Studiously, she ignored Eagle Jack and busied herself with the food.

But, after he'd dried his hands and started walking toward the table, he called to her.

"What kind of pie do we have, Susanna, dear?"

She glanced up. "No pie," she told him. "I've been packing the wagon."

Marvin and Tucker were right behind him, and at this news, their faces fell.

"We have bear sign instead," she said to them.

Not to Eagle Jack. She wasn't going to report to him.

He walked up to the table and picked up a plate from the stack. Maynell dipped him some baked beans.

"Miss Susanna's saving the dried fruit for the trail," she said, smiling up at him as she served his plate. "I tried my best, but I couldn't talk her out of any of it to make pie."

Susanna wanted to shake her.

"Maynell, this is Eagle Jack Sixkiller," Susanna said. "Eagle Jack, Maynell Hawkins. Jimbo's wife."

"Maynell," he said, with a gallant nod to acknowledge the introduction. "I thank you for trying. I'm already learning that sometimes it's mighty hard to get past Miss Susanna."

He gave her a big smile.

Maynell gave him another dipperful of beans. "Always did like a brown-eyed handsome man," she said, flirting with him. " 'Specially one who'd tell the truth and tell it straight."

They laughed together like naughty children.

"Yes, Eagle Jack told the truth," Susanna said, forcing a smile past her irritation. "So why don't y'all quit trying to get past me and do what I say?"

"No fun in that," they said, together, and laughed again.

Susanna sighed. Now they'd be buddies for sure. Thank goodness, Maynell wasn't going with them up the trail.

Eagle Jack gave her a great big smile, too, as she served him potato salad and then he served himself some sliced beef and biscuits. "This food looks delicious, Susanna dear," he said.

"It is," she responded. "Maynell and I are both good cooks."

"And very sure of yourselves, too," he said, with a retaliatory gleam in his eye.

Fine. Let him try to boss her around some more. They might as well get this settled before they hit the trail.

The men ate quickly and in silence, as was the cowboy custom, then, one by one they finished and threw their plates into Maynell's big washpan.

"Come get another one of these bear signs," Susanna called. "I made 'em for y'all to eat."

"Thank you, ma'am, for the meal," each man said, as he came by the table for another one.

Except for Eagle Jack. "Hope you get your wagon packed," he said. "Tomorrow's gonna be a busy day."

By the time she finally finished the work and started to get ready for bed, Susanna didn't even care what he'd meant by that. This had been a day to end all days.

And the last thing she would even consider doing now was set up her tent and sleep on the ground out there in the dust.

She pulled the brush through her hair one last time. Then she laid it on the dresser and smiled at her reflection.

Eagle Jack would learn that if he persisted in

giving her orders in front of the men, he would be the one who ended up embarrassed. He had better not be giving her orders at all.

Except maybe in times of danger on the trail.

Those images floated through her mind again, cattle skulls and dry marches, outlaw rustlers and swift rivers like Tucker feared. Then she'd be glad to let Eagle Jack take control.

She wasn't afraid, not really, but she shivered a little. The spring night was turning chilly.

There might even be times when it was cold on the trail, even though it would be full summer before they got out of Texas. There might be hailstorms, too, and with them the temperature could drop thirty degrees or more in only minutes.

She'd packed a slicker and Everett's old jean jacket jumper, but not her one wool shawl. She got up, went to the armoire in the corner, and began to look through its meager contents.

What she ought to take along in case it hailed was one of the board shelves. A hailstorm had come up when her neighbor Walt Terry's men were up by the Red River with not one scrap of shelter for miles. Finally they had held their saddles over their heads—it was the only protection they could find.

She stood still for a minute and tried to imagine how that would be. It would need to be a very fast-moving hailstorm if she were in that situation because, strong as she was, a saddle would get very heavy in a very big hurry. Maybe they would be lucky and not be in a hailstorm.

Or any other kind of storm. Everybody said lightning storms could make cattle and cowboys both go crazy and it was a fact that they often caused a stampede.

Her stomach tightened and she closed her eyes, but against the black of her eyelids she saw the cattle running beneath a wild, dark sky full of white flashing lightning. She could just hear their hooves pounding, loud as the thunder.

Living out under the sky for months at a time was going to be a risky thing. Besides the weather, there could be rustlers and toll-taking farmers and other herds trying to get the same grass. Besides deep rivers to cross, there could be wild animals and prairie fires.

She opened her eyes, straightened her shoulders, and stiffened her spine. What she had to do was quit worrying and start gathering her strength because she was surely going to need it.

"Reckon you can find me an extra blanket or some kind of soogan in there?"

Eagle Jack's low voice.

"Dear Lord," she cried, whirling to face him, "you nearly scared me to *death*! What are you *doing* in here?"

He was near enough to touch and she hadn't heard the sound of his steps. He filled her bedroom. His shoulders were broader than she'd even realized and his head nearly brushed the ceiling.

But it was *he* who made her private space his, with his pulsing, unbounded, impetuous energy. And his boldness.

And his own wonderful smell, mixed with those of horse and leather and dust and sweat.

"I'm in my *nightgown,*" she said, clasping her hands across her breasts.

"Yes, you are," he said. "And even more beautiful with your hair all long and loose."

But it wasn't only her hair that he was looking at. His gleaming dark eyes moved over her, head to toe.

She couldn't stop looking at him, either. The lamplight limned his face and threw it into high relief as it hit his high cheekbones and the haughty line of his nose.

A brown-eyed, handsome man.

And well he knew it.

"Eagle Jack," she said, as she forced her breathing to slow, "what are you doing in here?"

He grinned. He looked tired, he really did, but he grinned with a mischief that nearly made her grin back.

She couldn't. What if he, like Maynell, had decided he "might as well" be her husband for the next three months?

"Hunting a bedroll," he drawled, then cast a

lazy glance at the bed, already turned down for the night. "Mine got stolen."

Then that speculative glance of his came back to her and took her breath.

It was just because no one had ever looked at her like that, never in her whole life. As if she were the most desirable woman in the entire world.

Finally, she said, "Well, you don't have to sound so pitiful." She squared her shoulders and got hold of herself. "And you didn't have to invade my room," she added, a sharp tone in her voice.

She had to get him out of here or reach out and touch him. Like Maynell, she was losing her mind.

"If you'd pitched us a tent like I asked you to, I wouldn't even have had to come in the house and disturb your comfort."

That roused her hackles. But still she couldn't look away from him.

"Oh? Everything's always my fault, is it?"

"I'd say so," he said. "And it's because you're too damn stubborn to listen to reason. Now where can I find a bedroll?"

"In the wagon," she shot back. "Mine's already in there."

"Fine."

"Fine."

Neither one of them would break the stare.

"But I'm not going out there after it," he said. "Give me one of those quilts in that cabinet or I'm crawling into your bed. My headache's back with a vengeance."

Remorse stabbed her in the heart. He *was* hurt, after all, and he'd been working in spite of it, branding her cattle.

But she pushed the feeling away. She had to get him out of here.

Plus it was his own fault he was hurt and his own fault he was branding her cattle.

"From now on, maybe you'll stay out of drunken brawls," she said.

She turned her back on him and pulled out a quilt. Then another, her only other one.

He took another step closer, she could feel it.

"I wasn't in a drunken brawl," he said. "If you don't believe me on that, how can you trust me with your cattle?"

She spun around.

"And your life?" he said.

She thrust the quilts into his arms.

"Here," she said. "Go on and lie down. I'll fix a poultice for your head."

"No," he said. "Leave it." He turned away, walked to the lamp on the dresser, lifted the chimney, and blew out the flame.

"What are you *doing*?"

"Going to bed."

He walked past her to the windows on the

south wall, started spreading out a quilt on the floor beneath them.

"Well, not *here*, you aren't," she cried.

"Then where?" he asked.

He sat, toed off his boots, stretched out full length and pulled the other quilt over him for cover. The moonlight poured in and fell across his big form, peacefully, as if her heart weren't clattering in her chest.

"Out . . . side," she ordered.

"Why, darlin'," he said, in his teasing drawl, "we don't want the men to think we're havin' trouble, now do we?"

"Eagle Jack, sometimes you make me so mad."

"Sweet Susanna, don't worry. I won't bother you tonight."

He was asleep before she got to her bed.

For the longest ever, she couldn't even close her eyes.

I won't bother you tonight.

Tonight.

What had he meant by that?

Chapter 6

Did he mean that some night he *would* bother her?

After they were on the trail, after they'd left Brushy Creek far behind?

Susanna forced her body to lean back and lie flat. She sank her head into the pillow while she stared at the shadowy ceiling. Eagle Jack was a mystery to her, that was for sure. Only this morning she'd found him in jail, addled from drink and that blow on his head, yet on this same day he'd worked like two men with her cattle.

He'd been jailed as a drunk, yet he handled himself with the confidence of a land baron. He hadn't had the money to bail himself out, yet after he'd gone to the bank he'd bought a saddle and a horse and, after that, all the lease horses from Mr. Adams.

Eagle Jack Sixkiller. Who was he?

Susanna sat up carefully to look at him, as if studying his face would give her the answer. She needn't have bothered to be quiet. His breath came deep and slow, a little rough, as if he was very tired, which he must certainly be. The night wasn't a dark one and she could see that his head rested on one crooked arm.

She should've given him a pillow. That was the least she could've done—if for no other reason, out of old-fashioned hospitality.

Or, more basically, out of human compassion. What was it about him that unsettled her so completely that she couldn't think or find her manners?

His looks. The power in his dark eyes. The force of him—his smile, his voice, his implacable will.

I won't bother you tonight.

What if some other night he did? Would she be able to resist him?

Of course she would. What was she thinking?

She threw off the sheet and swung her legs off the bed. It was time to quit being fanciful and get to sleep, get ready for the hard day coming up tomorrow, but first, common decency demanded that she find the man a pillow. He'd have a terrible crick in his neck in the morning.

And a paralysis in his arm, which most likely had no blood circulation now. He would need his arms tomorrow to ride and rope and get her cattle ready for the trail.

That was why she wanted to make him comfortable. She really wasn't doing it just for him. He didn't deserve any consideration because he'd been too bold. Entirely too bold.

What a nerve he had—barging into her room like this and falling asleep on the floor! If Maynell ever found out, she'd never quit carrying on about it.

The other two pillows Susanna owned were already in the wagon, ready to go up the trail. She could do without one tonight.

Snatching hers from the bed, she padded in her bare feet across the plank floor. It would be easy to slip the pillow beneath his head without waking him since he was sleeping so soundly—it would take only a moment, and then, her conscience eased, she would be able to sleep.

He lay on his back, with his face turned toward her, his head resting on his bent arm. The other arm was flung out in utter abandon.

Like an exhausted child's. But there was nothing else childlike about him—he was the manliest man she had ever known. That undercurrent of power that she always felt in him was still there, even in sleep.

It sent her blood pulsing faster in her veins. He was silly and funny and he did impulsive things, like buying Adams's horses, and he was not half serious enough about life in general, but she'd known from the moment she'd laid eyes on him, from the moment she'd known he was honest, that whoever he was, Eagle Jack Sixkiller was a dangerous man.

The moonlight fell across his face. It lit the fierce curve of his nose and the sharpness of his cheekbone. It shone off his hair, long and black, spread underneath his shoulder.

It could have been paint, streaking across his copper skin as a declaration of war. She could just see him, naked and astride a barebacked horse, fitting a flaming arrow into his bow, riding at the head of a band of Cherokee warriors.

He was a big man, and, dear Lord help her, a handsome man. Maynell had reason to be besotted.

It was just a good thing that she, Susanna, was a much more practical, no-nonsense woman, a woman who'd had all the experiences with men that she ever wanted and more. Any entanglement with a man was a recipe for trouble. That was a lesson she'd learned at a very young age. She would never forget it.

She had just turned fifteen back in the mountains of her native Tennessee, when Mathias Hawthorne started hanging around while she did her outside chores at Uncle Job's place. He helped her chop the wood and carry water up from the river when the well went dry. They talked about running away to Chattanooga together.

He even kissed her on the mouth, so she really thought he loved her. She really thought he would take her away from there.

But the first time Uncle Job caught him carrying the water buckets and her walking alongside, talking and laughing, Mathias got so scared he set the buckets down and ran. He never looked back. He never *came* back.

Mathias turned out to be the biggest coward in the county. Mathias didn't love her and he never had.

And then, of course, there was Everett. Everett, who was older, Everett, who already had saved up a hundred dollars. Everett, who was talking about going to Texas.

He had gone right up to Uncle Job the second time he had seen Susanna at the general store and asked for permission to come calling on her. The third time he came to the house and sat on the porch with her, he had asked Uncle Job for her hand.

Susanna had felt a terrible disappointment that he hadn't asked her first, but she was desperate by then. Everett treated her well enough, she supposed, and he could get her out of there. He could take her away from being the poor orphaned relation with no home.

At least he wanted her to go with him to Texas.

No one else had ever wanted her to go anywhere or to do anything except the hard work.

It hadn't been three days on the road until she knew that Everett wanted her for that same reason. She could do the hard work. And besides that, she could cook his meals and keep his bed warm.

Everett had done more than kiss her on the mouth, but he hadn't loved her, either.

Her arms tightened around the feather pillow.

She didn't want to get tangled up with any man, ever again, but she did want to try to make Eagle Jack more comfortable. He had a bad headache and he needed this pillow.

When she put it under his head, she would have to touch him. She *wanted* to touch him.

The moonlight moved then, danced gently across his face as the branches of the big live oak tree moved outside the window. The breeze, cool and sweet, drifted into the room and brought the night with it to fill her senses.

No, her senses were already filled with Eagle Jack. He had washed up but the smells of horse and dust were still on him and she could also catch the scent that was uniquely his. She couldn't look at anything else but his face in the moonlight.

His breathing was so close, so intimate, that the sounds of the cattle and the nightbirds seemed far, far away.

He turned then, shifted onto his side and toward her as if he felt her watching him. The moonbeam drifted back and forth over his lips. He had the most sensual lips in the world.

How did they taste? What would it be like to kiss him?

The thought came with such an overwhelming urge to find out that it shocked her. She had to get away from him, pillow or no pillow.

Yet she didn't move. The breeze strengthened. It lifted her hair that was falling all about her face and shoulders and brushed it against her cheek.

How would it feel if it were Eagle Jack's fingers brushing against her skin, instead?

Again, the little frisson of fear raced through her blood. What would it be like on the trail with him—with all the men believing that they were married?

Why, darlin', we don't want the men to think we're havin' trouble, now do we?

Would he come into her tent at night the way he had come into her room? What would she say or do if he did?

They needed to have a talk about that remark of his and reach an agreement before they ever started north.

But what would he say or do if she brought it up?

She shook her hair back and made herself stop imagining. She couldn't even think right. How could he do this to her when he was *asleep*?

Resolutely, she knelt beside him. Get this done, get back in bed, get to sleep. Get on the trail tomorrow.

One day. She had known this man for one day and he was taking over her thoughts and her imaginings. She would have no more of that.

Susanna lifted his head gently and, when he moved his arm, she began to slip the pillow into place. But a bruise ran from his cheekbone down across his jaw, and in the moonlight she could see that the knot on the back of his head had grown since Salado.

She should make a poultice for it. She had mentioned it, and he had refused, true, but she should've insisted.

Eagle Jack could've ridden off and left her the minute he was free and out on the street. Instead, he'd kept his word and, as Maynell had pointed out, he had not only worked her cattle but had risked getting shot for her sake.

Gratitude or not, though, she had no call to be sitting here on her knees all night, holding his head. Her fingertips brushed along the line of his jaw as she slipped her hand out from between his head and the pillow.

She let them touch him again and linger, then she skimmed them across the aristocratic rise of his cheekbone. His looks were a fascination to her.

That thought brought her scrambling to her feet. She was losing her reason, and that was no condition to be in while trying to drive a herd of cattle across a pasture, much less for hundreds of miles.

Silently, she berated herself as she made her way through the dark room and into the kitchen. She had been chary of her feelings for her whole life, she guessed. Especially since she'd been old enough to know that her mother died and left her when she was born. All her growing up, her cousins and aunts had called her the no-nonsense one because all her life she had kept a strict control on her emotions. Now here she was, on the eve of her biggest venture, going off into some dream world that didn't make a lick of sense.

Forcing her mind onto practical matters, which was where it almost always stayed, she went to the box of medical supplies that she'd already packed. She took out the jar of antipholgistine and set it on top of the stove, which was still warm enough to soften its sticky, waxy consistency. Then she cut a circle of cloth from the tough canvas scrap in the bottom of the box and held it against the stove to warm it, too.

As soon as she had doctored him, she'd get into bed. As soon as she got into bed, she'd go to sleep. Her conscience would be satisfied, and she would sleep.

This racing of her heart would slow to a normal pace and she would stop thinking about how his mouth looked in the moonlight.

She would forget about the feel of his thick hair falling like heavy water through her fingers and the feel of the impervious line of his jaw. That hard jaw was one more thing about him that was so at odds with the mischief in his eye and the silliness in his banter.

But she wasn't going to think about him anymore. She would sleep, and when she woke in the morning, she'd be herself again. He would be her trail boss instead of the fascinating, mysterious man who'd barged into her bedroom, and as business associates, they would start north with her cattle.

And his remuda.

To put a fine point on it, the horses that would be supporting all their lives, human and bovine alike, belonged to Eagle Jack.

While she spread a layer of the salve on the circle of cloth, she thought about that. It didn't worry her the way it should—the way it would if, say, Mr. Adams still owned them and was going along for the ride. Somehow, deep inside, although he'd barged into her room and talked about bothering her, she still trusted Eagle Jack implicitly.

He wouldn't hold the horses over her as leverage to demand sex or anything like that.

She stopped and took a deep breath, plus a firm handle on her wild thoughts. Hadn't she already decided that she wasn't going to let herself think about him anymore?

Desperately she forced her mind to everyday details and their place in the fight for survival. Yes, she had put an extra bedroll in the wagon in case one of their drovers lost his in a river crossing or some other disaster. Yes, she had her box of medical supplies ready to go. Yes, she had two spare sets of clothes for herself, plus a dress—her only good dress—for when they got to Abilene. It was for the meeting with the cattle buyer.

A vision of herself in the dress, dancing with Eagle Jack in the street in Abilene, flashed across her mind.

Foolishness. She didn't even know how to dance.

She scraped the residue off the broad knife and twisted the lid onto the jar.

This would teach Eagle Jack to come barging into her room for the night. He'd get poulticed whether he wanted to or not.

She carried the patch, sticky side up, into the bedroom through the moonlight, which seemed to be growing stronger by the minute. Eagle Jack seemed still asleep, although his breathing wasn't as deep. Thank goodness, he'd turned more to his side so it'd be easier to get to the wound.

Susanna knelt and used her free hand to hold his hair to one side. She bent over to study the swollen wound in the moonlight, centered the patch on her fingertips, and brought it forward carefully, so as not to get it stuck in his hair.

A hand caught her arm, she screamed, and the patch went flying. Eagle Jack sat up, narrowly missing bumping heads with her as he turned and she tried to pull away.

"What do you think you're doing?" he growled.

He looked so angry that it scared her for an instant.

"D-doctoring your wound," she said, forcing the air back into her lungs so she could speak. "What I should've done the minute we got here."

"With what?"

"Antipholgistine."

That widened his eyes again.

"Why don't you just shave my head? Or, better yet, you might scalp me."

"I was being careful not to get it in your hair," she said.

"Except that the *wound* is in my hair."

"It's at the edge," she said. "Sort of."

He gave her a narrow-eyed look that forced her to defend herself.

"Once the poultice dried out, in a day or two, it would come off without too much damage," she said.

"You hoped."

"I know it," she said.

"Susanna," he said, speaking slowly in a hard tone, "nobody touches my hair. My hair is my power."

She held his fierce gaze. The moonlight was streaming in now, yellow and wild, bringing out the copper lights in his skin.

"I didn't know the Cherokee believed that," she said.

"Most do. We of the Texas remnant of the Nation are said to be old-fashioned."

His eyes burned into hers. If he only knew it, his *eyes* were his power.

"I'm sorry," she said, "I didn't know that about your hair."

"But you did know that I didn't want a poultice. I told you."

She shrugged.

"I thought you were just being contrary. Just being a man."

The corners of his mouth lifted.

"All men are contrary?"

"All men I've ever known."

He did smile then.

"And all women aren't?"

She smiled back.

"Some are."

"But not you?"

"Not me."

He was still holding her arm. His fingers were burning their shapes into her skin and sending their heat through it into her blood. Her breath was growing short again.

His deep, brown gaze was holding her as surely as was his hand.

"Of course *you* aren't contrary," he drawled. "You've only contradicted me at every turn all day long."

"You brought that on yourself," she said, "because you were wrong."

His grin broadened. "No. Not when I said you'd argue with a fence post."

"I *won't*," she said, and that made them both laugh.

Then they suddenly fell silent, staring into each other's eyes.

Eagle Jack couldn't move. Her mouth was only inches from his.

It was all he could think about but he wouldn't let his gaze drift downward. If he ever so much as glanced at her sensual lips, he would taste them.

The thought took him over and wouldn't let him go.

He closed the distance and kissed her. A light brushing of her lips was all he meant it to be, just enough to sample the taste of her and satisfy his curiosity.

But that first touch of his lips to hers, when she gave a little gasp of surprise and then leaned into his hand, did him in. He kissed her fiercely.

It was moonlight streaming in across them but she felt warm as sunshine to him. She tasted like the dawn wind, a new day stirring its wings.

And she kissed him back like there was no tomorrow. The way she opened to him was so immediate that it struck his heart. The sweet shock of it sent desire surging through him like a river.

She must've been wanting this all along, the way he had. Her tongue entwined with his, her lips melted beneath his, and a shiver ran through him.

Susanna stayed still on her knees and begged him with long, throbbing caresses of her tongue and light whimperings in her throat not to stop. He didn't.

He had been right at that first sight of her this morning—she was a woman passionate in every way. This could turn out to be the greatest trail drive of his life if he took her with him.

Eagle Jack slid his hand beneath the weight of her hair and caressed the nape of her neck, cupped her shoulder, and then moved his hand down to cup the fullness of one perfect breast. A perfect handful to fit in the palm of his hand.

Her mouth went still on his.

He found her nipple with his thumb and caressed it. Once. Twice. She melded her softness closer into his hand in one, brief, silent demand for more, and he gave it. He began the kiss again.

But she took her mouth away.

She turned her head from him and a strand of her hair brushed his face, soft as a feather's flight.

"No," she said, very low, almost in a whisper.

Her voice sounded sad and scared, both. Stunned, he stared at her. She looked out the open window for an instant, then she straightened her shoulders and in one fast, fluid motion, got to her feet.

"If you think you can soften me up and convince me to stay home when you couldn't *order* me to do it," she said, in her normal voice, "think again."

The words were a slap in the face, made even worse by the way she turned toward him when she said it but didn't look at him. Anger stabbed through his surprise and frustration.

"What are you *talking* about?"

Susanna started to walk past him. He caught her hand as he got to his feet.

"Talk to me, damn it. You're insulting me for no reason."

She still wouldn't look at him.

"Damn it, Susanna, you led me on. You're the one who has to explain yourself."

He took her by the shoulders and turned her to face him. Her gaze met his, then slid away.

"Let me go, Eagle Jack," she said. "I need to find that poultice."

"No, you don't."

"It's good medicine going to waste. We may

need it on the trail and I don't have money to buy any more."

Her voice wavered on the last word. That sad, scared sound was there again, and it made him feel sorry for her. She hadn't just been leading him on—something else was at work here.

"What's going to waste is that good kiss," he said, more gently.

"I told you you can't control me that way."

"I'm not trying to control you, Susanna."

That made her look at him. Her eyes flashed in the moonlight.

"You are *so!* That's *all* you've tried to do since the minute you hired on with me."

She was trembling now. The undertone of fear was in her voice more strongly.

He let her go.

"What are you scared of, Susanna? I'd never hurt you."

"I know that."

She turned and walked to the window, set her back to him.

He wanted, powerfully, to follow her, but he waited instead. She didn't say any more.

"*How* do you know it? I could be a ruthless outlaw for all you know."

"I just know it."

He waited a moment more to let her gather herself.

"Was it your husband who scared you?"

"Everett didn't exactly scare me," she said. "But he controlled me in every way he possibly could."

"How?"

"By withholding money—for food and lamp oil. He never gave me personal money, anyway. By not letting me have a horse to use as I wished, by running off the neighbors and not letting them visit me." She whirled to face him. "In general, by being a mean and petty lowlife bum who never thought about anybody's feelings except to try to manipulate them."

She stopped talking and swallowed hard. He looked for signs of tears, but she only hardened her jaw and glared at him as if he were Everett.

"And sometimes he didn't even try to manipulate, he just trampled on people's feelings instead. That's what he did the first time I ever had a social caller after we moved to Brushy Creek. Letty Martindale. He told her harshly that we didn't entertain and we didn't want visitors."

She took a long, ragged breath.

"I never had another," she said.

He was struck, suddenly, by the depth of the loneliness she must have felt. She hadn't had a friend, ever, much less someone to love her.

A quick, sharp guilt stabbed at him. All that while she'd been as alone as an eagle, he had been happily living on the Sixes and Sevens, surrounded by parents and brothers who loved him and hired hands and friends who came and went in the big headquarters house like family.

But his life hadn't been all roses and he could know a little bit about what she'd gone through by remembering the people who had turned away or who had turned him away because they didn't want anything to do with an Indian. As his grandfather would say, The Apportioner gives good and bad to every person.

That was true and he mustn't let himself feel too much sympathy for her. He mustn't take it upon himself to make her feelings his responsibility.

Her *cattle* were his responsibility. That was all.

"And you think that's what I am? A mean and petty lowlife bum?" he said.

"No," she said.

She looked at him, really looked at him, while his heart made the strangest rhythm of fast beats.

"I'll tell you straight," she said. "I'm scared of you because you're just the opposite of Everett."

He listened. But she didn't go on.

"And . . . ?" he said.

"And right now I have no idea what a little bit of kindness and desire could do to me."

He stared at her as the words stabbed through him. That was the most pitiful thing he had ever heard. And she was entirely serious about it.

"Well," he drawled, as he fought the urge to go to her, "it couldn't make you stay at home, I can tell you that, right now." He sat back down on his pallet and reached for his other quilt. "I could've told you that the first time I saw you, so you needn't be accusing me of trying to seduce you into submission."

He lay down and pulled his cover over him as he turned away from her, then he made a show of a great yawn as he thumped the pillow. What he wanted to do was to get up and go put his arms around her.

But she would shy at that. He wanted her coming to him, not shying away.

He wanted to show her what a little bit of kindness and desire could do to her. What they could do *for* her.

For his own peace of mind, that shouldn't be what he was wanting. But it was.

"Go to bed, Susanna," he said. "Morning comes early on the trail."

That remark committed him and he'd have to take her along, but then, actually, that had been true from the start.

It was certain he wouldn't leave her here now. He had a feeling old Everett couldn't hold a candle to the smiling Mr. Adams when it came to control. Not to mention trampling on a woman's feelings.

After what seemed an age, she walked past him and went to her bed.

"Good night, Eagle Jack," she said, as calmly as if they'd slept in the same room all their lives.

"Good night, Susanna," he answered. "Pleasant dreams."

Then he lay there wide-eyed. The pillow held her wonderful fragrance and the taste of her was still on his lips.

He could hear her soft breath like a whisper in the dark.

What had he done here tonight? He'd said he would take her up the trail, for one thing.

And he'd proved out his suspicion that if he kissed her once he'd have to kiss her again.

Restlessly, he rolled onto his other side so he could watch the moon out the window. It didn't help. He could still feel Susanna in the room as close as if he were still touching her.

This was insanity, pure and simple.

He never, ever, should've taken her offer. Not even if he'd had to dig himself out of the Salado Jail with the spoon they brought with his coffee.

Could she even swim? The river crossings were what most of the drovers dreaded the worst.

And the dry drives. He'd hate to see her lips cracked and her eyes wild with thirst and not be able to do anything about it.

Not to mention all the men, of all colors, who might see her. He would have to watch her constantly.

How could he do that and look for Molly, too?

His head began to feel dizzy, the moon swam before his eyes, and his lids drifted closed. He was not a worrier, he never had been, but if it weren't for this concussion or whatever was wrong with his head, he would never sleep tonight.

Once it went away, he might never sleep again.

Chapter 7

The next day was so hectic that Susanna barely saw Eagle Jack, and she was glad. She had been on the edge of losing control of her feelings last night, and she needed a day to get her balance again. She needed a *week,* if she let herself think about kissing him again.

Which she would not. She had too many other, more important things on her mind. The packing was the most important, along with the branding, and when Eagle Jack rode up from the herd about ten o'clock in the morning to tell her to hurry it up, she was proud of how businesslike their exchange was.

She reported exactly how much more she had to load and that the mules were already in the catch pen waiting to be hitched. He told her that the branding was going faster than he'd expected and he wanted to head out in the middle of the afternoon and drive all night, since the crew knew the countryside and the moon would give plenty of light.

Maynell grumbled that that idea was nothing but foolishness, predicted that the cattle would spook easier at night—swearing that Jimbo would agree with her, as if he were the wisest veteran trail driver in Texas—foretold that they could never hold the herd together in the dark, and prophesied that somebody's horse would step in a hole and throw the rider to his death before daylight. She pushed and pushed but Susanna refused to take up the matter with Eagle Jack.

The sooner on the trail, the better, was the way she looked at it. The sooner on the trail the less chance for Eagle Jack to change his mind and try again to leave her at home.

May finally stopped agitating when her nephew, Daniel, who was expected for a visit the next morning, arrived around noon. Susanna was so relieved that May would be distracted she could've hugged his neck. She had no patience this day for anybody else's opinions—or their wants and needs—because her own were pulling at her every minute.

All her thoughts were of Eagle Jack. How could she have been wondering who *he* was? She didn't even know who *she* was, anymore. She still couldn't believe she'd behaved in such a fashion as to let him kiss her senseless and then kiss him right back.

Every time she thought about it, she felt that overwhelming desire for him again and she could not deal with it. She also felt an unsettling sense of betrayal of her new self—the new, independent woman who had come to life in her skin since Everett died.

Was this the kind of trouble that independent women got themselves into? Did a woman have to stay completely away from all men to preserve her freedom? Did freedom mean never experiencing kisses that created a whole new world, one that shook her to the core—because they only made her want to come back for more?

Really, that didn't sound like freedom at all. But then, coming back for more with any man led straight to servitude again, didn't it?

She didn't know, she couldn't say. She hadn't lived long enough to know the answers to such questions.

What she must do now was get her mind on her business and take her cattle to Kansas. What she must do now was forget last night ever happened and hope that Eagle Jack would, too. The important thing to think about was saving Brushy Creek. Eagle Jack was only a tool to help her accomplish that and once it was done, he would be gone.

But in the middle of the afternoon, when she looked up from putting the last item, which was the one ham they had left in the smokehouse, into the wagon and saw Eagle Jack riding up the hill from the herd, he looked like a knight in shining armor come to save her. He and his horse were both covered in dust and sweat, but his seat in the saddle and every movement he made proclaimed he was in control and he knew what he was doing.

She was so glad he was there.

Because he was helping her save her ranch, of course. That was the only reason.

It had taken her all evening yesterday and all day today—except for the necessary hours required to cook three meals and clean them up—to finish packing her supplies, load and organize the wagon and get it hitched to the mules. She could never have done all that and helped get the herd ready for the trail at the same time.

"Time to head out," he said, when he reached her. "You have everything you need on the wagon?"

His eyes were sparkling. He was eager to go.

"This is the last of it," she said. "Let me make one more sweep through the house to see if I forgot anything."

Eagle Jack's gaze moved to something behind her. She turned.

"You forgot me," Maynell said.

May was carrying a bucket full of early plums and her winter coat over her other arm.

Susanna stared at her. "What are you doing? You're staying here, May."

Maynell shook her head. "Nope. Me and Jimbo's goin', too."

It took a minute for Susanna to actually realize what she'd said.

"But who'll watch Brushy Creek? The trail drive is to save Brushy Creek, Maynell. What's the sense if we leave it abandoned?"

"Daniel's gonna be here. He'll take good care."

"So that's why you quit fussing when Daniel came," Susanna said.

"Yep," Maynell said, "I couldn't go off with the cattle tonight without nobody to do the chores and I'd thought the boy wasn't comin' till tomorrow." She stopped and set her bucket down beside the wagon wheel and began to fold her coat. "Scared me bad," she said.

"Serves you right," Susanna said, "for making plans behind my back."

Maynell flashed her birdlike eyes. "Only made 'em when I seen what the truth was."

Susanna waited but May pressed her thin lips together and said no more.

"I'm afraid to ask what that truth is," she said.

"Fine with me," Maynell said. "Cain't tell you anyhow, or you'd know as much as I do." She cackled with satisfaction at her own joke as she stood on tiptoe to lay the folded coat on the wagon seat. Then she looked Susanna in the eye. "Only kept 'em secret 'cause I knowed you'd tell me stay."

It was her most stubborn look. Susanna knew it well. When Maynell got that look, it was a waste of breath to argue with her.

Instinctively, Susanna turned to Eagle Jack, although she regretted it the minute she did. If she couldn't manage her own help here at the house, how could she expect him to share responsibilities concerning the drovers with her?

He sat his horse quietly, looking down at her with a thoughtful look in his eyes and the ghost of a grin on his lips.

"Eagle Jack doesn't like to be responsible for women on the trail," Susanna said, throwing the words over her shoulder to Maynell while she looked at Eagle Jack with a silent, desperate demand for him to back her up. Her stomach clenched.

Living with Maynell in such close quarters as a trail drive chuck wagon for weeks on end would not be easy. Jimbo would be riding with the men. Once Maynell got on a rant about something, Susanna would be the one beside her on the wagon seat, and therefore the one who'd have to hear it for hours and hours on end.

"Got my own slicker and my coat," Maynell

said, as if she'd read Susanna's mind by looking at the back of her head. "Got my sourdough jug and my own rolling pin."

Eagle Jack raised an eyebrow. "She's prepared," he said thoughtfully.

Susanna made a face at him. "Tell her she can't go," she said. "Just the way you told me."

"Oh, I don't know," he said, folding his arms across his saddle horn and relaxing to enjoy the spectacle. "You seem to be telling her that yourself."

"You can see she won't listen to me," Susanna said, her voice rising with every word. "She never does."

She turned around to see Maynell already perched on the wagon seat, her coat folded neatly beside her and the bucket of plums set carefully between her feet.

"It's for your own good," Maynell said. "Give up the fight, Suzy."

"You need to be here," Susanna said. "Daniel can't be more than sixteen years old."

"He'll be fine," Maynell said serenely.

"Jimbo's a homebody. Surely he doesn't really want to travel so far away."

"Jimbo's been actin' like an old man," Maynell said. "This here trip'll be good for him."

Susanna whirled around to look at Eagle Jack again. "Did you tell Jimbo he could be one of the drovers on the trail?"

He spread his hands in a show of innocence. "This is the first I've heard about it," he said, in an entirely too reasonable tone, "but I can always use an extra hand."

It made Susanna want to take his horse away from him and make *him* ride on the wagon seat with Maynell.

"Jimbo's too old to be a drover, and you know it."

"He can help wrangle the remuda," Eagle Jack said. "And dig your fire pits."

Can help, not *could* help.

Susanna turned her back on him and gave Maynell her sternest look. "May, you get down from there this minute and get to thinking about Daniel's supper," she said. "Who's going to cook for him if you're gone?"

"Daniel's been batching it since his mother died three year ago," Maynell said. "He'll do fine. It's poor Eagle Jack I'm cookin' for."

Susanna was incensed.

"*Poor* Eagle Jack? *I'll* be cooking for him!"

"Yeah," Maynell said sarcastically, "and not a pie to be seen for a hundred miles around your camp." Scornfully, she swept her gaze away from Susanna and smiled at Eagle Jack. "These here plums'll ripen in a day or two," she said, "and I packed a Dutch oven to make a cobbler in."

Eagle Jack gave her that irresistible grin of his.

"I can't wait," he said. "If there's anything I love, it's pie."

"Always did like a brown-eyed handsome man with good, common sense," said Maynell.

They got the herd headed north and strung out just right for the number of drovers they had and were five miles from Brushy Creek when the moon came up. Eagle Jack rode out a little way ahead of the lead cattle, but not very far.

Until then, he had dropped back often to ride beside one or the other of the drovers. He was beginning to watch all of them with an eye to whether he wanted to take them with him after they joined the crew from the Sixes and Sevens. He took only the best, most reliable, toughest men north—that was a hard lesson he'd learned from the drives of the past.

He felt his lips curve in a wry smile.

He was fooling himself. How could he even have that thought when this time he was taking two women and an excitable old man up the trail? No, obviously, he hadn't learned that lesson at all.

Actually, it wasn't his fault, though. He hadn't had a choice about taking Susanna along, not after he'd stepped into the middle of her deal with Adams and left her vulnerable, and if Susanna were coming along, he'd had to have Maynell and Jimbo to help him with her.

That was the only reason he had agreed to it. They'd be a burden in some ways—two people besides Susanna who were more or less helpless in case of attack or disaster—but Jimbo swore he was a crack shot, and he could do a lot of work around the camp.

Yes, it would definitely be worth doing a little extra baby-sitting, if it came necessary, to have them on the drive. Even if they couldn't keep Susanna entirely out of his hair, just by their presence they could keep him from trying to be alone with her.

He'd had to do *something* to protect himself. During this long, hard day of working cattle he had fought thoughts of Susanna and his desire for Susanna, and he'd decided not to follow his natural inclination to pursue her.

He wanted, as naturally as he breathed, to pick up that challenge of being the first man to introduce her to kindness and desire. But she was far too complicated a woman for him, and best left alone right now when he had so much responsibility to face.

And, since she was far too desirable to keep away from without a little help, Maynell and Jimbo would be just the help he needed.

"Eagle Jack, wait up!"

He turned in the saddle.

While he'd been thinking of her, Susanna had passed the herd and almost caught up with him.

Was it because she was beset with thoughts of him, too? Had she, too, thought of their kiss a thousand times?

"I need to talk to you," she said, slowing to a trot to match his when she reached him.

"I don't have time to talk," he said, teasing her. "I have a trail drive to boss."

"You don't have supper, either, until I give it to you," she tossed back, brandishing a small cloth sack, "and you won't until I've said my piece."

He grinned at her sassiness. He couldn't help it. "I'm not hungry."

Except for the taste of you.

"Eagle Jack, I want to get something straight before we go a step farther," she said. "You got in my business again today when you sided with Maynell, and I cannot have that all the way to Abilene."

There was something about her when she was so deadly serious that brought out the opposite in him. Maybe because her seriousness always seemed about to overcome her somehow. She needed help with it.

He stopped his horse. Hers stopped, too.

"What are you doing?" she said.

"Not going a step farther," he said, solemnly. "Only following your orders, ma'am."

At first he thought she was going to smile, but instead, she scowled at him.

"This is a perfect example of what I'm talking

about," she said sternly. "You don't take anything seriously enough."

"While you take everything too seriously," he said.

"It's my whole life at risk," she said. "It's whether I have a home at the end of this summer."

"All our lives are at risk every day," he said, "if we so much as get out of bed. Even if we don't, a tree could fall on the house or lightning could strike in through the window and kill us."

"I didn't ride out here for a philosophical discussion," she said. "I came to tell you to stop getting in my business."

"Is this still about your ol' pard, Mr. Adams?"

"That is another perfect example," she said, "but this is about Maynell and Jimbo. All you had to do was back me up and they'd be at Brushy Creek taking care of the place like they're supposed to instead of leaving everything I have in the care of a half-grown kid."

He shrugged and heeled his horse to start moving again.

"You knew I like pie," he said. "Maybe if you'd made me some for supper last night, I'd've been in a different frame of mind when Maynell starting bribing me."

She hit her saddle horn with her fist and the sack almost bounced out of her hand.

"Listen to me, Eagle Jack Sixkiller. We cannot both share the responsibilities and boss this trail drive if you won't ever take my opinion into account or let me make a decision."

He stifled a grin.

"Then I'll boss it," he said, in a reasonable tone. "It's the only way."

"Over my dead body," she said, from between clenched teeth.

"Now, now, sweetheart. No need to be so agitated. Everybody knows the first year of marriage is the hardest."

Her eyes flashed fire at him in the moonlight.

"I am so sorry I ever had the thought of pretending to be married to you, much less that I did it!" she cried.

"But someday you'll be glad," he said.

"You make me so mad I'd take your supper right back with me if I wouldn't have to listen to Maynell go on about it for the next three months—day and night, seven days a week."

"That's another reason I brought Maynell along," he said. "I was thinking I might never get fed, otherwise. Not anything, much less pie."

She threw the sack at him and he caught it.

"There," she said. "Maynell sent it to you, but I cooked it. Eat it if you dare."

"Childish threats don't become you, Susanna," he said.

She was turning her horse to ride away, but she paused to glare at him. In her fury, she was more beautiful than ever.

Her cheeks were dusted with moonlight, her hair was pulled back tightly and held in one long braid, her shirt was too big for her. It fell away from her neck to show the delicate wing of her collarbone. He wanted powerfully to lay down a line of kisses along it and nestle his mouth into the hollow of her throat.

"Susanna," he said, "put your mind at rest. I couldn't be more serious about this drive."

"Empty words do not become you, Eagle Jack. I know we've hurried like mad all day and now we're driving all night only so you can look for your stolen horse."

He sighed. Beautiful or not, she would try anyone's patience. Sometimes the things she said and did would even try the forbearance of his grandfather, who was imperturbability itself.

At those times he wished he'd never left the comforts of home for adventure. He wouldn't have, if he'd known he'd find such aggravation, too.

Or would he? Words and behavior aside, she looked like an absolute angel in the moonlight. Maybe just looking at her would be worth all the vexation.

"Have a little trust in me, won't you, Susanna? Last night you said that you trust me."

That stopped her for a minute.

"I do," she said, slowly, "deep down. But in little things I don't. You're good but you're selfish, too, Eagle Jack. You're out to get what you want."

"And *you're* not," he drawled. "That's what I like best about you, Susanna."

"No need for sarcasm," she said. "Just remember that you'd better consider my opinion and let me share in making the decisions or . . ."

"Or . . . what?"

She went still in the saddle, sitting there with her horse waiting to head back to the herd and the moon rising behind her.

"I don't know yet, Eagle Jack." Her voice was flat with discouragement, almost despair. "I have no choice now but to go on with you but I cannot stand to be helpless and powerless. Now I don't even have free rein in the cook's job—Maynell will be meddling every minute in what I cook and how I cook it."

She stopped and looked at him very straight.

"And a miracle would have to happen for me to have the slightest chance of influencing even one decision about the trail."

"At the jail, you said whoever you hired as trail boss would make the trail decisions."

She nodded.

"I know. But this trip will last for a long time and I have no place in it. What am I, the errand girl? That's what I always was to Everett—errand girl and servant girl."

Eagle Jack thought about that while he turned his head to check on the herd. It was a crying shame that she'd been so young when she met Everett, so desperate to get out on her own that she had married him.

That was one of the big injustices of life because she didn't deserve to be scarred this way. It would affect her for the rest of her life. It might prevent her from ever trusting another man.

Her cattle were moving into view now, coming steadily closer.

"Turn your horse and ride ahead with me," he said. "If you were a man who owned this herd—a man who had never been up the trail before—things would be no different."

She threw him a doubtful look.

"It's true, Susanna. The trail's a dangerous place. A greenhorn can't make the decisions because too many lives are at stake."

"The first person who ever went up the trail had never done it before," she said.

He nodded and they rode along in silence for a while, the cattle lowing behind them.

"Here's what I'm thinking," he said, finally. "Why don't I teach you? Once you know some things, then your opinion will be worth considering."

The grateful look and the smile she gave him made him wish he'd thought of that a long time ago.

"I'm not saying we'll always agree on what to do, Susanna, but I can use another set of eyes and ears. This is a big country and nobody can notice everything all the time."

The moonlight fell across her face. Her eyes were shining.

"You mean to take me on scout with you?"

"Whenever you're not needed with the cooking, yes. Feeding the men is still the most important."

"Eagle Jack, I could kiss you," she blurted. "I would *love* to scout with you and learn to be a trail driver!"

That made him smile. It also made him smile that she held his gaze as if to say her word was good, even though her sheepish grin told him she hadn't meant to say that.

He could not resist that combination. Of course, when could he ever resist the offer of a kiss?

"Then I'll collect right now," he said, and stood in the stirrup to lean across the narrow space between their horses.

She blushed beneath the moondust on her cheeks. "I . . . it was just a figure of speech . . ."

He grinned. "I feel the same way," he said confidingly. "I could kiss you any time at all, Susanna."

"I said it, I guess I'll have to pay up," she said playfully.

"Right. You wouldn't ever want to go back on your word."

Her eyes twinkled as she leaned out of the saddle to meet him.

"You are the best at acting sincere of anyone I've ever known," she said.

"No acting," he told her, and brushed her lips with his. "I am the soul of sincerity."

"I only meant I could just kiss you on the *cheek*," she amended.

He kissed her lightly on the mouth.

"Maybe that's just what you *thought* you meant," he said, "but don't you like this better?"

He held her gaze with his. She had the most beautiful eyes.

"Yes . . ." she said.

He kissed her again, just a friendly peck, then he sat back down in the saddle. It would be best to leave her wanting more.

What *he* really wanted was to pull her off her horse onto his, into his lap, and kiss her with a long, burning kiss that would tell her exactly how sincere he was about wanting her. But that would scare her again. She might not kiss him back with that same unhesitating instinct as she had done the first time.

This time, whether she'd just been teasing with him or not, she might tell him not to take such liberties again.

But he couldn't believe how much he wanted to

do exactly that. He wanted to start it all again and hold that sweet weight of her breast in his hand and take up exactly where they'd left off the night before.

He could hear the echo of that tone in her voice, though, that ring of fear that had made him hate Everett who had hurt her in the past. And that other boy who had kissed her and left her, too.

Even if it would be good for her to lead her into that kindness and desire she had talked about, this wasn't the time. He wanted her to come to him.

No, he didn't. That wouldn't be good because it'd complicate everything too much.

And she was the most desirable woman he'd ever met, bar none.

Who was she, anyway, this independent, jail-invading rancher, Susanna Copeland? This beautiful person who played kissing games but talked to him as straight as any man would have?

What other woman on the face of the earth would have come right out and told him what she needed and how she felt about her job just now, instead of pouting and playing some kind of emotional game to try to make him figure it out on his own? Certainly not Talitha Gentry, whom he'd been seeing these last few months while he'd been living at home on the Sixes and Sevens.

Talitha was the queen of pouting and game playing, especially since he'd danced so many dances with Emma Dooley and Agnes Burke and all those other girls at the Box O Ranch social last month. Talitha was just like all the rest—she wanted to rope and tie him and make him settle down.

That thought brought him back to himself. There was no comparison between Talitha and Susanna. Susanna and he were in a business arrangement, not a personal one.

That was a fact he had to remember.

He had thought, during those first moments when she'd come to the jail, that he might have a dalliance with her, but not anymore. Her feelings ran far too deep to risk that.

And *that* was the real reason he hadn't truly kissed her tonight.

But he still wanted to, and knowing him, he usually did what he wanted, sooner or later.

It had done him absolutely no good to bring Maynell and Jimbo along. They wouldn't be a bit of protection to him if he was going to invite Susanna to scout with him.

They rode along in comfortable silence with Eagle Jack wondering, every step of the way, why he had invited her to be his companion for a large part of every day. That hadn't been necessary. Not at all. She herself had said that she had no choice but to go ahead with this drive, and he could've kept it on his terms.

He'd probably done it because of Cookie. When they threw this bunch in with the Sixes and Sevens crew and Cookie saw that he had two other cooks—and women, at that—for competition, he'd throw a wall-eyed fit. Maybe one woman wouldn't be so bad. If Susanna went on scout, it would just be Maynell vying with Cookie for the reputation of best cook on the trail.

Deep in his heart, though, he knew that wasn't the only reason, if it was a reason at all.

The true explanation was that he wanted to spend time with Susanna. And he really did have good intentions of teaching her some skills she needed to survive.

He could only hope those good intentions weren't the ones that paved the road to hell.

Chapter 8

Susanna rode along beside Eagle Jack, rocked by the slow, rhythmic motion of the horses. The moonlight seemed to reach out around them and pull them in, as it was growing stronger by the minute. It filled her with a whole new mystery—how could it open up the night over the whole prairie and wrap them close in a golden cocoon at the same time?

She ran the tip of her tongue over her lips. Yes, she could still taste Eagle Jack and feel the quick, sweet pressure of his kiss. He had abandoned it far too soon, yet, she would not—she could not—provoke him to finish it because it would only make her want more.

What she needed to do right that minute was go back to the wagon and help Maynell, because she was supposed to take supper to the other men, too. Maynell would be waiting for her and getting impatient.

Instead, she let the reins go a little looser in her fingers and kept on riding beside Eagle Jack. Spring was coming in, stronger on every moonbeam. The smells of grass beneath their feet and fresh rain way off somewhere mingled with those of the cattle and horses. A nightbird called.

Her heart rode higher on the sound.

The wagon creaked along, somewhere behind them, the mules' harnesses jingling. A cow bawled on one side of the herd and another, on the other side, answered.

Susanna stood in her stirrups and twisted in the saddle to look back. It was like a dream to see them moving through the night—the great sea of horns flashing, the white on their hides catching the moonlight, their hooves making a low rumble against the ground. She watched awhile, then sat down and looked to the north again, to the market, to the place where she'd get the money to save her home. Her goal was up ahead and she was on her way.

Her cattle were on the road at last! The realization came to her, into her skin like the moonlight's shine, into her blood like the sweet night air. Suddenly, for the first time since she couldn't remember when, she was there, there in only that moment, and a new sense of hope was filling her up, body and spirit. The thing she had dreamed of for months and months was happening.

And it would end well, too. Everything would be all right.

It gave her an instant of rare peace.

Eagle Jack began to whistle softly, a jaunty, happy melody that she recognized but couldn't quite name. Then she knew—it was "Oh, Susanna!"

She turned to look at him and he inclined his head and winked as if to confirm the tune was all about her.

As if her glance had asked that question. Sometimes he could be so full of himself.

Shaking her head wryly, grinning at his silliness, she held his gaze for a minute. He was the reason she was feeling such hope, such security, for once in her life. And that, in itself, was one of the scariest thoughts she'd ever had.

He could draw her into a whole web of hope and imaginings if she would let herself go there. She needed to turn her mount around and go back to Maynell.

But Eagle Jack wouldn't let her look away and they rode through the spring moonlight side by side for another little distance. He stopped whistling and just smiled at her.

"I have to go," she said finally. "Maynell will have the other men's food ready and I have to take it to them."

He nodded and raised his bag of jerky and biscuits in salute.

"Thanks," he said.

She turned her horse around and skirted the edge of the herd to get back to the wagon. Her heart was stirring with such a real confusion of feelings that she could hardly sort them out. She was scared and happy and excited and hopeful and uncertain and at peace and a whole lot more, besides. All she knew for sure was that Eagle Jack Sixkiller somehow was part of every emotion she had right now.

They drove through the night, just as Eagle Jack had planned and, although they stopped for breakfast and to water the cattle, they kept moving on north, slowly, during most of the rest of the day. Susanna had expected they would rest most of the day but he wouldn't hear of it. Finally, in the late afternoon, he stopped his horse, indicated a grassy meadow in the bend of a big creek for the bedground, and the crew threw the cattle off the trail at last.

Eagle Jack seemed to Susanna to be everywhere at once, but he was mostly with the cattle, showing his inexperienced men how to fan them out and push them slowly to the water to drink and how to gently hold them together and circle them as they grazed to get them, later, to bed down. She was glad he was so occupied because it meant she and Maynell could put up her tent in an unobtrusive spot in the trees without his notice.

Maybe he'd feel he needed to sleep out with the men to be nearer the cattle tonight. Maybe he'd forget he was supposed to behave as if they were married. Maybe he had already made his point by sleeping in her room at home.

She hoped so. She didn't even care if the men thought they were fighting. The last thing she needed was to share a tent with Eagle Jack—what would follow if they happened to kiss again? What would she do if he did decide to "bother" her? Would she be strong enough to resist him? Something was wrong with her. She had barely been able to keep her eyes off him all night and all day.

Even after they got the tent up, he kept coming into her mind while she was helping Maynell cook supper, but that was only because she was too tired to think straight. Or maybe it was because Maynell kept up a running chatter about what Eagle Jack would like for supper, and whether Eagle Jack liked dried apple pie and what Eagle Jack would want for breakfast.

"Maynell," she said, "why don't you worry about what Jimbo would want?"

"Because I know what he wants," Maynell said, with a sigh. "Jimbo wants to be off to hisself to chew his tobacco in peace."

Sure enough, when Eagle Jack and most of the crew rode up and stopped to dismount far enough from the fire not to get dust in the food, Jimbo wasn't with them. He and Rodney, one of Marvin's partners, had stayed with the herd.

"Remember, boys, let's keep a sharp lookout while we eat," Eagle Jack called to them. "That herd's nowhere near trailbroke yet."

Somebody said something she didn't catch and Eagle Jack's rich laugh rang out. He seemed to certainly be in fine fettle for someone who'd spent a sleepless night horseback.

That explained it. That was why her mind was such a mess. It was tied in knots just like her body after being in the saddle for so long. Her constant awareness of Eagle Jack was only caused by being so tired and being in this new world of the trail. He had been here before. He was her guide north. That explained why she kept watching him.

As the men walked up to the fire, Susanna turned, bent over the pot hanging there, and began stirring the stew she and Maynell had put on to cook the minute they had a fire. She would keep her back turned until Eagle Jack passed by and went to the wash bench to clean up for supper. She was exhausted. One look into his dark eyes and she'd forget all these chores and fall into his arms. She'd been thinking about how it would feel for him to hold her. She'd been trying to forget the taste of his kiss.

A big hand slapped her lightly on the bottom.

"What d'you think, honey?" he said in his low, rich voice. "Is supper ready?"

She sprang upright and whirled to face him, brandishing the long-handled wooden spoon, heat rushing to her face from embarrassment.

"Eagle Jack!" she cried.

Susanna couldn't help glancing around to see who had noticed the familiarity. Marvin's face was nearly as red as hers and his friend, Lanny, was grinning. Both of them quickly looked away from her and Eagle Jack. Over by the wagon, Maynell was watching, her eyes gleaming with satisfaction.

"You stop that," Susanna said, lowering her voice so only Eagle Jack could hear. "Good heavens, Eagle Jack, you're scandalizing the camp."

He pretended to be hurt. "I don't know why," he drawled, "they all know a man has every right to give his wife a little love pat once in awhile."

His eyes were twinkling with mischief. His contagious smile was as broad as the prairie.

"What's the matter, darlin'?" he said. "Have you forgotten our wedding ceremony? Remember—when the preacher asked if you would obey me, and you said you would?"

"I will *not*," she said, and swatted at him with the spoon.

He dodged the blow.

"Now, now, love," he said, "let's not set a bad example. Some of these boys might think about gettin' hitched some day. We don't want to discourage 'em."

"What in the world is the matter with you?" she said. "For a man who's spent all night in the saddle, and one with a wound on his head, to boot, you're certainly in an expansive mood."

He pretended to misunderstand. "It's not that expensive, sweet Susanna. It'll only cost you one little kiss."

She lowered her voice even more.

"Listen, Eagle Jack," she said, "I'm sorry I started that about playing kissing games. We've got to keep in mind that this is a business arrangement."

He shook his head, his eyes still twinkling.

"I'm all business, all the time. You know that." He reached out and brushed her hair back from her face. "Don't you? And you know that I'm only doing what you told me to do, sweetheart—just keepin' up appearances."

He grinned and looked her up and down in an overdone imitation of a lecher. His heavy-lidded gaze lingered on her breasts for a moment. Her treacherous nipples hardened in anticipation of his touch.

She looked him in the eye and hoped he didn't see the condition he'd put her in.

"You're overdoing it," she said. "A little bit of pretending goes a long way, Eagle Jack."

"Not far enough, Susanna," he said. "Not yet."

He leaned forward and gave her a quick kiss on the lips, then he followed the other men to the wash bench.

After supper, as soon as the dishes were done, Susanna went to her tent and made two separate beds. If Eagle Jack truly did intend to share her tent, when he came in from night guard he could clearly see that he was meant to use the same quilts he'd slept on in her room. And he'd also be able to clearly see that she was sound asleep.

Her purpose had been accomplished. They had all the men believing that they were married. That was all she needed or wanted, so that was all there would be, no matter what he had implied when he said, "Not far enough, Susanna. Not yet."

It sent a thrill through her, even now, when she remembered the low, intimate way he had said it. Her hands trembled as she washed up and changed into clean clothes. Eagle Jack had told the men to take off no more than their boots at night until the herd was well settled to the trail and she was going to do the same. They were so short handed they needed everyone watching the cattle just going down the trail and that need would be magnified if there should be a stampede. She was staying dressed, not because Eagle Jack might come in here—she wasn't going to let him have that much control over her—but so she could ride at a moment's notice.

She brushed her hair, crawled into her bedroll, and left all her anxieties behind. Exhausted as she was, she fell into a dreamless sleep the minute her head touched the pillow. She didn't even turn over until Maynell's loud voice brought her back to reality.

"Come and get it," May yelled, loud enough to waken Daniel way back there at Brushy Creek, "before I throw it out."

The sun was nearly up—pink light was filtering in through the canvas walls of the tent and the whole camp was stirring. Incredibly, it was morning already.

Eagle Jack. Where was he?

She sat up and turned to look at his bedroll. It was rumpled. It had been used. He had been here, he had been sleeping nearby and she hadn't even known it.

Something velvety and wet touched her hand as she reached down to throw back the covers. She jerked back her hand, looked to see what it was and then picked it up, her heart pounding harder than it had even when Eagle Jack had kissed her.

A flower. One beautiful bluebonnet, covered with morning dew.

The first flower anyone ever gave her.

"Dear Lord in heaven."

She breathed the words as a prayer. She had to

have help because if Eagle Jack gave it half a try, he could make her fall in love with him.

Susanna wasn't alone with Eagle Jack until that afternoon when they rode ahead on scout together. All day she had stuck close to the wagon and Maynell. All day she had been thinking what to do.

What could she do to protect her heart? What could she do to build a wall between them? She could never trust any man enough to let him into her life as a husband. Yet a fantasy of Eagle Jack in that role had actually flashed across her mind when she'd held the bluebonnet in her hand.

By the time he called her to scout ahead with him for the night's bedground, she had thought of only one course of action.

"Eagle Jack," she said, when they had left the herd behind, "don't bring me any more flowers."

He whipped his head around to look at her.

"What the hell kind of a remark is that?" he asked.

He looked and sounded so surprised that her heart tripped over itself and then pounded, hard.

"The . . . bluebonnet," she said, suddenly wondering whether he'd brought it or not, trying to think if someone else could have.

He stared at her with such an insulted look, such an incredible expression that she couldn't look away, even when she wanted to.

She felt her cheeks get hotter and hotter. Her mind chased every glimpse of a thought. Had she made a mistake? Could *she* even have torn the flower from the ground in her sleep? They were camped on grass. Yet it had been touched by the dew.

"Aren't . . . you the one who left that bluebonnet on my bed?" she asked.

"I wondered if you found it," he said.

"Yes, I did," she said.

He pushed back his hat while his hard, dark eyes searched her face.

"And you didn't like it," he said flatly.

"I didn't say that."

He gave a disgusted snort. "You better start saying what you mean, Susanna, or I'm gone down the road. This is craziness."

It struck her then how much she was hurting him.

"Acting like we're married to fool the men is one thing," she said stiffly, "but in private, that's another thing entirely."

"You've kissed me in private."

"I know," she said miserably, "but this is different."

"Yeah," he said sarcastically, "it is. I've never given flowers to a woman who said 'Don't bring me any more flowers', instead of 'Thank you, you are so thoughtful, Eagle Jack.' "

He glared at her harder.

"None of 'em ever said, 'No, I won't marry you but thanks for the flowers,' either. I didn't bring you that bluebonnet as a proposal of a real marriage or anything like that, Susanna. You sure know how to insult a man."

He was furious. *That* was how much she had hurt him.

"I *know* that," she cried. "What I'm trying to say is . . ."

"Spit it out," he interrupted. "I thought you didn't like to be slapped around—from what you said about Everett—so I thought you might *like* a flower."

"I did! I do! What I mean is . . ." she began, but it was too late. He had figured it out for himself.

"All right, I remember," he said, "you're scared of me because I'm *not* like Everett. Well, that's just too damn bad, Susanna. I am who I am, and you can just get over it or give me my pay."

He kissed to his horse and galloped on ahead. When she caught up to him, he had cooled down but he would talk only about the lay of the land and the grass and the water and where they might bed down that night if no other herd had that bedground. He had drifted all over this country, he said. He knew it well.

But when she tried to get him to tell her more about his life as a drifter, he wouldn't. A terrible loneliness moved through her. She had done it now. They weren't even going to be friends anymore, and she'd built the wall she'd wanted between them.

Now that she'd done it, she hated the way it felt.

She also hated that she had hurt him so much over one small gesture he had made, which was a small flirtation to him, nothing more. She had overreacted by a mile.

Her cheeks flared even hotter, she was so embarrassed. Eagle Jack had known lots of women and she was only another one on the string to him.

But the trouble was that she didn't feel that same way about him. He was special to her and when the drive was done, she would never forget him. She already knew that without a doubt.

So it was best that he was hurt and mad at her and they'd be only business partners. That was for the best, by far.

But that evening, when Eagle Jack rode away right after supper, it tore a hole in Susanna's heart to see him leave. He told her good-bye as her good public husband but the look in his eyes was as dispassionate as it had been all day. She watched him out of sight, then turned to their supper guest, a rider who claimed to be out looking for strays from a herd already gone up the trail.

Susanna and Maynell agreed that he had the demeanor of a grub-line rider who didn't want a job, but she'd thought of testing him by offering him one. They needed more help. Yet she didn't like the fellow. She didn't like much of anybody today, including herself. Especially herself. She didn't like for Eagle Jack to be so cool and businesslike, was the main problem. That was coloring her every minute and she had to learn to forget it.

"Did you see the little running mare yourself?" she asked the visitor. Her tone came out sharper than she'd intended.

Startled, he looked up from his coffee.

"No, ma'am. I done told your husband that. All I know is the Bar 20 crew was saying they've been winning money when they race her."

"Did they tell you what color she is?"

"No, ma'am. They never said."

Susanna sensed his relief as she turned away and left him. She knew he'd already told his stories, but she'd been helping Maynell and she hadn't heard the details. All she knew was that Eagle Jack had bolted his food and called to her to say he was going to see if the little running mare with the herd coming along behind them could possibly be Molly.

He'd called her Susanna, not any endearment. In private, he probably wouldn't even speak to her at all.

Now he was gone, the sun was sinking slowly to the close of the hottest day they'd had since last summer, and the sky was starting to flash with lightning. There were heavy, dark clouds to the west. The cattle were restless. Maybe she should try to hire this man on, after all.

But just then he stood and threw his tin cup into the wreck pan. "Thanks for the grub, ma'am," he said to Susanna. Then he looked at Maynell. "Ma'am," he said, and tipped his hat to her.

"Sayin' thanks won't cut it around this camp," she retorted. "Git over here and wash these dishes to pay for your supper like a visitor with any manners would already be doin'."

Sheepishly, he did as he was told.

Susanna smiled to herself as she walked out toward the remuda. She might as well save her breath on the job offer. No way would a lazy man hire on with this outfit with Maynell cracking the whip.

She chose a fresh horse and saddled it. Eagle Jack's absence made her too restless to sit still and left a man missing from the herd. She would take his place and pray that the weather wouldn't cause the cattle to run.

At first, it was almost relaxing riding slowly around and around the herd. Marvin was riding in the other direction, and they passed each other each time they made a circle. Most of the cattle had lain down and, although some were bawling and moving around, Susanna had hopes they'd all go to sleep as soon as darkness fell. The air was heavy and humid, though, and some of the clouds were getting heavier. It was raining to the north, she could tell.

She rode and listened to Marvin singing to the cattle and thought about Eagle Jack. Five miles to the herd behind them and five miles back would take a while. He had left camp on a fresh horse at a lope but he'd have to slow him to a trot part of the time or wear him out. Maybe he could ride Molly back. For his sake, she hoped so.

For her sake, she hoped so. Then maybe he'd get his mind on her cattle and not leave them when it was stormy weather. A shard of fear sliced through her. He had accepted her offer so he could get out of jail and look for his stolen horse. He had come up the trail because he was keeping his word to her, yes, but also because his horse was rumored to be headed this way.

That race horse was probably the most important possession he had, probably the source of the money he'd withdrawn from the bank in Salado. So what did it mean if the horse he found tonight did prove to be Molly? Would he take her and leave Susanna and the herd?

If he did, who would blame him, after her rejection of the simple, friendly gesture of a flower? The embarrassment and chagrin were too much to deal with, yet again, so Susanna tore her thoughts away from that memory.

Surely he'd be back by midnight. Surely the storm wouldn't hit until then. But she knew she was fooling herself. It would storm within an hour or two, the clouds were moving so fast.

She watched the sky, which was stunningly beautiful, as if she could predict the exact minute trouble would start. Scattered shafts of sunlight were shining here and there in the dark gray and blue of the clouds. The paler yellow of the lightning cut through them, too, and thunder rumbled somewhere far off in the distance.

It was coming closer. She turned to look toward the sound, which seemed to be in the northern sky. Or in the cloud of dust rolling toward them from that direction.

A herd? Was an outfit up ahead on the trail losing their cattle? She stared, amazed, as the cloud came closer and closer, then she turned her mount and rode for camp. Whatever it was, it coming right at her cattle and she needed all hands if they were going to have a prayer of holding them.

She rode in at a high lope, yelling for them to get horseback, only to see that they'd already heard the noise and were running for their night horses, saddled and tied to the wagon wheels. Streaking back to the herd, she stood in her stirrups to get a better view and saw that the approaching trouble was in the form of horses, a bunch of wild horses who were running full out.

There was no time to wonder where they'd

come from or where they were going. They burst into the herd as if it weren't even there and ran through it without altering their course one bit. The cattle were already starting to move. Fast. They were running as soon as they got their feet under them, fleeing from danger as if they were one.

She made it to the south end of the herd and glimpsed Marvin coming, aiming to meet her, but she knew in a heartbeat there was no hope of turning them now. Could they have held them if she'd stayed with the herd? It was impossible to know, but probably not.

That was the last coherent thought she had, because from then on it was nothing but a race for survival. She and Marvin rode only to keep clear of the onrush. The cattle pressed them hard but their mounts kept the lead.

Susanna held on to her mount and tried to stay in the saddle. That was all. Just stay in the saddle and out from under the thousands of hooves trying to catch her. She rode as she'd never ridden in her life before.

Finally, when she was thinking only that she'd never be able to take a full, deep breath of air into her lungs again, the pace began to slow. Thank God, running was not a natural gait for cattle. Through the din, she could hear nothing but as she glanced to her left, where she'd last seen Marvin, she saw two distinct flashes. He was firing his six-shooter into the air to try to turn the cattle. It hit her like a blow that she should be wearing hers also. From now on, she would.

The leaders did begin to turn to the right, Jimbo and one of Marvin's men appeared out of the dust to help, and gradually they pushed the herd around to head to the north again. When it was sure that they were all under control and there were men on both sides of the herd, Susanna slumped in the saddle and let herself take it all in.

Pride flowed through her with the overwhelming relief. She had done a man's work and she had ridden like a cowboy in spite of her fear. She had helped lead her herd and because of what she and Marvin had done, the cattle were mostly all still together, as far she could tell in the fading light.

She had gambled everything she had that she could take these cattle to Kansas. Now she knew that she could. She also knew she could have died here tonight.

Around midnight, when Eagle Jack rode back in, Susanna was sitting cross-legged on a saddle blanket outside her tent, smelling the fresh-washed world on the wind. It had rained, finally, but mostly the storm had passed over them dry.

He still had only the horse he rode out on. By the light of the fire, which was always kept going for coffee, she watched him unsaddle and take his mount out to the remuda. Then he strode toward her as if he could see her sitting there in the dark shadows.

As he got closer she could tell that he did know she was there, even before he spoke. She couldn't have said how she knew it, but there was no doubt.

"So," he said, "I hear you had a little run."

His voice had lost its anger. Or at least most of it.

"How?"

"I stopped and talked to Rodney. He says they're ready for a rest now."

"It was a bunch of horses that started them," she said. "Looked like some mustangs running crazy."

"Probably got separated from their main herd," he said, and then, with a weary sigh, sat down beside her. He took off his hat, laid it on the grass, and stretched out full length, leaning on one elbow. Looking at her.

A thrill ran down her spine. It was a speculative look that spoke of far-reaching possibilities.

"Was the mare not yours?" she said.

"No. She couldn't hold a candle to Molly."

"I'm sorry."

He nodded.

Susanna swallowed hard and thought how to say what she needed to say.

"I'm sorry about something else, too," she blurted. "I was rude about the flower."

He just kept on watching her. Then he said, "What brought this on?"

"I could've been killed tonight," she said. "I would've hated that to happen with your feelings hurt and you mad at me."

He grinned. She could barely see his face in the sporadic light from the moon riding in and out of the clouds.

"I would've hated it, too," he said. "I was arrogant, thinking I could give flowers to any woman I wanted."

"It's all right," she said.

"I'll get my blankets and sleep out with the men," he said. "I'll tell them it's so we won't disturb you when they call me for night guard."

Susanna felt a sudden deflation, as if all the air had gone out of her. But why? She didn't want him in her tent. She really didn't. This was what she'd been trying to accomplish this very morning, was it not?

"From now on, don't worry about anything more than keeping up appearances," he said.

"I'm not," she said quickly, too quickly. "I don't."

The words hung in the air between them.

"Because," he said, in a tone that assumed that wasn't the end of the conversation and they both knew it, "I was thinking about you tonight. I'll just wait for you to come to me."

Surprise, no, shock, actually made her mute for a minute. Then anger stirred her tongue.

"Arrogant is right," she said, bristling. "What makes you think I will?"

He smiled and the moon showed her the glint in his dark eyes.

"The way you kiss me," he said.

Then, in one fluid motion, he got to his feet, picked up his hat, and ducked into the tent. When he came out with his bedroll under his arm, he walked away without so much as one glance back.

Chapter 9

For the next two weeks they made good time, considering that the cattle were only slowly getting broke to the trail and the drovers had to watch constantly to keep the herd together and not let them turn back to their home range. All the crew had almost more than they could do but Eagle Jack, as usual, worked as if he never needed rest and he kept pushing to hold their position on the trail.

Eagle Jack and Susanna, while scouting ahead for water and bedgrounds, had come across an old drifter who told them that he knew of four herds that had gone before them, and word had come from a rider who took a meal at their fire that there were more cattle not too far behind them. This would be a record year for the number of cattle driven north. That had been the prediction, and it seemed to be proving true.

Susanna worked like two persons, too, helping Maynell prepare and clean up the meals, and riding with Eagle Jack (both of them behaving in the most businesslike fashion) every hour she was free. She began to be grateful to him, not only for the knowledge she was gaining but also for the relief from drudgery. Stepping up onto a horse and riding away into the open country after bending over the cook fire and the dishpan for hours was a lift to her spirits every time.

And it wasn't *only* because she was with Eagle Jack. At least, that's what she kept telling herself. But she had to admit that she wouldn't look forward to those hours out in the beautiful countryside nearly so much if she weren't with him.

Eagle Jack was unfailingly cheerful, no matter how tired he was, and his conversation was a welcome respite from Maynell's chatter about the drovers and the meals and her constant directions about how Susanna should take advantage of her time with Eagle Jack. Maynell could be downright tedious sometimes.

Now they were within thirty miles of their first really hazardous big river crossing, the Brazos, and Susanna's trail-driving lessons had been on that subject for the last couple of days. There had been lots more of the rain to the west, they had heard that by word of mouth, and they'd also seen lots of faraway thunderheads since the night the mustangs had run through their herd. More rain had fallen on them, too, and all the smaller streams they'd crossed within the last week had been swollen more than usual.

That night, Eagle Jack and Susanna found a bedground early and then, side-by-side, rode back toward the herd. She was the one who had considered all the possibilities and made the decision of where to settle the herd for the night.

"You did a good job," he said.

"Thanks. I'm learning."

"That's 'cause I'm such a good teacher," he said, in his mischief-making voice.

"Oh." She teased him in return, "I see the way it is. The fact that I'm a fabulous student gets no credit at all. Is that right?"

He just rode along, relaxed in the saddle, giving her that irresistible grin of his. "I reckon so."

"And the fact that I have, inexperienced as I am, brought this herd for all these miles without losing a one gets no recognition at all?"

"That's right."

"You are so conceited, Eagle Jack."

She couldn't keep the affection out of her tone when she said it. He was, as Maynell pointed out at least once daily, the most lovable man in Texas. There was just something about him.

It didn't mean that she was going to go to him for more than friendship, though, as he had predicted. She had herself totally under control.

"There you go insulting me again," he said, in his careless way. "That's what started us out all wrong, Susanna. You made some similar remark right there in the jailhouse in front of everybody on the morning we met."

She chuckled. "Did I embarrass you in front of your friends?"

"Well, yes, you did. That's why I was so glad to leave them behind. Now I just live in fear that you'll do it again in front of the men."

That made her laugh.

"Yeah, yeah, sure you do. I couldn't embarrass you, Eagle Jack, if I stole your jeans some night and you had to ride all day in your underwear."

He lifted an eyebrow and widened his grin. "And how do you think, Miss Susanna, you can steal my jeans off me when, like everybody else, I crawl into my bedroll every night with them on? Have you been peeking out of your tent and spying on me, hoping I'd take them off one night?"

Her cheeks grew warm. She should not have said that. Hadn't she learned by now that Eagle Jack could take one remark and make jokes out of it all day?

"Certainly not. That's just another example of how conceited you are, E. J."

He ignored that while he leered at her.

"I surely do hope you *are* watching me, Annie. I might just return the favor if I get half a chance."

She didn't really know when or how they'd

started calling each other by nicknames, but it seemed natural to do so now. They had become better friends than she'd realized.

Or maybe it wasn't friendship, maybe it was simply fun to pass the time on the trail.

"I hate so much to disappoint you, but I *couldn't* be spying on you. Don't forget it's dark when you crawl into your bedroll and there's a lot of men out there doing the same thing."

He drew back and clapped his hand over his heart.

"But there's no comparison, is there, Suzy girl? You'd know me from those other guys even if the night was pitch black, wouldn't you?"

The sad truth was, she probably would.

She heaved a theatrical sigh. "I'm afraid you've a terminal case of self-admiration, Eagle Jack. We may have to shoot you to put you out of your misery."

He flashed her a flirtatious look. "Kiss me first," he said. "Don't let me die, beautiful Susanna, without a kiss."

He slowed his horse and leaned toward her from the saddle.

Without hesitation, she leaned to meet him.

His lips brushed hers, once, twice. He kissed her, lightly. And with such a piercing sweetness that it brought tears to her eyes.

With such a splendid affirmation that it made her proud to be exactly who she was.

I like you, Susanna. You're all right. I like to be with you.

She fancied that was what the kiss was saying.

He tasted like the smells on the warm wind, like faraway pines and close-by sage and the open sky.

He tasted like Eagle Jack.

She could have stayed there forever, exactly like that, moving with him on the slow-walking horses, with his mouth on hers.

When he took it away, she felt bereft.

And traitorous to herself, as if she'd taken a step toward walking into his arms. He'd said she would come to him. She had promised herself she wouldn't. She couldn't afford to, with her heart at stake where he was concerned.

She could not believe she was so *weak-willed*, where he was concerned.

But his gaze was holding hers, sure and steady, and she felt connected to him.

"We'd have to say we're partners on this drive, wouldn't we?" he said.

"I guess so." She laughed a little. "Neither one of us ever rides with anybody else."

"Then that means we stand night guard together," he said, teasing her. "When I roll out at midnight, you'd better do it, too."

"No. The cook doesn't stand night guard."

"The cook and the trail boss are exempt," he said.

"Then how come you're doing it?"

"We're shorthanded," he said.

"Sorry," she said. "I can't sing very well at all."

"The cattle don't care," he said. "All they need is the sound of a human voice." He grinned at her as the horses quickened their pace. Mention of the cattle was drawing them both back toward the herd. "As the segundo, you need to set a good example," he said.

"Oh, yeah. As if a woman could ever be the segundo."

He held her gaze with a long, straight look.

"Keep on like you're doing, and you could."

"Tell that to the men. I couldn't even hire them on my own, remember? They won't follow orders from me."

He smiled. "By the time we cross the Red River, you'll be able to take the herd on to Abilene all by yourself."

A shaft of fear sliced through her. An old fear, one she knew well, although she hadn't felt it for a while.

Not since she'd wondered if he would leave her if he found Molly. Was he hinting now that he might leave her and her herd after they crossed into the Territory?

She shot him a quick glance. He was riding relaxed in the saddle, still smiling at her.

Could she trust him? Had her instincts been right these past two weeks?

Or not?

* * *

By late the next afternoon, Susanna's herd was within twenty miles of the Brazos River crossing and Eagle Jack went scouting ahead, leaving her to select the bedgrounds. They had passed two yearling herds whose drovers said the river had been impassable for a week, and it was urgent to find out if they should go on closer to it or not.

"Take the wagon with you," he said, "and make sure Maynell has her shotgun loaded. If there's any trouble, use it."

"I'm wearing my handgun," she said. "Don't you think I can shoot?"

"Use it, too," he said.

The minute he was gone, she had the strangest feeling. What if he didn't come back tonight? What if he didn't come back ever?

She knew she was letting fear get a hold on her again when she said as much to Maynell as she rode beside the wagon.

Maynell replied with her famous skeptical look. "Eagle Jack's not gonna run out on you, girl," she said. "He's as good at heart as he is handsome."

"I really don't think he will," Susanna said, "but—"

"—but you ain't known nothing *but* people runnin' out on you, one way or the other, since the day you was born, and that's what you expect," Maynell finished for her.

Maynell had known her for only a couple of years, but she knew her well. She knew Susanna's mother had died birthing her, that her father had run off shortly after, that her relatives had passed her around from one family to another.

They were all too poor and too overworked to take another mouth to feed, and it seemed that as soon as she would even begin to think she was going to stay in one place they sent her to another. That had gone on during all her years of growing up, from the time she was born until she'd married Everett when she was seventeen.

"I suppose so."

"Ain't no supposin' to it," Maynell said. "It's a hard-down fact, that's what it is."

In a flash of insight, Susanna realized that that was another reason Maynell had insisted on coming along. Making pies for Eagle Jack was only one excuse.

Maynell loved her even more than she'd realized. Cooking out on the ground for a bunch of men three times a day and then cleaning up, packing up, and moving on, only to do it all over again, was much more work than Maynell's usual chores at Brushy Creek. Susanna resolved to help her more and ride with Eagle Jack less.

They rode along in companionable silence for a short way, then Maynell hit a rock and began a long story about a wagon wreck she'd been in before Susanna was born. She was just building up to the cause of it when the sound of hooves drumming announced a rider coming.

"From the east," Maynell said, and she was right.

It was a short, stocky bay mare with a tall rider. When he was within earshot, he slowed his horse and called to them.

"This the wagon for the Slanted S herd?"

"Yes," Susanna called back and turned to ride to meet him.

"Stay by," Maynell said. "Let him come to us."

Discreetly, she felt for the shotgun beneath the seat.

The horse bore a brand that looked like a staggered six and a seven, a brand that Susanna didn't know. Both the little mare and the rider looked well-fed. This wasn't a grubline drifter looking for a free meal.

He swept off his hat and gave them each a bold smile. "Nat Straight," he said, by way of introducing himself. "What a stroke of luck to come across two such beautiful ladies out here so far from town. I hear it's better to be born lucky than handsome, and this proves it right down to the ground."

With all that talk of luck he might be a roving gambler.

Or with that talk of beautiful ladies far from town, he might be the kind to try to take advantage of women.

Susanna didn't give him the encouragement of smiling back at him. "My husband will return momentarily," she said. "Do you have business with the Slanted S?"

"So I've heard," the man said. "But that might depend on what your husband's name is."

"Eagle Jack Sixkiller," she said.

Surprise flashed across his face, then it was gone.

"Congratulations must be in order," he said. "I wasn't aware that Eagle Jack had finally got himself roped and branded."

"Yes," she said, and then didn't quite know where to go from there.

"Well, he always did pick the prettiest ladies," Nat Straight said. His weathered face reddened a little as he realized that might not have been the most tactful thing to say. "But this time he's gone and outdone himself," he said heartily. "You're the most beautiful of them all, by a long shot, ma'am."

He fell silent, twisting his hat in his hands, obviously wondering whether that remark had been a mistake, as well.

"Thank you."

How many beautiful ladies had Nat known Eagle Jack to have? There must have been lots. Did he love any of them? She wondered if Nat would know that.

"I reckon I'll ride on back to my herd now," he

finally said. "How much farther you reckon to go before you make camp?"

"Not far," Susanna said. "I'm looking at that grove of trees over there to the northwest. That meadow next to it may be just right."

"I'll find y'all, then," Nat said. "We can hold my herd all the way back here tonight if you don't have enough room and not throw 'em all together until we head out up the trail." He started to turn his horse, then stopped. "Tell Eagle Jack we'll be here directly," Nat Straight said, as he wheeled his horse.

"Will you be here for supper?"

Again, the tip of the hat.

"Yes, ma'am," he said, "along about that time. But thank you kindly, we got our cook wagon with us."

Susanna watched him ride away. Surely she had heard him wrong about throwing the herds together to go up the trail. Eagle Jack would have said something to her about it if he had plans like that.

Wouldn't he?

By the time Eagle Jack got back from the river, Susanna had picked the bedgrounds where the drovers were beginning to settle the herd—she'd done a mighty fine job of it—and she was sitting on a log somebody had dragged up to the fire, scooping more coals onto the top of the Dutch oven. Evidently, she was in charge of the sourdough biscuits again, and he was glad. The ones she made were the best he'd ever eaten. Maynell was frying steaks.

And some cowboy was walking from his ground-tied horse into camp, clearly headed toward Susanna. He took another look. It was his trail boss, Nat Straight. He'd know that swagger anywhere.

"Nat!"

At Eagle Jack's shout, he turned and came out to meet him.

Eagle Jack dismounted and they shook hands.

"We're holding the herd a couple of miles back," Nat said. "Figured you'd wanta wait and throw 'em together when we head on out."

"Sounds good," Eagle Jack said. "How's their condition?"

"Fat 'n' sassy," Nat said. "We took it slow after we got your message." He gave Eagle Jack a look. "Wish *I* was in as good a shape as the herd."

"What's the matter with you?"

"Nearly had a heart attack a while ago."

"What happened?" Eagle Jack asked.

"That pretty lady over there told me she's your wife. I swear, it was a shock to my system, Eagle Jack. I come within a hair of swallowing my tobacco."

Annoyance stabbed at Eagle Jack, irritation that this silly marriage farce had carried over to his home territory. Nat was one of the best cowboys on the Sixes and Sevens and there were eight or ten more men from the home ranch with the herd. He hadn't thought about them and the married-up story he and Susanna were telling.

He'd pay hell if his mother heard it—she'd been hoping and praying he'd get married and settle down for so long that this would make her hysterical with happiness. She'd never believe that it was only a tale for the trail.

He needed to correct Nat's thinking.

"Aw, that's just—" He bit his tongue.

Nat would be with all them the rest of the drive. The man was a big talker and he could never keep a secret, no matter how trivial.

Besides, talking and gossip and jokes and foolishness were about the only entertainment for everyone on the long, hard journey. No sense providing any ammunition.

The men who were with him and Susanna believed they were married and if they heard differently now, their trust in him as a leader would be broken.

Trust meant life or death on the trail.

Besides, he couldn't make Susanna out to be a liar. She was the one who had told this to Nat.

". . . just somethin' I did on the spur of the moment," Eagle Jack said.

Nat laughed. "Well, she must be as quick as she is beautiful if she could get you hog-tied and branded before you could get home from one short jaunt to Salado," he said. "Did you know her very long?"

"Nope," Eagle Jack said, and started them walking toward the fire. "Just met her that trip."

He needed to get them into the middle of some more people. Enough of this heart-to-heart. Nat always was as curious as a cat, no matter what the subject or the situation.

Now he'd have to try to send word, somehow, to his mother about what the real situation was. There'd be opportunities, from time to time, to send and receive letters at trading posts and towns they might visit, and Nat had a lot of girlfriends back home. One of them even worked for his mother.

This news would travel fast because nobody had ever thought that Eagle Jack would settle down.

His mind was spinning. It was too late now, since they'd already spread the story, and he guessed all this intrigue was necessary. Even with Maynell and Jimbo along as chaperones, it would save a whole lot of problems if everyone believed Susanna was married to him.

She stood up and turned to them as they approached. "Well, hello," she said. "I see y'all have found each other."

"Yes, ma'am," Nat said, with a tip to his hat. "I hope you won't hold it against me none for appearin' here at your fire after I declined your offer of supper."

"Not at all," Susanna said, giving Nat a bright smile, "you're more than welcome."

Now that was a smile that was totally unnecessary, in Eagle Jack's opinion.

The men were coming in by twos and threes to eat and she began helping get the food ready. Eagle Jack watched her bend over and brush the coals off the lid of the oven, thinking how small her waist was and how lush the curve of her breasts.

The heat from the fire made her face glow.

He saw that Nat was watching her, too.

A shaft of resentment stabbed through him. He turned to Marvin and his cohorts, who were picking up their plates from the tail of the chuck wagon.

"Men," he said, "I want you all to meet Nat Straight. He's trail boss for my beef herd that's joining us here. The two herds together will make us about four thousand head to trail to Abilene."

He saw, from the corner of his eye, Susanna's surprised turn toward him and felt her gaze on him. She said nothing, however.

They all shook hands with Nat as Eagle Jack introduced them each by name. Then he introduced Maynell and Susanna.

"You're throwing another herd in with ours?" Maynell asked bluntly.

"Yes."

"And they've got their own chuck wagon."

It wasn't a question, but Eagle Jack answered it anyway. "That's right."

He went to the wagon to get a plate for himself.

"Then who's the cook?"

Maynell's belligerent tone made him turn to face her. She planted her fists on her hips. In one hand she held a long-handled wooden spoon like a weapon.

Uh-oh. He'd expected a few fireworks from Cookie but not from Maynell. He tried to think fast.

"You mean on this wagon?"

"I mean on this trail drive where you're talking two herds in one. You aim for me to cook for another whole crew of men?"

"No, Maynell," Eagle Jack said, keeping his tone calm. "In fact, you don't have to cook at all if you don't want to. The other herd has a cook who's been up the trail several times and he can cook for everybody."

Maynell snorted.

"Hmpf. Never seen a man yet who could cook vittles fittin' to eat. I ain't looking to starve nor t' let y'all starve, neither."

Eagle Jack picked up a tin cup and went to the coffeepot. He tried to make sure of what Maynell was saying.

"If you want to keep on doing what you've been doing, Maynell, that'll be fine."

Cookie would throw one of his famous fits at the very thought of competition, not to mention the waste of building two fires for every meal, heating two pans of water to clean the dishes, and maybe some men getting better food than others. Darn! Why hadn't he left Maynell at home?

He thought of the right thing to say just in time.

"You think about it," he said. "If you want to specialize in such things as pies and cobblers and fluff-duff and raisin pudding and bear sign and such, you can." He finished filling his cup and turned to give her a smile. "Nobody can make pie like you can, Maynell, no matter how many times he's been up the trail."

She smiled back at him.

"Always did like a brown-eyed handsome man who appreciates a little something sweet," she said. "It's pudding tonight."

Then she carried her spoon to the fire and used it to stir the beans.

Pleased with himself, he finished serving himself some of everything and walked to a spot out on the grass between Nat and Marvin. He crossed his feet, balanced his plate in one hand and his cup in the other, and let his knees move outward to lower himself to sit.

But he felt Susanna's gaze on him again. It was so strong it seemed to hold him up in the air. He looked at her, but he couldn't see the approbation there that he had expected. She looked angry, as a matter of fact.

Why, he couldn't possibly say. She should be happy that he'd saved her from having to listen to Maynell's tirades for the rest of the trip. And he'd done it pretty darn smoothly, at that.

Yep. That was one small problem solved.

Now, if he could only have the same good luck with the big ones.

Chapter 10

Eagle Jack balanced his plate on the calves of his legs, set his coffee cup on the ground beside him, and began to eat. He had plenty more pressing problems to think about than who thought he was married and who didn't and who was going to be cooking what for the two crews of drovers.

They were two crews now but they'd have to mold themselves into one and do it in a hurry. A river crossing, no matter how easy it looked, was always one of the most dangerous undertakings on the trail. A million things could go wrong and every man of them had to be alert and willing to do what had to be done. If they didn't work together, somebody could die, a lot of valuable cattle could be lost, or both.

He glanced around while he cut another bite of

his steak. Nat was a good swimmer, so he ought to send him to look for another spot. If a place looked likely, Nat could swim it to judge the depth of the water and the strength of the current.

If they couldn't ford it, though, the wagons would be the trouble, and he might as well accept the fact right now that that would be the case. If there was another good, shallow crossing on this section of the Brazos, he'd never heard of it, and he'd lived in the area all his life.

His only hope for the wagons would be the ferry near a little town called Sycamore. He glanced at the western sky. There was still a lot of daylight left, and a man on a fast horse could get to the ferry and back by midnight. The evenings were steadily getting longer and there'd be a big moon.

He looked around the fire. Marvin's buddy, Rod Cooper, would be a good choice. He was young and full of vinegar and always wanting to horse around and play jokes at bedtime, no matter how hard he'd worked that day. He could put some of that energy to good use.

Everyone ate fast and in silence, as was the custom. When each man finished eating, he went to the wreck pan and threw his dirty plate in. Some kept their coffee cups and refilled them and then gathered again to talk a little. Supper was the only meal of the day that they could ever linger at the fire.

They would be expecting Nat to tell what news he'd gathered coming up the trail and the happenings that had befallen his herd. A new man in camp was expected to offer entertainment in exchange for his food, but they were out of luck tonight because he had a job for Nat to do.

Eagle Jack spoke to Nat quietly and then to Rod. Both of them started for their horses.

As Eagle Jack turned back to the other men, he noticed that Nat gave a smile and a farewell tip of his hat to Susanna as he passed her and that he said something to Maynell. Nat would leave no stone unturned when it came to finding favor with the ladies.

Of course, he had to admit that Nat had a powerful sweet tooth, so he had a reason to be friendly with the cooks. He wasn't necessarily flirting with Susanna.

And he himself had a soft spot in his brain. What the *hell* was he doing noticing who talked to Susanna—who was *not* his wife—when he had big trouble ahead and more decisions to make than a Philadelphia lawyer?

A shocking thought struck him. When Nat arrived and mentioned the silly fake marriage, he'd thought about that so much that he hadn't even thought to ask Nat if he'd heard anything about Molly!

Molly was fast enough to be famous throughout the Southwest. Horsemen all over Central

Texas knew she belonged at the Sixes and Sevens. Nat might've heard something about her whereabouts, but now he'd have to wait until Nat came back to even ask about her.

He sighed as he walked back to the fire. Damn it. He was losing his mind and he needed every bit of brain power he'd ever had to get these herds across the river.

"Men," he said, "I'm sending Nat to look for another spot where we can get across the Brazos. I just got back from the ford and there are five herds already holding there."

"Then we'd have to hold here," somebody said.

"Right. The grazing near the ford is already taken up by the waterbound herds, so we can't crowd in there and we'll be behind them all the way if we stay on the trail."

"How long they been there?" Marvin asked.

"The river's been impassable for a week." Eagle Jack took a minute to look each man in the eye. Swollen rivers were as sure as stampedes to make drovers nervous and on edge. They'd have to trust him on this and he'd have to make the right choices to get it done with no loss of life.

"We gonna swim the wagon over?" Maynell asked.

She sounded as calm as if this happened to her every day.

He turned to look at her. "I'm hoping the Sycamore ferry's running so I can send the wagons around that way. Rod's gone to find out if they are."

"My mules are swimmers," Maynell said, and turned back to her work.

That surprised Eagle Jack. He'd expected her to get into one of her famous swivets at the thought of floating her wagon on a swift-running river.

Susanna didn't even glance at him. She went to the wreck pan and picked it up, then took it around to the other side of the wagon. Eagle Jack followed her.

"We'll know when Rod gets back," he told her, "but if the ferry's not operating, you'll have to get the wagon ready to go in the water. Break the supplies down into packages that can be carried by a man horseback and lash the bedrolls to the top . . ."

She set the pan on the fold-down shelf and turned to face him. "Don't give me orders, Eagle Jack. I'll just take my herd and boss it myself and go on, since Maynell's not scared to swim the river."

He couldn't believe he'd heard her right.

"What are you talking about?"

"We'll be short a man without you, but I'll take your place."

She turned her back on him, picked up the hot water bucket, and poured some onto the dirty dishes. Anger blossomed in his gut like a fire on the prairie.

"Did you ever think that if you can't hire men, you can't boss them, either? Now stop this nonsense and listen to me. We've got to get ready to cross this river."

She flashed him a look that would singe the paint off a barn. "Oh, yes. When it comes time to give orders, you can talk to me just fine."

"I don't have the patience for riddles," he said, and turned to go.

"Stay right where you are," she said. "And *you* listen to *me*."

Grudgingly, he stopped.

"Don't ever try to feed me that line of palaver again, Eagle Jack Sixkiller," she said. "All that about how much I'm learning and how skillful I'm becoming and how I'm your valued segundo and your right-hand, trail-driving woman."

Stunned, he thought about that. He whirled on his heel and faced her.

"What do you mean, line of palaver? I meant what I told you."

"But you didn't tell me you had another herd coming to meet us."

Perplexed, he stared at her. "It was my business."

"Mine, too. Another herd thrown in with mine affects my business plenty."

"It's the other way around, Susanna. Your wet herd slows down my beef herd."

"You still should've told me."

"I told you tonight."

"When you told everybody else."

He held her steady gaze. "Yes."

"Well, what about that promise way back there before we got to Brushy Creek? The promise that we'd make decisions together?"

He lost all patience. "Susanna, get a handle on this. The decision that we'd trail these herds together was already made—the minute I accepted your offer in the jail."

"You never said a word about it to me when you were calling me 'partner' and you had every opportunity to do so."

"I would never have agreed to your deal if I hadn't already been going up the trail. You're just lucky, that's all."

She rolled her eyes. "Oh, yes. Lucky that I hired someone who lies to me. Lucky as a four-leaf clover."

"Save your sarcasm. Get this wagon ready to cross the river." He wheeled and started to walk away, then stopped and turned back. "And I've never lied to you. I don't take kindly to your saying that."

She advanced on him, dishcloth and tin plate in hand. She shook them at him.

"You most certainly have lied to me. Lies of omission. Those are lies, too, you know."

"You've been out in the sun too long. Wear your bonnet tomorrow."

"I'll wear what I please. You're the one who's sun-addled if you think you can relegate me to sitting underneath a bonnet on the seat of the cook wagon. I aim to cross my own cattle tomorrow—my fate and my fortune are in the hands of no man."

He was so mad he didn't dare speak to her. Despite the blood roaring in his head, he made himself bite his tongue and walk away.

All he cared about was that she didn't do something foolish tomorrow and cause a disaster. He didn't care what she thought of him personally. This was nothing but strictly a business deal, pretend marriage or not.

It was hard to imagine how she could be any more trouble to him if the marriage *were* real.

Nat came back around midnight and Rod an hour or so after that. Susanna knew, because she didn't fall asleep until the graveyard shift came in and the bobtail guard took over duty to watch the cattle for the tail end of the night until breakfast.

Eagle Jack was still up, sitting by the fire drinking coffee, when Nat came in. She heard the low murmur of their voices but she couldn't catch a single word, which added to her frustration.

It made no difference. Frustration wasn't important. What was important, what made all the difference, was determination. She had learned that from a thousand different lessons since Everett had been gone.

She had meant every word she had said to Eagle Jack. Maybe the men wouldn't take bossing from her and maybe she couldn't split her herd off and go her own way to Abilene, but she could *lead* the men in taking care of her herd and that was what she was bound and determined to do.

Let them think they were working for Eagle Jack—she didn't care—but she was going to oversee every detail about her cattle. Eagle Jack had another cook with his herd, Maynell didn't need help to make only desserts, and she, Susanna, might as well do what she'd set out to do in the first place before she found out men were so all-fired stubborn about working for a woman: drive a herd up the trail to Kansas.

So, when she heard Maynell climb down from the wagon at dawn to wake the wrangler in charge of the remuda (usually that was Jimbo), Susanna rolled out, put on her clothes, and then strapped on Everett's handgun that she'd been wearing ever since their short-lived stampede. She'd also be scouting on her own sometimes, now. No telling what danger she might meet.

Quickly, with the ease of a growing habit, she tied her bedroll and got everything ready to load on the wagon.

She had just stepped out of the tent when she heard a rider coming in from the west.

The newcomer was at the fire drinking coffee with Eagle Jack by the time she'd stowed everything in the wagon. Susanna joined them.

"Tolly Walters, ma'am," the man said, as he stood and tipped his hat, "of the Rafter W."

"Susanna Copeland with the Slanted S herd," she said, and briskly filled her coffee cup before she sat down on the log beside him.

Eagle Jack gave her a horrified look, raised his eyebrows, and waited for her to leave, but she ignored him. Anything the stranger had to say that could affect her herd was imperative for her to hear.

It didn't seem to bother Tolly that she was a woman inviting herself into men's conversation.

"So what we're doing is building a bridge across a slough upstream where the river's already gone down," Tolly said. "That gets us across to the bank of the shallowest part of the river without bogging in the mud."

"As long as it'll take to build a bridge, the whole riverbed will be down to a trickle," Eagle Jack said. "And it's a day's drive to get there. We might as well just sit around the fire and wait for the water to go down if we're gonna hold up here that long."

That didn't even dent Tolly's enthusiasm. "It won't take more than a day if you'll bring your men to help," he said. "We've already got our outfit and the Broken O boys."

"You've got cowboys working on foot, felling trees and stacking brush so you can drive your cattle across a bridge, onto a little spit of land and then you still have to swim them across the river," Eagle Jack said. "Could be low enough we could even ford it by tomorrow or the next day."

Tolly grinned and shook his head. "Buildin' a bridge beats heck out of hundreds of cattle gettin' drowned or scattered plumb to kingdom come."

"Have to be a heck of bridge," Eagle Jack said.

"We'd have to keep them moving at all costs," Susanna said, "onto the bridge and into the river. No hesitating."

"Yes, *ma'am*," said the cheerful Tolly. "Once the leaders take the bridge, we can't let 'em even think about stopping. Especially with two more herds behind them."

"But we can't crowd 'em, either," Eagle Jack reminded them.

"Nope," Tolly said, and he took a sip of coffee, "then we're liable to have 'em mill and that'd be hell on the bridge *or* in the water."

While Maynell finished cooking breakfast, the three of them talked about it from every angle they could see. It felt good. Susanna loved it. Both men were listening to what she said and taking her ideas into consideration.

"It'll take you a day to drive your cattle up

there, and another day, probably, for us all to finish the bridge," Tolly said. "That'll still put our herds way ahead of the five waterbound outfits. This ford's not going to be passable for another week."

Susanna held her breath. Tolly had convinced her and she thought they ought to do this but she was afraid to say that in so many words. Then Eagle Jack might feel she was pushing him and do the opposite. At least, that's the way Everett had been.

"I'm in," Eagle Jack said finally.

"So am I," Susanna said.

He looked at her, surprised, as if to say he'd already spoken for both of them.

But Tolly took her for her own boss. "That's the both of your crews, then," he said. He slapped his leg and stood up. "We're in business. We'll all be north of the Brazos and on our way to the Red in two days' time. Very well, then, boys and girls, let's eat our breakfast before we hit the trail, 'cause we never know where we'll be for dinner."

That made Susanna smile. Not only that Tolly, who was the visitor, was calling everyone to eat, but also because he'd fully accepted her. It would be Tolly bossing the building of the bridge, so she'd get a chance to show Eagle Jack what she could do.

Susanna had quit scouting with him and started riding out alone in front of her herd. Eagle Jack kept thinking of the old joke about the snuff-dipping woman in church who, when the preacher began to condemn that habit, called out, "You've done quit preachin' and gone to meddlin', now."

He had ridden back to talk to Nat and the boys as they drove the Sixes and Sevens herd up behind the Slanted S, and Susanna had just gone right on out of sight without him. Without a word. Come to think of it, she hadn't given him very many words after Tolly left them.

Or while Tolly was there, for that matter. She'd been talking to Tolly, not to him, Eagle Jack.

The one thing certain was that Susanna had quit listening and gone to meddling, now—sitting in on his talk with Tolly and speaking right up like she knew what she was talking about—and it was liable to have dire consequences for her. He couldn't allow it. He absolutely could not. Whether she wanted it to be true or not, he was responsible for her and he had to make the big decisions, like whether to help with the bridge and cross their cattle over it or not.

Thank goodness, they had agreed on what answer to give Tolly, but next time things might not work out so well.

There might not even *be* a next time if she wandered off and got herself killed or kidnapped by some lowlife or else hopelessly lost.

His stomach clutched and he lifted his horse into a slow lope.

He had to go find her, whether or not it made

her even angrier with him. *He* was the one who should be angry with *her,* anyhow—this kind of behavior just to pay him back for not telling her every detail of his business in advance was too petty for him to endure.

He loped up to Nat. "I'm going on to pick a nooning place," he said.

"Right, boss." Nat grinned. "Tell that pretty wife of yours I hope she's the one doing the cooking this time."

Eagle Jack answered with a noncommittal wave of his hand and rode off. That was another thing. If she was going to keep on spreading that story around, she had better start acting like his wife.

By the time he caught up with the wagons an hour later, he had a dozen things ready to say to her, but Susanna wasn't there. Unfortunately, both Cookie and Maynell were.

What had looked, from a distance, like a normal scene of two chuck wagons peacefully setting up in a shady meadow to cook a meal for a couple of outfits was, up close, a battle of wills and a war of words, all guaranteed to leave a bunch of drovers as hungry to ride out as they were the moment they rode in.

Eagle Jack rode into the meadow, crossed behind the wagons, and pulled his horse up in the shade of the low-growing limbs of a big live oak tree. He got down. He loosened his cinch and dropped his reins for a ground-tie.

He walked toward them.

All that time, neither cook so much as glanced at him. Maynell had a fire going with a coffeepot hanging over it and hot coals in a trench to one side. She appeared to be guarding her handiwork with the spade she'd been using to move the coals.

Cookie stood facing her, legs apart, heels dug in. "That'd be the dumbest waste of wood I ever seen," Cookie was saying. "I ain't takin' orders from nobody and I ain't buildin' no second fire."

"Suit yourself," Maynell said, "but you won't be usin' mine. If you're such a cook, you oughtta know to carry wood on the wagon."

"I do," Cookie said, "and we'll use it for supper." He stared her right in the eye.

She stared back.

"Women should never go up the trail," he said.

"Men should never be cooks," she said.

"And meals should never be late," Eagle Jack said, "or the three of us might have to drive four thousand head of cattle from here to Kansas."

Finally, they both turned and looked at him.

"I know it's dangerous for me to get in the middle of this," he said, "but I reckon I can take a chance since there's two cooks on this drive."

"Is that a threat to fire one of us?" Maynell said.

"Take it any way you want to," Eagle Jack said.

Maynell and Cookie exchanged a glance.

"Well, fire away," Maynell said, "but I can tell you right now neither one of us is leavin'." She looked at Cookie for confirmation.

"Damn straight we're not," he said. "This outfit'd starve to death down to the last man if I rode away from here."

Maynell nodded at Eagle Jack triumphantly, then she realized exactly what Cookie had said. She rounded on him, hands on her hips. "If you rode away from here? That sounds like an insult to me, old man."

He repeated Eagle Jack's words. "Take it any way you want to."

"Then I'll take it as a dare," she said, and hit her spade against the leg of the cook rack for a ringing note of emphasis. "Put your best foot in the soup, Mr. Cookie, and we'll see whose fire them boys comes back to for second helpings."

That was all it took. Cookie started building his fire, Maynell started a skillet heating on hers.

Eagle Jack set his jaw. He'd thought he brought this whole situation under control when he'd had his brilliant idea to assign all the sweets to Maynell. Now they'd be cooking more than could be eaten at one meal and the men hated leftovers with a passion.

But he certainly didn't want to get crossways of them again—either or both of them.

Damn it all! *Where* was Susanna? If she was going to insist on coming along on this drive, and then insist on trying to be the one to take her own herd across the Brazos and do the scouting all by herself, why didn't she take care of the cooks?

If she wouldn't *be* one, she could at least keep them straightened out.

"Why don't y'all pick one thing a day?" he said, trying for an offhand tone. "It could be a contest of coffees one day and sourdoughs the next."

"And stew the next and steak the next," Maynell said.

"And fluff-duff the next," Cookie said, in a tone that brooked no disagreement. "I ain't lettin' you be the only one makin' sweet stuff."

"Fine," Maynell said, "but it still won't do you no good. You're jist scared they'll all vote fer my food if I'm the one givin' 'em sweets, but they will anyhow."

Eagle Jack's headache was trying to come back. It seemed that his peacemaking idea hadn't been such a good one, after all. Listening to these taunts and threats every day might be a whole lot worse than eating leftovers.

"They'll vote with their feet and their empty plates," Cookie said. "We'll see whose wagon has a path beat to it in a hurry."

Eagle Jack turned toward his horse. He had to get out of there. "Have y'all seen Susanna?" he said.

"She'll be back in a minute," Maynell said. "She's gone up the river a little ways to see if it's out of its banks up there."

"I'll go meet her."

He walked faster, eager to get to his mount. Anything to have a little peace and quiet and figure out what to say to Susanna to keep her around the camp. One more skirmish like this and he'd have to knock Cookie and Maynell's hard heads together and then he'd have no cook at all.

The horse he was riding was the youngest one in his mount and, ground-tied or not, the gelding was moving around, edging out into the sunlight from the shade of the tree, throwing its head around and acting as if it wanted to run. Eagle Jack broke into a trot, trying to keep it slow and easy so as not to encourage the horse to bolt.

That was all he needed on top of everything else today—to have his horse run off and leave him afoot and that be the subject of all the hoorahing and laughter for the next couple of days. Or until something funnier happened, which could be a while longer than that.

He slowed back into a walk as he got closer and began saying, "Whoa, now, bay horse, whoa now."

The bay pricked its ears and looked upstream. It nickered.

A horse nickered back and Eagle Jack turned to

see that it was Fred, with Susanna in the saddle, coming toward them at a nice long trot.

He lifted his hand, thinking it was best to be as friendly as possible if he was going to have any hope of talking her into better behavior. She returned the greeting and he went back to trying to catch his horse, who was truly dancing now.

It would be even worse for him to run off with Susanna watching.

"Now, now," he muttered, "come on, now."

Finally he had the reins in his hand and he stepped around to put his foot in the stirrup. As his seat hit the saddle, he turned his mount to go meet Susanna, who was coming on much faster now.

As soon as he saw her, he froze.

She was almost to him and she held a gun in her hand. Somewhere, way back in the recesses of his mind, he recognized it as the old hogleg she'd been wearing when he'd seen her that morning. It was leveled, pointing straight at him.

Before he could even take a breath, she fired.

Chapter 11

Something slapped him in the face right after the old gun roared. There wasn't the hot sting of a bullet, though. A musty odor and a cold roughness tickled the one thin edge of his mind that was still working—a snake fell across the withers of his horse.

The bay broke apart in a heartbeat. It got its head down and bowed its back faster than Eagle Jack could blink. Then it was all high jumps and hard licks and the world going up and down into the sky.

Eagle Jack's instincts took over—at least *this* was an understandable, familiar thing that was happening. For one long minute he rode the horse. He stayed in the saddle and in both stirrups just long enough to think that when the bay got tired, Eagle Jack would still be on top.

But the snake stayed with them and the bay began to sunfish so desperately to be rid of it that it turned sideways and nearly upside down in the air and Eagle Jack lost his center of gravity. He hit the ground as hard as he ever had, landed on his bottom with a force that jarred his teeth and made him bite his tongue and that knocked the last scrap of breath out of his body. The snake fell, too, not far away, and the bay lit out across the prairie, headed straight for the herd with the force of a strong, straight-line wind.

The boys had better be paying attention, or else they might be fighting a stampede there in a minute.

That was his last sensible thought for what felt like a long, long time. He collapsed full length onto his back, his head hit a lump of dirt with enough force to addle him—if he wasn't, already—and all he could do was try to draw breath.

Futilely, *helplessly*, try to draw breath.

After what seemed an age with no air, faces appeared above him: Susanna. And Cookie and Maynell.

Eagle Jack stared up at them with eyes he couldn't close and saw Nat, Rod, and Marvin appear, too. Above Cookie and Maynell. At Susanna's height.

Those four were mounted. They ought to be riding the other direction, trying to stop the bay before it bucked its way into the herd and scattered it all over Texas. He tried to open his mouth to say so, but he couldn't even do that.

His mind began to work again, though.

A shot fired meant a call for help or a predator near the camp or lethal trouble in their midst or even a man already dead. More men would be there in a minute—if they weren't trying to keep the cattle from heading back toward the Rio Grande—and here he'd be, laid out in the dust like a greenhorn by a horse scared by a snake that he didn't even see.

The boys would hoo-rah him about this one for days to come.

Before he could get enough air back into his lungs to move a hand or sit up, much less give an order of any kind, the whole bunch was talking about him as if he were dead, or something.

"I take it that he ain't shot or he couldn't have rode that horse that long."

Dimly, Eagle Jack realized that was Nat's voice.

"You mean for thirty some-odd seconds?" Cookie said, with a chuckle. "He sure didn't stick with him for a whole minute, I know that."

"*Of course* he ain't shot," Maynell said. "Susanna ain't gonna shoot our brown-eyed handsome man."

"I reckon I've got brown eyes, too," Nat said, always having to draw a woman's attention to himself, the whiny baby.

"But I reckon nobody's callin' you handsome," Rod said. "So watch out, Nat, you're liable to get shot."

Eagle Jack would've said something similar himself if he could've talked.

And it was good that Maynell acted like she didn't even hear Nat and so did Susanna. Maynell was bending over, poking around on Eagle Jack's person, searching him over for damage. He wished Susanna would.

No, he didn't. She'd made him look like a tenderfoot fool.

Then Cookie made it all even worse. "That snake must've scared Eagle Jack as much as it did the bay," he said. "I never seen that boy buck off quite so soon."

If only he could talk. He'd tell that mouthy old cusie he'd stayed on the bay for a whole lot longer than a minute.

"What snake? What happened?" Marvin said.

"That there cottonmouth was on a limb right at Eagle Jack's head," Cookie said. "Miss Susanna shot it, it fell across the pommel of the saddle and that was all she wrote for the bay horse. Eagle Jack only rode 'im the first couple of jumps."

He didn't have to keep saying that. Eagle Jack wanted to tell Cookie to shut up more than he'd wanted anything in a long, long time.

Nat, Marvin, and Rod chuckled at the vision he'd created.

"Always heard 'if it was a snake it woulda bit you,'" Nat said. "Sounds like the boss woulda been snake bit if you hadn't've been quick and accurate, Mrs. Sixkiller."

"Thank you," Susanna said.

Hmpf. Prissy as an old maid schoolteacher. She oughtta know it wasn't a woman's place to be running around camp shooting at everything that moved.

The least she could do would be to show a little concern and get down from that horse and see about him. After all, she could've killed him.

"He's just got the wind knocked out of him," Maynell pronounced, as she finished looking him over and lifted his head off the ground.

She crooked his neck so much it would've cut off his air, even if his lungs had been working.

How come nothing was like it was in the storybooks? How come some bad guy hadn't shot at him and Susanna wasn't down here beside him on her knees, softly soothing his brow?

She owed him that. After all, she'd bought him a world of aggravation with the men.

He tried again to move his lips, but he couldn't speak.

"Good thing that horse is a pioneer bucker," Cookie said, frowning down at him. "If he hadn't a-kept on lookin' for new ground, he mighta bashed your head in on that very tree limb the snake fell off of."

At least somebody was talking *to* him, now, instead of about him. They must be expecting him to live.

"Good thing your head is hard as a gourd, boss, is what I'm thinkin'," Nat said.

A whole new heat suffused Eagle Jack's limbs. Those two wouldn't stop teasing him about this until the Judgment Day. Drat Susanna, anyhow.

He thought about all the possibilities of jokes they could make about him, since he was powerless at that moment to try to stave them off.

Eagle Jack Sixkiller himself, sitting under a tree limb with a snake on it—a big snake—and he hadn't known it was there any more than a greenhorn would've. A woman had saved him from it.

And then he'd let a broke horse throw him, like he was the biggest tenderfoot in Texas.

Now he was lying prone in the dust, helpless as a kitten.

Who *wouldn't* hoo-rah him?

All he could do was glare at Susanna. If she'd minded her own business, as she'd been trying so hard to do this morning by going off and leaving him, none of this would ever have happened. He'd have ridden out from under the tree, no worse off from never knowing that the snake was there.

Every bit of this fiasco was all her fault. And, dear God in heaven, shooting at him with that relic of a gun! It was a miracle that it could be sighted in enough to hit the broad side of a barn. She could just as easily have sent a bullet through his head.

"Damn it . . . Susanna," he said, with the first ragged breath he was able to take, "why couldn't you . . . have just hollered a warning at me?"

"I didn't have time to holler," she said, with a complete lack of concern that he could have been mortally wounded and no apparent joy whatsoever that he had recovered enough to speak at last. "He was starting to come off that limb, unwinding there beside your head."

Nat chuckled. "You're lucky you married, boss," he said. "You need somebody to take care of you, it's plain to see."

She didn't have to *say* right out, plain and simple, that the snake was hanging down practically in front of his face. She was, without a doubt, the most aggravating woman alive.

"Yeah. What's the matter with you, anyhow?" Cookie asked, lighting into him with a frown on his face that would scare a bear. "Instead of cussin' at her, you oughtta be *thankin'* your wife for savin' your worthless hide."

Damn it. Here was entertainment for the outfit for miles to come.

Eagle Jack gritted his teeth. He'd bitten his tongue when he landed and that made him even madder. Every bit of this misery was totally unnecessary.

"Oh, darling," Susanna said, sweet as sugar, "I just couldn't let anything happen to you. I was so scared that snake would bite you right on your handsome nose."

Great. *Now* she chose to play up the pretend marriage. Well, two could play at that game.

"Thank you, sweetheart," he said, with his sore tongue from behind his clenched teeth. "You saved my life."

He gave her a heavy-lidded look.

"I can't wait to show you my appreciation."

Her cheeks pinkened, which gratified him. And nobody else said anything, which was even better.

Cowboys weren't accustomed to any such innuendo in the company of a lady, married or not. But it didn't faze Maynell.

"Fine, you do that," Maynell said, supporting his shoulder as he tried to sit up, as if he were a helpless baby, "but you're not able for any such shenanigans right now, mister." She looked at Nat and Rod. "Boys, he's weak as a cat. Let's get him into the shade over there by my wagon. We've got to eat dinner now."

As if he were holding up the whole drive just for the amusement of lying on the ground. His anger blossomed.

"No. Y'all had better be riding out to the herd," he said, forcing more air into his body so he could try to take control again, "last time I saw my horse he was headed that way."

"That young boy, Johnny, with your beef herd turned him," Rod said. "Got to him soon enough he didn't spook the cattle."

"Yeah," Cookie said. "That's another thing to be glad about, Eagle Jack. Your horse coulda caused a stampede, you know."

Without a doubt, when the strength came back into his arms and legs, he'd strangle Cookie into silence. He'd stuff a bandana into his mouth and tie it so tight behind his head his eyes would squeeze shut. He'd make him wish he'd never learned to talk at all.

Then Susanna smiled at him and he forgot about Cookie. She had a beautiful smile when she chose to use it—maybe it was because she had such a beautiful mouth.

But then, when she spoke, she had to go and ruin it.

"We may be driven to shoot the brown-eyed handsome men in this outfit or run them off," Susanna said, looking straight into his eyes and grinning, "but we're not letting the snakes bite them. No, sirree."

So she was going to join the others in rawhiding him. Little vixen. He didn't *care* if she rode away all by herself straight into trouble.

But first he was going to teach her a lesson.

"Honey, I need you to hold my head," he said. "Maybe instead of riding scout this afternoon, you oughtta make me a bed in the wagon."

She gave him a long, straight look. "Of course, darling. Let's just get you into the shade for right now." He pulled away from Maynell. "I don't need to be carried," he said. "Bring me my horse . . ."

The world started spinning.

"You're in no shape to ride," Maynell said, her tone suddenly sharp.

"Yes, I am."

She tried to guide him back down. "You ain't even ready to sit up. Lay back down."

He resisted the pressure of her hand. "Somebody get my horse . . ."

Everything faded before his eyes. The sun went down and the world went black and, in front of all of them, he fainted like a tender girl. Flat out onto the hard, ungiving ground.

When Eagle Jack came to, he was alone in the back of the jolting, swaying wagon with the bedrolls shifting under him. There was a cloth on his forehead that had dried and stuck there in the heat, but no soft hand stroking his skin.

He thought of the poultice Susanna had tried to apply at her house that first night, but there was no tell-tale medicinal smell of antiphlogistine. There were smells of dust and cattle and leather and sweat, but no faint scent of flowers, either.

No fragrance of Susanna.

A sharp disappointment stabbed him. A feeling of hurt, really. Didn't she care what was wrong with him? What if he'd been hurt inside and become sicker and sicker while unconscious?

He sat up, ripped the cloth off his head and threw it out the back of the wagon. The sun was halfway down the sky. He'd been out for two or three hours.

This also meant that his little plan to get back at Susanna, his *wife*, hadn't worked.

"Hey, hey, easy there, mules!"

Maynell's voice. Maynell was driving the *bed* wagon?

He turned and saw, through the front opening, that it was, indeed, Maynell on the driver's seat. Susanna was riding up to meet the wagon as it slowed.

He'd make her think twice about scouting alone. He wasn't going to let her out of his sight.

Eagle Jack started scrambling toward them, over the bedrolls and other claptrap of the bed wagon.

"I need a horse," he said, the instant he emerged from under the canvas top. "Where's the remuda?"

Startled, Maynell glared at him. "Lay back down," she said. "I didn't risk letting Cookie's helper drive my chuck wagon just so's I could watch you ride a horse."

He glared back at her and turned to Susanna. She had turned her mount and was riding alongside.

"Where's my horse?" he said.

She grinned in the most maddening way. "Surely you don't want the *same* horse," she said. "Remember you couldn't stay in the saddle the last time you tried to ride him."

"I don't care *what* horse," he said, every word clipped by cold anger. "I'm getting out of this wagon and I don't intend to walk."

"All the horses are back with the cattle right now," she said. "A half mile or so."

"How far are we from the bridge?"

"Our crews are already working," she said. "I came back to point Maynell to that clump of cottonwoods over there."

She did so, and the two women talked for a minute about the camp site. Then Susanna turned to him again.

"And, of course, I came back to see how you're doing," she said. "How do you feel?"

"Now that you so thoughtfully ask," he said, in his most sarcastic tone, "I feel as damn good as I ever felt in my life. Now get me a horse."

"You'll have to wait until the wrangler brings them up. It shouldn't be too long."

He glanced at the distance between the wagon and her mount, ignored the slight dizziness plaguing him, and stepped out. He threw his leg over and landed behind her on the rump of her horse.

Not a perfect feat but a respectable one that cheered him a little. He put his arms around her and took the reins before she recovered from the surprise of his move.

"What are you *doing*?" she said.

"Eagle Jack Sixkiller, you get back in this wagon," Maynell said. "I've gone to a lot of trouble to take care of you and you're gonna do what I tell you."

"Go on, May," he said. "Start supper. Tolly said his cook is a hell of a hand with an axe, so you and Cookie'll have his crew to feed on top of ours."

Thank God, his memory was still there. His brain was still working.

And so was his temper. He'd spoken in a sharper tone than he normally ever used with a woman, but, damn it, he'd had all of this babying he could take.

"All right, then," Maynell said, her mouth tight with anger. "But don't you be expecting any pie."

Susanna laughed. "Now you've done it, Eagle Jack. You've gone and offended your strongest supporter."

"That's right," Maynell snapped. "Handsome is as handsome does, brown eyes or not."

She raised the lines, slapped them down across the mules, and took off across the rocky ground at an alarming clip.

"Now," Eagle Jack said, laying the rein against the horse's neck and turning him around, "we're going to see about the cattle. I can't believe you're so doggone loco over that infernal bridge that you've taken the crew away from the herd."

Susanna stiffened in his arms. He hated that. She absolutely just fit against him, he'd noticed during these fleeting moments.

"We've got two big herds to make into one, in case you've forgotten, Susanna. They need to be held together."

She jerked her head around as far as she could with him so close behind her and her eyes flashed blue fire. She grabbed for the reins but she didn't have a chance against his greater strength.

"I am *not* loco. I am perfectly capable of bossing this drive any time you choose to faint and fall over, Eagle Jack."

Hot fury chased the worried anger out of his veins.

"You had no call to shoot and scare my horse," he said, through gritted teeth. "This is what comes of a woman carrying a firearm and shooting at random in the middle of camp."

She butted him backward with her head, slamming painfully into his breastbone.

"This is what comes of a man falling off his horse," she said, also through gritted teeth. "If you'd stuck, you wouldn't have been knocked silly at all."

"I haven't been knocked silly."

"Then what is your excuse for making such ridiculous, outlandish remarks?"

She tried again for the reins back, but he wouldn't let her even get close. He held them down against his thigh with one hand and grabbed both of hers with his free one.

These gloves she wore were still the ones with the holes in them. He'd forgotten all about the new ones he'd bought her.

Well, he might just save them for some girl in Abilene. He couldn't remember now why he'd ever bought Susanna a gift in the first place.

"You turn me loose," she said, her husky voice sounding downright dangerous. "I'm warning you, Eagle Jack Sixkiller, that I will not abide being treated this way."

"Well, I will not abide my cattle being scattered all over Texas and Mexico."

"They aren't! They won't be! I left enough men with them and they're perfectly calm and they'll be here soon."

"You hope, Susanna. Let's just go and see for ourselves how they're doing."

"You brute!" she said. "I promised Tolly I'd come right back and help drag brush to the bridge."

That made him angrier.

"You have no business promising Tolly anything," he said.

First Nat and now Tolly.

"Don't be promising anything to any man," he said, before he thought, "tell them they'll have to deal with your husband."

Her sudden laugh was almost a snort. "Oh, yes, how could I forget?" she said, in a sarcastic tone. "Especially when you're kidnapping me while I'm on my own horse. That's just exactly like something my first husband would've done."

That remark stung. It was an insult to be compared to the evil Everett, but now he'd be embarrassed to turn her hands loose in response.

Her wrists were resting now in the tangle of his fingers. However, her pulse was beating fast, as fast as his heart was.

It was anger that was causing that. Anger and concern about the herd.

His blood was not pulsing through his veins like a freight train because he was so close to her, feeling the curve of her breast against the inside of his arm. Smelling the lemony scent of her hair in spite of her ridiculous leather riding hat.

But what about her? Was her pulse drumming like this beneath her smooth skin because she was angry, too?

Or was it because of his nearness?

"I'll promise whatever I like to whomever," she said.

With a sudden jerk, she pulled her hands free. He let them go.

"Now you turn this horse around, Eagle Jack Sixkiller, or . . ."

"Or what?" he demanded.

"Or I'll . . . I'll take my herd and go off on my own as soon as we cross the bridge."

One thing that was totally consistent about Susanna was her yearning for independence. For self-sufficiency. It was admirable, but it could kill her, too.

The other consistent feature he'd noticed was her tendency to do the opposite of what she was told.

"Make that a promise," he said. "You go right ahead, Susanna, and do what you have to do."

She stiffened even more and tried to sit up away from him but there wasn't room in the circle of his arms.

"I will," she said. "And I'll take Maynell with me."

"Fine," he said. "She's already cut off my supply of pie."

"Oooh," she said, narrowing her eyes as she twisted around to look up at him, "that's all you can think about, isn't it, Eagle Jack? Your desserts and your cattle."

He used both hands to hold her there, splaying his fingers twined with the reins over her slender body just beneath her full, soft breasts. Slowly, he brushed the underside of them with his thumbs.

"No," he said. "Sometimes I think about this, Susanna."

She looked at his mouth as if she already knew what he meant.

He kissed her, light and easy.

Somewhere, deep inside, he intended to leave it at that. Somewhere, deep inside, he knew he should leave it at that.

But her lips parted beneath his and they tasted like honey. Her tongue touched his and desire shot through him in a lightning bolt of wanting.

More. He wanted more.

He let the reins drop and caressed her hungrily, running his palms over her back, feeling the heat of her skin through her shirt. Her hat slipped off to hang around her neck on its stampede strings, and he thrust his fingers into her hair, cradling her head in his hands.

She wanted more, too, and she told him so with a helpless little whimpering sound deep in her throat and the silent messages of her tongue and her lips. She wanted to know him, they said, all of him, and she wanted this kiss to last forever.

So did he. That was all he knew for certain at that moment. So did he.

She broke the kiss at last, broke it with no warning at all, and turned her face away from him.

"Susanna?"

"Eagle Jack," she whispered, "don't kiss me anymore. Just don't do it, okay?"

She leaned forward, away from him, and bumped the horse with her heels to move him from a walk to a trot. Eagle Jack realized he hadn't even known they'd slowed down.

Without turning, Susanna spoke out loud. Solemnly.

"This is a business arrangement," she said seriously. "We can't either one afford to forget that."

Eagle Jack realized how much he hated solemnity.

"I know you like to kiss me," he said.

He leaned sideways to look at her face. For a minute he thought he had made her smile.

But she didn't. And she didn't even glance at him.

"I like it too much," she said.

He relaxed and squeezed their mount with his knees, lifted them into a slow, rocking lope with Susanna still in the circle of his arms.

"That's no way to think—quittin' somethin' because you like it too much," he said, murmuring the words into her ear. "Life's too short for such foolishness."

She didn't answer.

He smiled to himself. That was exactly the reason she stayed in his mind all the time, the reason she had such a power to draw him to her. She was the greatest challenge of any woman he'd ever known.

That was probably the reason, too that he felt the most passion for her that he'd felt for any woman. It had been there even when he'd been lying on the ground looking up into her laughing eyes.

He might as well admit to it. And he might as well go ahead and make love with her, which would be very good for her because she was way too constrained in her life. Maybe he could teach her to enjoy life more.

He had changed his mind. He wouldn't wait for her to come to him. After they had crossed the Brazos, he would go to her, he would take her in his arms and make her beg to stay there.

She would beg him to make love to her.

And they would let the passion that shimmered between them like a light live in all its glory. They would let it run its course and die out and then she wouldn't have such a hold on him anymore. Then he could forget about her.

Then he'd be fancy free again and Susanna would be just one more of the many women in his life.

Chapter 12

The place Tolly had chosen to build the bridge was a miry slough that oozed with only a few inches of water. That water was steadily getting deeper, though, because of the rain to the west, and all the men were working as hard as they could to fill in the last of the turf and dirt in the logs that rested on top of the sixty-foot-long, thick pile of brush that they'd laid down first.

A bridge was the only way to approach the river here, because a man could tell by looking that this swampy mess would bog cattle right and left. Tolly was right about that.

Eagle Jack sat his horse and looked it all over. He didn't like it.

Yes, it had solid banks on either side—he had already ridden across to check that out. And yes, the river did flow more slowly and more shallow just beyond it than at any place they'd looked at downstream. But he still didn't like it.

Something in his gut had told him the very idea of a bridge was a lost cause as soon as the word came out of Tolly's mouth there at the campfire that morning. But he'd been desperate to get across and desperate to get ahead of the five herds already waiting at the ford. He had let that desperation drive him.

And now the bridge was nearly completed and he had given a day and a half of his and his crew's strength to the task. Like it or not, he was in it now.

It was either use the bridge or swim the thousands of cattle and all the men—not to mention the two women—across a deeper, faster part of the river. That'd be dangerous as sin right now, with it freshening even more from the new rains. They might as well take the bridge.

Tolly rode up to him.

"Bring up your herd," he said. "Mine is two miles out and scattered more. You can cross while we bring them up."

"We have no right to go ahead of you," Eagle Jack said. "This bridge was your idea and your crew did most of the work."

"No time to argue," Tolly said, turning to look at the sky, "it's raining harder to the west."

A few sprinkles splattered onto the brims of their hats.

"And moving this way," Tolly added. "Besides,

your cattle aren't as wild. Mine need a good example to follow."

"My beef herd's not too bad but Susanna's wet herd is," Eagle Jack said.

Susanna. He didn't even know if she could swim.

He couldn't decide which he'd rather do: go first and get it over with or hang back and see how the bridge held up.

"So we'll send your beef herd first," Tolly said, as he started to ride away. "Head 'em up."

This was Tolly's project. That made him the boss. Which was why Eagle Jack hated getting involved in something like this.

He sat straighter in the saddle and banished every hesitant thought. Too late for that now.

"All right, Tolly," he said. "Let's get it done."

Eagle Jack had the men bring his and Susanna's herds around in a circle, more than a mile in diameter, and as the rear end of the cattle—made up of his beef herd—was passing, they turned the last hundred head, put their usual leaders at their head, and pushed them toward the bridge.

The cattle balked and wouldn't even consider it.

"Let's try it again," Eagle Jack said, "and bring them up slowly, keeping them in a solid body until we get them opposite the bridge. We'll round them up slowly, just like we were going to bed them down."

He turned to looked at Tolly, who was waiting to help.

"Then how about you put a long line on one of your oxen, Tolly, and lead him through them and onto the bridge?"

Tolly thought about that. "That'll work," he said. "I'll bet you money your leaders will follow Old Whitey."

"Go get him," Eagle Jack said. Then he turned back to his men. "Careful not to crowd them, boys. We all know if we get them milling, the jig's up. He swung his horse around and came face-to-face with Susanna, mounted on Fred. "I thought you were crossing with the wagons," he told her.

"I am. Cookie said we'd use saddle horses instead of the mules to swim them across the river, so I can help y'all until then."

His heart thudded once, hard, against his ribs. He had to be careful how he put this or she'd do just the opposite. Except she had promised, way back there at Brushy Creek, to follow orders in matters of life and death.

"Yours doesn't need to be one of the ropes on the wagon," he said. "Is Fred a good swimmer?"

"The best," she assured him, patting the horse's neck. "Now what do you need me to do?"

He hesitated thoughtfully. "Mainly just to get yourself and Maynell across safely. Cookie will insist on managing the wagons. You know how bullheaded he is."

She cocked her head and looked at him.

"I need all the men on this herd right now," he said. "So y'all will have to wait a little while."

"I'm not going to just sit around and watch," she said.

"All right. Help push the cattle onto the bridge. But once they're moving, go back to the wagons."

"You'll need every hand you can get when the cattle go off the end of the bridge and hit the river," she said. "Cookie and Maynell can take care of the wagons."

He bit his tongue and tried to hold his temper.

"That's not the question," he said, proud of himself for the calm tone that came out of his mouth. "I'll send men back to help them with the wagons."

She gave him her narrow-eyed, dangerously stubborn look. "So then what *is* the question?"

His control snapped. "Your safety, damn it. This is one of the life-and-death times you promised to take orders from me."

"I can swim like a fish," she insisted. "But we're not in the river now. Where do you want me to get this herd moving?"

So he gave her a position and went back to the cattle. He'd watch her like a hawk when they got onto the bridge.

The men worked the herds perfectly, keeping the beef herd nearest the bridge, and Tolly caught up his white ox. A few small bunches tried to mill, but Susanna rode through one of them and Marvin another and after about a half hour, they all quieted down.

Then Tolly, whistling, rode into the herd leading his ox on a long rope, heading for the bridge. He led the ox onto it, giving him all the time he needed and stopping every few feet.

A few cattle started to follow them. Eagle Jack held his breath. They shied and turned back.

Tolly waited but it was no use. He led the ox back in among the cattle and tried again. He tried the trick again and again but the herd was having none of it.

The heavy clouds were coming closer now from the west and the sprinkling rain was becoming more frequent.

"Let's try a different bunch next," Eagle Jack suggested. "And if they won't go, we'll force them."

He was going to have to do something. Tolly's herd was coming up behind his now.

So they shifted the cattle, but these new ones were just as sulky as the others. They were having no part of such a strange contraption as a bridge.

Next, Eagle Jack tried forcing them, running the remuda back and forth across the bridge several times and then trotting them onto it ahead of the cattle. The cattle turned tail at the last minute and would have none of it.

It began to rain in earnest.

They tried cutting out a small group and running them from a distance so that they couldn't turn back but even that didn't work. Everyone was looking to him, and Eagle Jack was out of ideas.

He was fighting despair, trying to hold on to his temper, and reaching for his sense of humor all at the same time.

"Well, boys, we may have to hold them here until they cross or starve to death," he said, only half joking.

He was furious. First the snake and getting bucked off a broke horse and now this. Pretty soon he'd *have* to let Susanna be the boss because the men would take orders from a woman before they would from him.

He had run the length of his rope. His head was as empty of solutions for this problem as the lowering sky was of sunlight.

Eagle Jack Sixkiller, the trail boss who can take a herd to the Brazos, but no farther. Forget about Kansas. Not only would the men scorn him, but so would Susanna.

Susanna.

It floated into his head from the gray clouds overhead that Susanna's herd was a wet herd. Nothing on the face of the earth would stir range cattle like a bellowing calf.

He reached for his rope.

Everybody within sight watched him ride

through the stubborn cattle. It was only minutes after he reached a bunch of Susanna's wet herd until he had his rope around the neck of a calf.

As he came back through the herd, the frantic mother cow followed her baby. In turn, a string of steers followed her, becoming more and more frenzied at the sound of the bawling pair. Eagle Jack dragged the calf, caterwauling at the top of its lungs, straight to and then onto the bridge.

The crazed mother cow came right along.

The excited steers stayed tight on her heels.

The commotion spread through the herd and more cattle moved toward the bridge. And onto it. They gathered and pushed at the entrance until the riders could barely hold them back—three or four men, plus Susanna, had all they could do to let only few enough pass to keep the chain of horned beasts from breaking.

Susanna looked up from the work and met his gaze over the sea of horns forming between them. She sent him a smile that would rival the sun.

It warmed his blood so fiercely he could feel it moving underneath his skin. He had done it, that smile said. He had done what no one else could do. He was the hero of the hour.

He'd felt good before in his life. He generally always felt good about himself. But Susanna's smile made him feel the best. In her eyes, he was ten feet tall and bulletproof.

That beautiful smile stayed before his eyes

when he reached the end of the bridge and hit the river, all the time he swam his horse and the calf across. They climbed out onto the far bank and got out of the way of the wave of cattle following as Eagle Jack looked back to see some of his drovers already in the water, swimming their horses downstream to the cattle to keep them from drifting too far.

He had good men. He was thankful for that.

As soon as he'd driven the leaders far enough onto the north side of the river to settle down and graze in the direction of Kansas, he got down and took his loop off the calf. Mother and calf reunited joyfully and finally quit bawling.

Eagle Jack coiled his rope and dropped it over his saddle horn as he rode back toward the river. Now if he could get back over to the south side before Susanna left her post at the bridge entrance and swam her horse into the river full of clashing horns and flailing hooves, he would've done a fine day's work.

Susanna turned her horse and started for the river when she noticed her chuck wagon rolling that way. All she could see of it was the back as it went down the bank toward the water with the boxes of supplies lashed to its wooden top.

The cattle were moving in a continuous stream now, all of them steadily determined to stay with the herd, and two drovers at the entrance to the bridge were plenty. She was needed more with the wagon.

Maynell always had been the impatient sort, and at first she had thought the older woman was intending to swim her beloved mule team across on her own, but as Susanna trotted her horse nearer, she saw that some of Tolly's men had tied their ropes to the wagon and were planning to pull it to the other bank with their saddle horses. Everybody in both the outfits was helping everybody else, eager to get the crossing done after all the waiting.

"We're gonna get me over yonder to start the supper fire," Maynell yelled, when she saw Susanna. "These men need some hot coffee in their bellies with this cool drizzle soakin' 'em through and through."

"And some steak and biscuits," one of the drovers called as he looked back, "*plus* a gallon of coffee."

"You got it," Maynell said.

Susanna rode up to the wagon and looped her rope over the brake handle. "I'll help keep you upright," she said. "I'm craving some coffee, too."

The horses moved swiftly over the swampy ground of the slough south of the cattle-covered bridge and out into the river. For fear of bogging down and of horses balking, they never let up speed as they pulled the wagon in behind them a few yards downstream from the drovers on swimming horses who formed a line between them and the cattle.

It was raining harder, now, and Susanna pulled her hat down against it as her horse began to swim. She wished that she'd taken time to find her slicker because Maynell was right, as usual. They'd all be wet to the skin by the time they reached the other side.

Wherever on the other side that might be. Even with the water no higher than her saddle skirts, the current was strong enough to take all of them drifting a little more downstream every minute.

"Don't let 'em slow," one of Eagle Jack's drovers yelled. "Push them cows, men, push 'em!"

The river was colder than the rain, way colder than Susanna had expected, and she wished, suddenly, that she had chosen to sit up high and dry on the wagon seat with Maynell. She glanced up to see how her friend was doing. Maynell had her neck cranked around to watch the cattle.

Susanna followed her gaze. There seemed to be trouble of some kind in the middle of the river.

One of the men—it was Tolly—took off his hat and waved it at the cattle. He yelled an order that got lost in the commotion, and then he was standing up in his stirrups, shouting again.

"Break 'em up," he said. "Push 'em! Don't let 'em slow like this! Watch it, boys, they're about to mill."

He never should've said it. It was like his words

were prophecy because the moment they came out of his mouth was the moment the cattle in the middle of the river began to swim in circles. On both sides of the tightening mess, some cows ignored it and kept swimming for the north bank but others were caught up in it.

The sound of horns clanking together rang out over the water and more men began shouting.

"Hey ya!! Hi yay, *cows!*"

"Somebody git a bullwhip!"

"Watch out, now, there's one goin' under!"

A high, shrill whistle rang out but the cattle in the middle paid no mind to any of the racket. Frantic for a firm footing, they were on top of each other, hooves and horns, and thousands of pounds. More cattle were being drawn into the maelstrom.

The men tried, but the horses weren't going into the melee and they honestly couldn't get room between the cows anyhow. The next specific thing Susanna saw in the confusion of white horns and spotted hides against dark water was Tolly, standing on his saddle now and stepping out onto the backs of the cattle that covered the river thick as moss.

More and more cattle were pouring off the bridge and into the river, it was becoming solid with thrashing bovine bodies. Tolly started walking on them toward the mill, his quirt in his hand.

Susanna watched him with a sinking heart.

What good would a quirt do? Those cattle would hardly even feel it in normal circumstances, and they were panicked now.

She looked ahead to see that the way was clear and then to the far shore for Eagle Jack. He might know what to do but, even on the ground, if cattle got to milling, it was next to impossible to break them up.

Eagle Jack was nowhere in sight. Maybe he was already back in the river, helping with the crossing on the upstream side.

"Oh, no! Hey, men, let's see if we can reach him . . ."

The general shout of dismay brought her around in the saddle. The wagon was moving even faster now and she leaned across her saddle horn to see as best she could.

Tolly was gone from the backs of the cattle. Vanished. The stricken looks on the remaining men told the tale. He had been sucked into the maelstrom.

Susanna's heart plummeted, too. She strained her eyes at the bawling, milling mass as if she would only look long enough, hard enough, she could bring Tolly to the surface again.

He couldn't survive that, could he? Nobody could. But if he were a very strong swimmer, he might dive underneath the cattle, mightn't he?

But was the water deep enough? Was there enough room for a man to move free of the cattle?

Her thoughts scrambled frantically while her blood pounded with a roar in her head. The wagon jerked against her rope and brought her back to herself.

She had a job to do and she'd better do it. They didn't need a second disaster on top of the first one.

But she couldn't actually do anything but watch the water now, the strongest river current that was running in the middle of the stream, now just ahead of the men pulling her chuck wagon. An incoherent shout from the men tore her eyes away from it and she lifted her head to see several of them staring at the opposite shore.

Eagle Jack was racing his horse along it, and at the sharp bend, he headed it out toward the water and sent it leaping into the river. A huge relief surged through her. Eagle Jack could save Tolly if he was still alive.

Susanna searched the surface of the river between her wagon and Eagle Jack, she scanned the churning water between her and the other shore, then she drew her gaze back nearer to settle on the strongest current again. A flash of blue caught her eye—Tolly was wearing a blue shirt—and then she realized a scattered glimpse of a pale hand.

The sight galvanized her in the saddle for the space of two heartbeats. "Here!" she screamed. "Over here!" She waved her hand high, then dropped it to point. "Here!"

She couldn't get another word out of her mind or out of her mouth and she couldn't get her rope loose from the wagon and she couldn't let Tolly go by because she was the only one who'd seen him. Eagle Jack was barely in the water on the other side of the river, and the men nearest her would only turn and stare.

So Susanna threw away the reins, kicked loose from her stirrups, grabbed a huge, ragged breath, and dived headfirst into the river, struggling for all she was worth against the dragging weight of her boots and the divided riding skirt she wore. Oh, if only she had put on a pair of Everett's breeches today as she had so many mornings!

She tried to think about that, she tried to think about anything at all except that Tolly had vanished again and she wasn't finding him. Maybe he'd gone up for air!

Struggling against the weight trying to hold her down, trying to *pull* her down to the bottom, she fought her way to the surface, broke it, and took air in in great, gasping breaths while she scraped her hair out of her eyes and looked around for Tolly.

No sign of him.

One more gasp and she let herself sink back down, forcing her eyes open, fighting panic so she could search.

There! The blue again.

She tucked her head down and began to swim

with the longest, strongest strokes she'd ever made. Images flashed across her mind of one miserable summer spent with her aunt on Spunky Mountain. That house had been such a hateful place and her aunt so lazy that she didn't care if Susanna did any work or not, so she'd spent her days in the creek, learning to swim.

Now she was glad of it. This must've been the reason for all that tormenting loneliness—now she could use that old amusement of hers to save a man's life.

She got to him, she actually got hold of the back of his collar. It was Tolly, and he was alive because his hand moved. His face was turned away. She had to get him some air and herself some air. She had to get to the surface, so she twisted her fingers into the cloth, twisted in the water to get his weight up and started upward as best she could.

It was the hardest fight of her life but she'd gone too far to turn back now. She was saving this man's life. She was not giving up because Susanna Copeland never gave up. That's how she had survived in her life.

She never gave up.

She would not give up now.

This man was going to have some air if it took her the rest of the evening.

Tolly was not going to die because she was not

going to let him. Sometimes in life, things happened anyhow, but sometimes a person let them happen.

This time she wouldn't. She would not let it happen that Tolly died because the stupid cows had started swimming in a circle.

The water wasn't all that deep, it wasn't all that far to the top of it, she was almost there. Almost. She was there.

Her head broke the surface and the rain pelted her face and ran into her open mouth that was gulping for air. Tolly. She had to get air for him.

Tugging on him with both hands, she realized she was using the last of her strength. Then Eagle Jack's voice in a panicked shout broke through her consciousness and she realized one more thing—a thrashing, wild-eyed steer was barreling downriver straight at her and Tolly, its horns already hooking.

She found a new strength she didn't know she had and started swimming again to get out of its way, dragging Tolly along. Susanna made it out of the current and past the steer's path but it hit Tolly with a sickening sound she would never forget. The force ripped him from her hand and turned her onto her back in the water.

Looking upstream.

The water was full of cattle coming at her, struggling, bawling, fighting the current. Her cattle. Scattered thick all over the river like enormous fish.

They had lost them. The men had lost control of the herd.

She had thought she could never lift her arms or move them anymore, but she turned onto her stomach and began to swim again, this time to try to save herself.

The sounds came to her from far away, fading in and out, but they were still loud, too loud for anything. The cattle bawled unmercifully. One bellowed so loud it made echoes come back from everywhere.

Men hollered and yelled.

"Grab the rope!"

"Heads up, boys, tend your wagon!"

Water was splashing, loud, too, in with clacking sounds and snorts, but she was safe.

All this noise was making her foot hurt, though. It was a hard, throbbing pain.

"Hey, here's Tolly."

"Alive?"

There was no answer.

Susanna snuggled deeper into the blankets with the barest motion she could manage, so she wouldn't disturb the deliciously perfect dream she was in. It held her safe and warm and happy, with the fragrance of a sweet wood fire mixing with Eagle Jack's scent and the call of a faraway night bird floating on the wind.

She could hear his heart beating, right against her ear. His arms held her there, her cheek against his chest and his arms loose and relaxed around her.

He was lying on his side, turned to her, snoring gently. Every time he did, his breath blew her hair. It lifted and then fell across her cheek, lifted and then fell, in rhythm with his low, rumbling sleep noises.

She snuggled a little closer into the warm curve of his body.

His arms tightened around her. The noises stopped. He kissed the top of her head.

Her eyes flew open. The dream was gone, yet Eagle Jack was still there.

"Susanna," he said, "are you awake?"

"Yes."

She didn't move.

Eagle Jack had been holding her while she slept. He had been sleeping beside her.

They both lay very still.

He didn't even breathe in her hair. She couldn't feel him breathe at all.

"Are you hurt?" he asked, at last.

Instantly, the wild mirage of images flooded her, mind and body. The horns clashing all over the water, the cattle coming down the river at her, the bellowing and bawling, Eagle Jack jumping his horse into the river, a horse rearing, its rider sliding out of the saddle. And Tolly's pale hand underwater.

Dear God.

"Tolly?" she whispered.

"You have a cut in the side of your foot," he said. "Maybe from a tossing horn, maybe from a sharp rock. Is there anything more?"

She did feel a vague throbbing pain in her right foot, now that he said that.

"Did you save me?"

"No, you saved yourself. You were out of the river before I could get to you."

"I can't remember anything past the cattle coming at us and that steer barreling right into Tolly."

"That's because you hit your head on a log in the slough."

Then he did move. He took her in his big hands and turned her onto her side and lifted her a little so that they lay face-to-face. He did it gently, more gently than anyone had ever touched her in her whole life.

"I haven't made your poultice yet," he said, "but I will as soon as I can get my hands on some antiphlogistine."

She smiled, in spite of the tears gathering in the back of her throat.

"Don't bother," she said. "I'll only throw it across the room."

"Careful not to knock a hole in your tent," he

said. "And you don't want the canvas smelling like that medicine all the time, either."

"Eagle Jack," she said, "I know Tolly died or you would've already answered my question."

"I hated to tell you," he said.

Her tears spilled over.

"I should've held on to him," she said, with a sob. "I should've seen that steer coming. I should've swum faster."

"You did more than most men would've done—or could've done," he said. "They're all talking about it. You'll do to ride the river with, Susanna."

"But I wanted to *save* him," she cried. "It was useless. I did all that for *nothing.* I came so close . . ."

More and more tears, coming faster with every memory of that horrible afternoon, choked off her words.

Tenderly, he pushed her hair back from her face.

"You've got to get hold of yourself," he said. "Listen to me, Susanna . . ."

She threw her arms around him and buried her face in the hollow of his neck.

"Hold me," she said.

And Eagle Jack did.

Chapter 13

Facing each other, the length of her body fit even more perfectly against his than it had done back-to-front, spoon-fashion, and he wished he hadn't been so gallant as to wrap her in a separate quilt when he'd lain down beside her. But, with both of them naked while their clothes dried at the fire, what else could he do? He was a rounder, yes, he'd admit that in a minute, but he wasn't low-down, not the kind to take advantage of an unconscious woman.

Not even if she insisted on pretending to be his wife.

Now he wished he'd never been the one to strip off her wet things in the first place, but he'd had no choice. By the time he'd swum his horse back across the river with Susanna limp and unconscious in his arms and had finally found Maynell and the wagons and the tent and the fire, Maynell had been far too busy treating the gash on Rod's head and trying—with what equipment she had left—to get hot coffee and jerky into the bellies of the men so they could be gathering cattle while they dried out from the river.

He could not have asked May to quit all that and get Susanna out of her clothes when, after all, everyone thought he was her husband, and there was no reason a husband couldn't do that. But he did wish he hadn't had to do it because, try as he would, he couldn't get the brief—he had tried, gallantly, to keep his glance averted—glimpse of her naked beauty out of his mind.

Which was a travesty and totally unworthy of him as a human being, considering the upset state she was in.

He cradled her head in one hand and pulled her closer with the other, caressing her back in circles. She was shaking all over, more than just trembling, clinging to him as if *this* were the moment she could drown.

As if he, and only he, could save her from this river of tears.

It made him feel helpless and all-powerful both at the same time.

"Poor Tolly," she said, muttering the words against his neck, "he worked so hard on the bridge."

Her lips moving against his skin stirred him, made him gather her even closer.

"He was always so cheerful," she said. "He shouldn't have died."

"Tolly was going up the trail," he soothed. "He knew there'd be rivers to cross."

She tilted her head back suddenly, to look at him. In the darkness of the tent, he couldn't see into her eyes, but he could see them flash.

"I don't care," she cried. "I've spent five years learning how to be strong."

Her vehemence surprised him.

So did the fact that she pulled away and scrambled to sit up. She pulled her quilt around her and sat looking down at him. He sat up, too.

"Everett always tried to make me think I couldn't live a month without him, but I have done *everything* and I have survived on my own." A deep sob racked her but she wouldn't let it stop her. "I have even held on to my ranch," she said, in a fierce tone he'd never heard before, "and I know now that I can take my own cattle up the trail. But I couldn't save Tolly."

"Susanna, you're not God," he said.

"I *know* that," she cried, "but I had him in my hand! And he was good to me! He treated me like an equal. I should've been able to . . ."

The tears began again, in earnest.

He wanted to hold her again. He ached to take

her into his arms. He felt lonesome without her closeness.

He reached out to brush back her hair. Loose and wild, her hair was beautiful. Even here, with no light, it caught some moonlight through the wall of the tent.

"You did all you could," he said. "It's ridiculous to blame yourself."

She hit her knee with her fist.

"I saved myself, didn't I? Well, then, I should've held on to him . . ."

He touched her cheek, beneath the swinging curtain of her hair.

"This isn't like you," he said. "Usually you're pretty sensible. Like when you hired me. You knew that you had to hire a man for your trail boss."

"That *wasn't* sensible," she said. "It was nothing but sheer, stupid necessity because nobody would work for me . . ."

He tried to look at her, but she hung her head and her hair swung down.

" '*Now* I know I can take my own cattle up the trail,' " he said, quoting her. "Don't you agree that it was sensible to hire someone who'd been up the trail before? Isn't that the reason you think you know how to do it now?"

She looked up and tossed her hair back over her shoulder.

"Well, yes. And I *am* a sensible person."

"I know you are," he said.

"But I should've saved him," she repeated stubbornly.

Eagle Jack wanted to shout his frustration. He wanted to grab her and kiss it away.

He wanted to hold her again and kiss all the words in the world away.

"This conversation's going nowhere," he said roughly. "It's stupid. You nearly got *killed* trying to save Tolly."

She began to cry again.

"I just . . ."

"It's a terrible thing when any man dies," he said impatiently, "especially a good man. It unsettles us all. But you didn't even *know* Tolly."

"That's not even the *point*," she cried. "That's not it."

"Then what is? *Why* are you blaming yourself for his death?"

She looked down again and shook her head.

"I just think that . . ."

The answer hit him then, coming together from the echoes in his head. Everett. Her ranch. She'd survived. On her own.

He thought about that for a minute.

"Susanna," he said softly.

She turned her face up to his.

"You can still survive on your own," he said.

"You swam to the bank and saved yourself. No matter whatever happens, you can survive as long as you believe you can."

He leaned to her and cradled her face in his hands. "You just can't work miracles, that's all."

She made a tantalizing little sound, deep in her throat, like a cross between a laugh and a cry. "Oh, Eagle Jack," she said, "you're such a comfort to me."

When she threw her arms around his neck he was already kissing her, bending down to find her mouth with his, gathering her into his arms. He drew her onto his quilt and pulled hers around them with one hand, falling deeper and deeper back onto the grassy-smelling earth with her into the magical world of her bare skin against his.

Her warm, smooth body quivered against his, called to his, greeted his with the galloping drumming of her heart. And with the sweet, honeyed taste of her tongue.

Susanna's blood began a deep, vibrating rhythm in her veins that she had never known lived there before.

"Susanna," he murmured, "sweet Susanna."

The low, ringing tone of his voice stroked her body as surely as his hands were doing. It floated in the tent and wrapped around her like the smoke.

She let herself run her palms over Eagle Jack's

skin, as helpless to stop learning the rise and fall of his muscles and the strong, angled structure of his bones as she was to take her mouth away from his. His tongue, his lips, talked to her without words and she answered in the same ways, openhearted.

Then he pulled away, just far enough to speak.

"Susanna," he said, "are you sure you want this? Do you know what you're doing?"

"Yes! I need you, Eagle Jack."

He stroked her sides with his open hands, hands rough with calluses on the outside, yet gentle as a falling leaf. His thumbs brushing, barely brushing, her breasts, then his fingers warming her ribs and firmly caressing her hips, once and twice more, he seemed to be laying claim to her.

That's what she thought until his mouth left hers and his hands tangled in her hair and he began to plant a trail of kisses down her throat. Burning his brand onto her skin, it must be that, he was so deliberate about it.

Helpless, she arched her body up for more, her breasts begging for the touch of his hands, for the pleasure of his mouth, her whole self trembling beneath him. He trembled, too, then, and gave a great sigh of longing as he rose up above her, bending his head to take her distended nipple into his mouth.

She thrust her fingers into his hair and held

him there, she could not get enough of this closeness, this intimacy, this far-gone purest pleasure that she had ever felt. She would never move again because this, this was all she would ever want.

"Eagle Jack," she murmured, "yes. Oh, yes."

Her hands became voracious, wanting all of him, needing to explore every inch of him, demanding to claim him as he was claiming her. Dimly, a thought flashed that that might not be a good thing. Then it was gone.

Eagle Jack was hers and she was his.

This was right. She was more alive at that moment than she had ever been in her whole life before and that was true because she was with Eagle Jack. This was meant to be.

That was her last conscious thought. He moved his mouth to hers again, desperately, insistently, while his hands brought her breasts to ecstasy, and they went rushing headlong into the night.

His big body wrapped around her, his hands and mouth set fires intensely burning, and she was melting, flesh and bones, until she no longer had the strength or the sense to breathe. He slipped one of his long thighs between her own.

He gathered her to him, and held her closer than close before he pressed his mouth to her ear.

"I have to do this," he said urgently, and then

buried his face in her hair, kissing the side of her neck and then lifting the mass of it to spread across the blanket beneath her head. "Your hair is like moonlight and sunshine," he whispered. "The moon and the sun both let you wear some of their light."

He leaned over her, on his elbows, to kiss her again. The hard peaks of her breasts brushed his harder chest.

She moaned.

"Eagle Jack . . ."

"Not yet," he said, and planted a line of kisses down the side of her neck and over the curve of her shoulder.

It made her cry out. Her breasts needed his mouth, and her belly, and her thighs—they needed his hands.

"You're torturing me," she said, and he smiled against her mouth and kissed it again.

Then he stopped and looked down at her. Dimly, she could see his smile.

Vaguely, somewhere in the far reaches of her mind, she realized that it was lighter in the tent. The moonlight was getting brighter because the moon had dropped lower in the sky. Morning would be here soon.

It didn't matter. Nothing mattered but that she was aching for him and reaching for him and he was teasing her.

She lifted her head and nipped his lower lip,

then she traced its shape with the tip of her tongue.

His mouth fell onto hers and devoured it, her hand took his and put it on her womanhood. He traced his own golden fire there.

"Eagle Jack," she demanded.

He came into her as unerringly as that Grandfather Moon of his washed light over the land. They melded in that very same, sure and eternal way.

Susanna clung to him and buried her face in the hollow of his neck and moved with him to leave the earth itself. She wrapped herself tighter around him and they rose higher and higher to meet the moon in his path.

When it was over and they lay sated, gazing into each other's eyes, his leg thrown over hers as if to pin her to the earth again, she traced the line of his cheekbones with her thumb. She was cradling his cheek in her hand.

"The cattle drifted downriver," she said. "Where are we, Eagle Jack?"

He smiled a slow, slow smile.

"Together."

Her breath caught in her throat. Tears stung her eyes.

All she could do was drop a kiss into the hollow in the middle of his chest and smile back at him.

He gave a great sigh and gathered her to him and he held her while he began to drift off to sleep. She felt his heartbeat slow beneath her ear and his breath go deeper and deeper as his body relaxed against hers. All but the iron bands of the muscles in his arms, because those never wavered. They folded her close to him and kept her there as if they'd never let her go.

They suffused her whole body with what felt like a golden glow, a warm safety that she'd dreamed of all her life. Everett had never held her like that.

Everett had never made love to her like that, either. He couldn't have done so, even if he'd known that such a different world existed.

Eagle Jack had held her and touched her and talked to her as if he loved her. It scared her to even think the word, but it was the only one that even came close to describing this new experience that he had given her. This must be what it was like when people really loved each other.

He'd certainly been hurting right along with her about Tolly. Not only that, but Eagle Jack had looked into her heart and seen the fear that she was keeping silent—the fear that she was weakening, that she wouldn't be able to survive on her own anymore.

It seemed to her that one person would nearly *have* to love the other in order to sense something like that. It was definitely true that he'd been interested in who she was, that he'd been observing her and learning her personality all along, every day, or he'd never have known what else she was feeling.

But she shouldn't be thinking about love. She didn't want to think about love.

Loving someone, especially loving each other, brought on questions and decisions about the rest of people's lives and where they would live and it brought talk of marriage. She had her freedom now. She would never marry again.

Susanna smiled to herself. She didn't have to think about all that. She didn't have to think at all.

What she would do was close her mind to every future and past and just lie here and live in the present. Right now she would enjoy being safe and happy in Eagle Jack's arms.

The day was creeping up on them, for the camp was starting to stir. She heard the hiss of the fire and the jingle of spurs and somebody's low-pitched voice.

But none of it mattered. She was in a place that was safe and warm. She and Eagle Jack were together.

When Susanna woke, Eagle Jack was gone. The flap of the tent stood open to let in a little breeze, and if it hadn't been for that, she'd have been even sweatier beneath the heavy quilt. The sun beating down on the canvas felt as hot as the middle of summer.

She sat up with a start. It was noon or thereabouts. Why weren't they on the trail? Had the cattle scattered over a wide range?

A cold hand clutched her stomach. Had they lost more men than Tolly?

Wearing the quilt like a cloak, she scrambled up and looked for her clothes. The tent was empty except for the quilt Eagle Jack had used and Susanna's leather hat.

She ducked out through the open flap. Her chuck wagon was there beside the fire and the clothes and boots she'd worn the day before lay spread out on the grass nearby. She went to get them.

"Well, it's about time you got up, you lazybones," Maynell said.

Susanna turned to see her coming into camp with her apron full of wild onions. The smell of slow-cooking beef came from the pot. "Why didn't you wake me?" she asked, snatching up all her articles of clothing and turning toward the tent. "May, why aren't we getting back on the trail? How bad are they scattered?"

Maynell proceeded calmly to the back of the chuck wagon and began washing the onions.

"Bad enough," she said dryly. "We've got cattle scattered from here to the Indian Territories."

"Then I need to be helping to find them," Susanna said.

Giving a little to her sore foot, she hurried back

into the tent and started to dress. She pulled on her camisole and then raised her voice so Maynell could hear her.

"I can't believe Eagle Jack didn't wake me and you didn't, either!"

She thrust her arms into her blouse and started buttoning it up.

"He gave me strict orders not to wake you," Maynell called back. "He said that you came to once in the night but you were so worn out and torn up about it all, you had to sleep some more."

Susanna felt the heat of a blush flood her face and neck.

"I don't think that man slept a wink for watching over you," Maynell said.

Susanna stepped into her pantaloons and riding skirt, then pulled on socks and stepped into her still-damp boots. Her foot did hurt, but it wasn't really bad.

"That was very nice of him," Susanna said.

Her boot was cut in the same place as the gash in her foot, probably by a tossing horn, but it would have to hold together until the drive was over. She had another pair, but not with heels high enough to stay in the stirrup.

Ignoring the pain, she stepped outside again, fastening her waistband as she went.

"Listen to me, Missy," Maynell said, looking Susanna in the eye, "next time your husband spends the night in your tent, I don't care how tired and wrung out you are, if you want to keep him, you best stay awake and entertain him, you know what I mean?"

Susanna looked back at her.

"I haven't been liking it one bit for him to sleep out with the men for night guard," May said, "and now that we've thrown these two crews together he don't have to do that anymore."

Maynell was half teasing and half serious about what she'd said but she was also trying to see Susanna's state of mind. May knew her well enough to know Susanna was upset over Tolly and May was trying to find out how much so and to distract her from that.

Well, there was work to be done, so she would let herself be distracted. And she would return the favor, for Maynell herself looked pretty drawn around the eyes.

"Thank goodness you don't know everything, Maynell," she said.

Maynell stared at her. "Now, just exactly what do you mean by that, missy?"

"Only that if I told you everything I know, then you'd know as much as I do," Susanna said.

"Hmpf."

"I've got to get to work," Susanna said. "Where do I go to find the remuda?"

Maynell waited for more information, but when Susanna only smiled at her, she finally gave up. "Over that hill there," she said. "And once you're mounted, go in any direction you pick and you'll find cows running around and men chasing them."

"Two of my favorite things in the whole world," Susanna said. "It's a beautiful day for both."

She pulled her hat down and walked away, whistling for courage.

"Better watch out," Maynell called after her. "You know the old saying: 'A whistling girl and a crowing hen always come to some bad end.' "

Susanna laughed and waved good-bye without turning around. Somehow, today, the life force felt much stronger than death—maybe because of the bright sunlight and the fresh-washed fragrance in the breeze.

And . . . maybe because of Eagle Jack.

Eagle Jack was surprised—to tell the truth, he was shocked—by the unexpected lift he felt in his heart when he saw Susanna coming toward him with a little bunch of cows and calves she'd gathered. It wasn't anything to worry about, though.

It was only natural that he'd have feelings for her because, in the last day or two, they'd been through quite a lot together.

Including last night, which was really special. But he couldn't let himself get too carried away thinking about making love with her.

It didn't mean a thing, except that he admired

her for her bravery and he appreciated that she had so much heart. This thrill he was feeling was because he admired her. That was all it was.

"Hey," she called, as she came nearer. "Look what I found in that gully over there."

Her smile alone was enough to make his day. But every part of her looked beautiful. Even more beautiful than he had remembered it to be.

"Good job," he said, glancing at the dozen steers she'd found, which looked none the worse for what they'd been through, "throw 'em in with these."

"Where are you taking yours?" she asked.

"About a mile west to the main herd."

Her smile faded and some little lines appeared in her forehead as she looked over the cattle.

"Eagle Jack, do you think we lost very many?"

Now she was all business, as usual. Yet she was looking at him in a different way, today. Maybe she, too, was thinking about last night.

"Hard to tell," he said, as they let the cattle meld together and then began to push them toward the west.

Well, damn, he might as well tell her the bad news and get it over with. He just hated being the one to make her sad.

"We had twenty head of them drown in the mill," he said. "Maybe a few more. And a whole lot scattered. We'll take a count tomorrow when we get 'em separated from Tolly's bunch."

Her blue eyes widened. "You think we won't move on until tomorrow?"

"We can't if we don't want to leave some good beeves behind for the next drovers to pick up."

"That's the bad thing about being off the regular trail," she said, "there probably won't be anybody else coming this way who could bring them to us."

He glanced at her with a smile. "Right," he said. "You're learning, Susanna. Keep it up and you *will* be able to come up the trail as your own boss next year."

Right then he made a decision. He would try to bring a herd along at about the same time as she did, next spring. Not to watch out for her, exactly, although he could do that, too, but mostly just to see her again.

He'd have to keep in touch with her so he would know her plans about when she'd leave Brushy Creek with her herd. Come to think of it, they might even make plans to travel together.

It was the strangest thing, but somehow he knew that he couldn't leave her forever at the end of the trail. Somehow she'd become a part of him—someone to whom he would always feel a connection.

What kind of connection, he didn't know. It was more than friendship, yet he didn't know if it was love. It was different from what he'd felt for any other woman before.

But it wasn't that he wanted to marry her. It definitely was not that. Eagle Jack Sixkiller was not the marrying kind.

Susanna rode through the main herd looking at the condition of the cattle and trying to count them, roughly, although she didn't have the gift that Eagle Jack said Nat had, and that she'd heard other men had, which was to be able to ride through a herd or watch it pass in front of him and know to the cow exactly how many head were in it. There were many different gifts in people.

Eagle Jack's gift was to lighten the load. The tired, tired men had been laughing and perking up ever since he'd ridden up and started talking to them.

She gave in to temptation and glanced at him again, hoping that he wouldn't catch her at it. It wouldn't do to cause him to assume that she was thinking about him all the time or anything like that or that she might be giving more importance to what happened between them last night than he did.

He had meant to comfort her, she knew that. And he did. But for him, that may have been all it was.

She made another mark in her tally book and thought about that. What had it been for *her*?

That was something she wasn't going to think

about. There was no way she was going to let her life become tangled up with a man's. Not any man's. Not even a man as special as Eagle Jack.

No matter *what* Maynell said.

She smiled to herself and gave a determined nod as she made one slanted mark across four straight ones so that it meant five. Then she snapped the book closed.

Nope, she was on her own at last, she didn't have to answer to anybody, and she was going to keep it that way.

Across over there on the east side of the herd, Eagle Jack was talking to Nat and Marvin and making them laugh again. The men hadn't slept, except maybe a few winks in the saddle, for over twenty-four hours, but they could still laugh because Eagle Jack was laughing. He had already told them that he'd take the midnight guard tonight, which, as a trail boss he didn't have to do, since, as Maynell had noted, the outfit now had enough hands.

Did that mean he'd sleep out under the stars with the men tonight? She'd better hope he did. She didn't want to get used to having him in her tent every night, because someday they would come upon Kansas over the horizon and it would all be over.

She headed her horse toward him. All she wanted was to hear his voice, just talk to him for a minute to ask how accurate he thought her count might be, and then she'd go out looking for more strays.

He might even go with her.

A rider was coming from the east with a bunch of steers. It looked like Rodney or Lanny—at a distance, she always had trouble telling Marvin's friends apart. Generally they were known as Marvin's boys, although they couldn't have been more than a year or two younger than he.

When she reached Eagle Jack and the others, the new arrivals were blending into the herd. It was Lanny who had found them.

". . . brought 'em on in," Lanny was saying to Eagle Jack, "'cause we reckoned you'd wanta hear the news right off."

"What news?"

"Might be word of your race horse, boss," the boy said. He gestured with his head at the cattle he'd brought. "This bunch was nearly to the main trail at the ford," he said, "and over there at the store I met up with a button drummer tellin' about a little mare that could outrun a tornado."

Eagle Jack sat straight up in the saddle. His eyes drilled into Lanny's. "What'd he say?"

"Said she was short-legged and rough-lookin', so all comers us'ally bet against her. Said she's draggin' in the stake money by the sackful for her owners."

"*Owners*," Eagle Jack repeated, in a menacing growl. "Where'd this drummer see her?"

"Someplace south o' Fort Worth. He couldn't recall the name of the place exactly."

"Did he mention her color?" Eagle Jack asked.

Lanny pushed back his hat and scratched his head. "Reckon not."

"I want to talk to him," Eagle Jack said. "Where'd he go?"

Lanny shrugged. "Don't know. He was pointed at the ford when I headed out, but the river's still deep there. I reckon it's too deep to cross."

Eagle Jack asked for a description of the man. Then he could barely listen for it, he was so eager to be gone. He was already turning his horse to ride out.

"I'll be back by midnight, boys."

But he looked straight at Susanna when he said it.

She watched him go until he disappeared behind some trees.

"He'll be all right, Miz Sixkiller," Lanny said. "Eagle Jack, he can handle anything."

Surprised, she looked at him. What had the boy just seen in her face?

He smiled at her, touched his hat, and rode off. It didn't matter what he thought. Good grief, she was *expected* to love her husband!

Then she couldn't believe that she'd had that thought—especially not right out here in the daylight. Heaven help her, she was losing her mind.

She turned her horse and started back to camp. She needed to find out what supplies had been lost, if any. *That* would bring her right back to reality.

Chapter 14

At midnight, Susanna was sitting cross-legged on the ground outside her tent, as she always did when she couldn't sleep. Which, now that she thought of it, always seemed to be when Eagle Jack was gone from camp at night.

This time she was making a list by the light of the fire and trying not to panic. Maynell, who was exhausted and had to get up in a few hours to cook breakfast, had been persuaded to go to bed after the two of them and Cookie had found and organized every scrap of supplies saved from the river.

There hadn't been much.

And that wasn't even the worst of it. From what she'd gleaned from the stories told around the fire after supper and Cookie's and Maynell's recollections, the loss in cattle would turn out to be substantial. More than she would ever have guessed from what Eagle Jack had said.

One of Maynell's mules had died in a watery confrontation with a panicked longhorn cow. Cookie's wagon had broken a wheel, and they'd put the one and only spare one on it today.

Susanna's trunk had been lost, so the one change of clothes she'd carried in her bedroll was now all she had. The bedrolls had all been found, but some of them were still wet.

The medicine box was still with the wagon, thank goodness. But the harness-mending stuff was gone.

Everything considered, the three or four days—or maybe more—that they had saved by not waiting behind the waterbound herds at the ford in the river had cost them dearly. Knowing that scared her so much she couldn't think how to go on.

But they had to go on and they had to do it soon.

If only Eagle Jack hadn't gone chasing off after a useless racehorse this evening instead of staying here to make plans with her! They might even need to change direction and go find a town they hadn't expected to pass near, just to get food.

Which she had no money to pay for.

And now the thought of killing beeves on a regular basis to feed the men made her sick to her stomach. She couldn't spare them. If she didn't go into Abilene with enough cattle to sell, if she couldn't get enough money out of them to save Brushy Creek, then she was going through all this trouble for nothing.

She could not bear it if she lost her home.

She wrote "beans" on the list, with a pencil that trembled in her hand.

"Flour. Dried fruit. Rice."

Lots of shopkeepers gave supplies on credit to drives and trusted people to return in the fall with the money. It was done all the time. It was a long-standing practice. She surely would have no trouble at all.

Thank God, both sourdough crocks had come out of the river unharmed. Cookie and Maynell, like most cooks, were so attached to their favorite old pots they'd probably have turned around and gone home if they'd lost them.

She tried to smile. Right there was something really big to be thankful for.

But the sharp claws of panic wouldn't let her go. They wouldn't back out of her flesh even a little.

How, *how* could she have been walking around whistling and sleeping in for hours on this very morning?

She got up, thrust her pencil and paper into her pocket, and began to pace, in spite of her sore foot. One thing about it, she would never sleep tonight, no matter when Eagle Jack came home.

Came *back*. Not came home. This wasn't his home, or hers either.

She paced the length of the camp, turned and then came back again.

There by the fire, she stopped. The soft, rhythmic fall of hooves was on the air. She listened. Two horses. If it was Eagle Jack, he was bringing a visitor, or else he had found Molly.

If it wasn't Eagle Jack, then she should be careful. She was the only person awake in the entire camp, and trouble could come too fast for the sleeping men. The ones on guard were with the herd, at least a quarter mile away.

Her pulse began to beat even faster. She tried to slow it by thinking sensibly.

Another thing to be thankful for was that her old pistol had stayed with them, too, in a box lashed to the top of the wagon. It hadn't even gotten wet and it was now in her tent. She went in after it.

When she stepped out with it in her hand, Eagle Jack was riding up to the wagon. He caught her movement from the corner of his eye, and turned as the horses stopped.

For one, hopeful moment she thought he'd found Molly. Then she saw that it was a mule he was leading, a mule loaded with supplies.

Such a mix of savage feelings attacked her that she didn't know which to acknowledge first or what to say or do. He had gone right ahead and taken care of the supply problem without a word to her, and now she'd be in debt to him for the rest of her life.

She could've shopped much more wisely and probably bargained better than he did because she was desperate. She wouldn't have bought all those extras that he usually did. Why, Cookie's wagon even carried chocolate to drink.

No, Eagle Jack had gone gallivanting off and left her to find out all the bad news for herself and try to figure out what to do about it all by herself while he was wildly spending her money.

He stopped his little caravan and grinned at her.

"All I can say is, 'Thank God I'm not riding the bay horse'," he said. "Put up your gun, won't you? I promise, Susanna, there's not a snake within miles."

The firelight on his face lit his gorgeous cheekbones and made his eyes sparkle.

"I don't limit myself to snakes," she said. "Lots of other wild critters run at night, too."

He chuckled. "Yeah, and me and ol' Jasper, here, are wild as they come," he said, as he stepped down off his horse. "That's why we're a little nervous when we see that hogleg in your hand."

She didn't move. "A mule named Jasper, hmm?" she said.

"So the man says. He can move right on through the country, too, can't you, Jasper?"

"Eagle Jack," she said frostily. "Did you ever think that the owner of your beef herd may not want to pay for all these expenses?"

He turned from untying the mule from his mount and gave her a funny look. He raised his eyebrows. "The owner of my beef herd?"

"Right. And that I, the owner of your wet herd, cannot afford to pay for extras like a pack mule?"

He kept on giving her that strange look that she couldn't read. "You lost a mule yesterday," he said.

"Which you didn't bother to tell me about," she said.

He went back to unfastening his rope.

"I wasn't about to start listing all your losses with you in the fit you were in," he said. "I knew you'd find out soon enough."

He sounded so calm and matter-of-fact that she tried hard to use the same tone and not sound like a hysterical woman.

Which was what she really wanted to be. She wanted to scream and throw things and have a tantrum at the unfairness of it all. Hadn't she worked like a hired hand for all these years and planned and scrimped and saved and sacrificed, and now she couldn't even buy food?

"So is that the same reasoning you used to buy all these supplies without asking me? That I'd find out soon enough?"

He shook his head. "You don't have to pay for a doggone thing," he said. "It's taken care of."

"You can't make love with me *one time* and then start taking care of my debts," she blurted.

She hadn't known she was going to say that.

Despite her efforts to sound calm, her voice trembled a little. And she fought them, but tears filled her eyes.

He turned and looked at her, then he left the mule tied to the horse and came toward her.

Slowly, with that flowing panther walk that proclaimed he owned the world. That walk she loved so well.

"Annie, baby," he said, "I'm not going to start taking care of your business. I know how you love to plow through life all on your own hook."

That startled a chuckle out of her.

"You need to know that's more than fine with me, because I'll never settle down anyhow," Eagle Jack said. "The whole idea of getting hitched scares me plumb silly."

That remark relieved her. But somehow it pricked her pride, too.

Then she forgot it.

He stopped in front of her, close enough to touch her, but he didn't. He held her perfectly still, mesmerized by the power of his burning dark eyes.

"I know how you like to make love with me,

too," he drawled, speaking very, very softly. "So I promise you now it won't be just one time."

She looked up into his twinkling eyes, heavy-lidded now with the memories of their time together and she wanted nothing so much as she wanted to touch him.

But the tears took her then and stopped her hand. They even stopped her tongue.

Eagle Jack smiled at her and reached out to cup her chin in his big, rough hand. He tilted her head up to look even more deeply into her eyes.

"I can't make good on that promise right now," he said, "because I'm standing guard. But you listen to me. You're stronger than you've ever thought you were and you're gonna buck up right now and set a fine example."

She could only look at him, wide-eyed and questioning.

"You're my wife for the duration of this drive and I'm the trail boss. We're gonna band together and lead these good men and all the cattle we can gather straight to Kansas and have a good time while we're doing it."

She expected him to kiss her then, but he didn't.

He fanned out his long, callused fingers and stroked her neck. A trembling thrill took her—it ran through her whole body.

"They're more shaken up by all this trouble

than you know," he said. "Some of them believe a bad river crossing can jinx a whole drive. Believing that can make it happen."

He drove that truth into her with his hard gaze.

"I've been fightin' that superstition all day," he said. "I'll have to fight it for days to come. Help me here, Annie."

"I will," she said, and somehow she had the feeling that she was promising more than he asked.

"Don't worry about money and debts," he said. "Remember—right now it's life and death."

"All right."

He did kiss her then—on the lips. A light kiss but long.

All the panic vanished as the heat from him spread through her veins.

The heat and the strength of him.

"I'm the one who first agreed to cross at the bridge," she said, when he pulled back. "I can't stand it if I don't make the decisions but now I'm scared to death I can't make the right one."

"Hey," he said, "it was me, too. I wasn't gonna wait at the ford if I had to teach them damn longhorns to fly."

She smiled. It felt really good to relax inside herself.

"I've got to stand guard," he said. "Get some sleep. Tomorrow we'll have a lot of decisions to make."

She nodded.

Finally, his gaze released her. He turned away and started back to his horse and his mule.

No. He couldn't go. She couldn't bear to let him go.

"Was it Molly?" she asked. "That the drummer saw?"

He chuckled. "It was. We'll find her soon." He turned to flash a grin at her over his shoulder. "There's your chance for money, Annie girl," he said, walking backward so he could look at her. "Win you a bundle with Molly."

"First I have to have something to bet," she said.

"I'll stake you," he said, and held up his hand to stop her when she opened her mouth to protest. "For ten percent of your take."

She laughed. "It's a deal," she said.

Then she turned, lifted the flap, and ducked under it into her tent. If she didn't get away from him she would run after him and throw herself into his arms.

It was a miracle how much better she felt. It was incredible that the awful panic was gone.

There never was a man who knew her the way he did.

The next day, while she was helping Maynell peel some of the potatoes that Jasper the new mule had hauled in for breakfast, Susanna figured it out. She would think of this trail drive as a time out of time.

Even if she did get attached to Eagle Jack, she would do it with the hard, cold truth firmly in mind. Once they reached Abilene and sold the cattle, that would be the end of their dalliance and she would be entirely on her own again.

Eagle Jack was right: he wasn't trying to take over her business, and she did have to have his help to make this drive, so she should be sensible. The sensible thing to do was to take pleasure where she found it, to make this a wonderful time that she'd remember forever, but not to let him into her heart.

She didn't even know what that was, actually, which would probably be a natural protection to keep her from falling in love with him. She didn't know how to love anyone, for she'd known the minute she decided to marry Everett that she was doing it only to get away from Aunt Skeeter and Uncle Job and out into a home of her own.

Little had she known the perils in that kind of thinking. It had been Everett's home and not hers.

What she must do with Eagle Jack was take and enjoy the fun and excitement he gave her—both of which were so rare in her life—and give only the same. The main thing she had to do was watch herself so that she didn't fall back into her hateful old habit of always wanting to please the other person.

All her life, from the minute of her birth, she'd been trying to persuade someone that her existence was a good thing. From her mother who deserted her at birth by dying, to the father who'd lit out for the hills soon after that, to the succession of resentful aunts and cousins who raised her, to Everett who used her instead of loving her, to the banker who'd dogged her for two years for the deed to her place, nobody ever wanted her to be wherever she was.

Or to do whatever it was that she wanted to do.

When the word came that Everett was dead, she had promised herself, "Never again."

Never again would she fall back into those ancient habits of trying to please. Never again would she depend on somebody else for her livelihood. Never again would she let anyone else control her.

Eagle Jack Sixkiller wasn't demanding any of those things and now that he'd gotten used to her being on the trail, he seemed perfectly happy for her to be there. He was different.

He was a fun-loving sort, and the Good Lord knew she needed some fun.

She would take his advice. She wouldn't think about what the cattle would bring in Abilene or whether she could keep Brushy Creek. For the rest of this drive, she would concentrate on staying alive, she would take life one day at a time—it could as easily have been her instead of Tolly who'd drowned—and she would remember every single minute of every one of those days.

And those nights.

It took until the middle of the afternoon to cut their cattle out from Tolly's, but when it was done, Eagle Jack pushed their herd north anyhow, just as he had when they left Brushy Creek. Now, as then, Susanna had mixed feelings about it.

Not because driving part of the night would lessen the time she and Eagle Jack would have in the tent alone. No, it was because camp was already set up and it seemed a waste of effort to take it down and put it back up later the same day.

She and Eagle Jack rode ahead to scout and found a way that was grassy, mostly open land with not too many trees. There had been so much rain that water for the cattle wouldn't be a problem.

At the end of the second day, they struck the Chisholm Trail again, miles north of the ford where so many herds were waiting to cross, and began making good progress toward Fort Worth. Their scouting ahead of the herd every day became as much a search for Molly as for a place to camp, because Eagle Jack made sure to talk to everybody headed back down the trail.

Finally, when they were within a day's drive of Fort Worth, he found someone who had seen Molly run.

"I'll never fergit it, neither," the gap-toothed man said. "I personally lost ten dollars and I never woulda thought that mare coulda run fast enough to beat a lame mule to the feed trough."

"Where'd they run her?" Eagle Jack asked.

But the old man was lost in the memory. He shook his head in wonder. "Like greased lightning," he mused. "Never seen nothin' like it."

"Was it in Fort Worth that you saw her? In town? Tell me now."

Susanna looked at Eagle Jack. He was so anxious she thought he might lean out of the saddle and grab the man to shake the information out of him.

Evidently that thought also occurred to the man, for he spoke quickly. "If you wanta see for yerself, they'll run her again tonight," he said. "Not far on up the trail. There's boys in that Slash Double D outfit refusin' to believe their own eyes."

"The mare's owners are traveling with the Slash Double D?" Eagle Jack asked.

"Reckon not. That trail crew's jist layin' over one more day fer another race. They's a race track down by the Deep Fork where they run." He gestured to the northeast.

Eagle Jack was already turning his horse. "Thanks, old-timer," he said, "I know that track."

The man ambled his horse to the south, on down the trail.

"Let's run on over there and just see if she's there yet," Eagle Jack said to Susanna. "It's not far."

"It's great you know where it is," she said, nodding her agreement.

"I've used that track myself," he said.

They rode at a lope the whole way there, avoiding everyone they saw.

"Somebody might notice my hair," Eagle Jack explained. "Don't want word to reach those worthless horse thieves that I'm anywhere around—not until I've set my eyes on Molly."

His voice vibrated with unbridled excitement. It made Susanna smile.

"Once you set your eyes on her, what are you going to do?" she asked.

"Oh," he drawled, "I haven't really thought about it."

Susanna grinned at him. "Don't try to tell me that," she said. "You've been in a fit about this horse ever since I met you."

"Depends on what kind of shape she's in," he said. "If she hasn't lost weight and her haircoat looks good and her eyes are bright . . ." He grinned back.

"What?"

"For starters, I may just steal her back again."

They looked at each other for a moment, then burst out laughing.

"Let's do it!" Susanna cried. "It'd serve 'em right."

Eagle Jack nodded. "It would. They can go crazy looking for her, riding off in all directions, and then if they find out and challenge us, I'll—"

He stopped.

"You'll what?"

He ignored that. "They may find out I have her but they won't have the guts to come after me," he said. "They're horse thieves, pure and simple. That's a hanging offense."

"They've been getting rich off her," Susanna said. "Stealing her will hurt them worse than a hanging."

He pretended to study her. "You're a hard woman, Susanna. I believe you'd like to see them suffer."

"I would," she said. "I may have to look them up and mention the little mare they used to win with, every time."

He chuckled. "Remind me not to cross you," he said. "I think you actually would torment them like that."

She laughed.

His gaze held hers. She saw laughter there and something else—affection. It gave her a little thrill.

Only Maynell ever looked at her that way. Very few people in her life had given her true affection.

"Don't ever underestimate me," she said.

"I won't," he assured her. "I'll be on my guard."

About a mile farther on, he signaled for quiet and they slowed their horses to a soft, ground-eating trot.

"It's a track some farmer built," he said. "He collects a few dollars from every racehorse owner who uses it."

"I hope the thieves have already paid their fee for tonight," she said.

Eagle Jack chuckled quietly. "Mean as a snake," he said. "I'm surprised you shot that one."

She made a face at him.

Then, suddenly, through a little grove of pecan trees, she saw the white rail fence and then the straight stretch of beaten earth.

Eagle Jack gave a hand signal to stop the horses. When they had dismounted, he came close and spoke into Susanna's ear. "Hold the horses," he whispered. "Over there, under that low-hanging tree. Watch for me and keep them quiet."

He helped her get the horses arranged in the shadows, then he vanished.

Susanna shifted her position to try to keep him in sight and she could see him drifting from tree trunk to tree trunk, silent as a falling leaf. But she heard the sound of hooves and then a man's voice.

Beyond Eagle Jack, on the other side of the

fenced track, a tall man sat a tall gray horse. Beside him, there was a loafing shed in the shade, open to the south. At first, she didn't notice the second man—he was near the fence to the track.

"Let 'er be," the mounted man said loudly. Then he dropped his voice and said something that might have been, "Quit foolin' with her."

Or maybe it was, "I'm not foolin' with you."

He moved his horse to the left and Susanna could see that the man by the fence had another horse—a small one with a scruffy mane and pricked ears, tied to a hitching rail on the far side of the white fence. Could this be her first glimpse of the famous Molly?

The second man stooped over, raised her right forefoot, and began, apparently, to pick her hoof. He didn't even look up when the other man spoke to him again.

"I want you to time Prince," the tall man shouted. "Right now!"

He was holding out something in his hand, which must be a stopwatch.

Still no response.

Molly pinned her ears and stretched the rope she was tied with just enough to bite the hoof-picking man smartly on the bottom.

The horseback one threw back his head and laughed. The other one dropped her hoof, slapped his hand over his wound, and headed away from the track, hobbling toward the trees on the far side of the track. Susanna glimpsed a tent farther on, back in the shadows. They must be living there at the track.

The man on the gray horse followed the one on foot, saying something now and then, all of it unintelligible from this distance. Susanna looked through the pecan grove for Eagle Jack again, but he had disappeared.

She glanced back at Molly, if Molly it was.

The hitching rail, the green grass and blue sky met her eye. The shaggy little horse was gone.

Susanna blinked.

It was impossible. Not even a whole minute had passed since the horse had bitten the man.

Had it? Maybe she'd lost her sense of time.

But no. It hadn't been very long because the gray horse had not yet reached the trees.

She tried to take in what had happened. Instinctively, she wrapped her arms around the muzzles of the two horses she held.

No sense letting them speak if they should see a new horse coming toward them through the trees. She concentrated on scanning the grove, both in and out of the shade, for a glimpse of Eagle Jack and Molly.

Could he have Molly in hand? Could he have untied her that fast?

"Let's go," he said, from behind her.

She startled and bit her tongue to keep from crying out as she whirled to face him.

Sure enough, he was leading the horse she'd seen tied to the fence. He was holding his other hand out for the reins of his saddled mount.

Susanna handed them over and threw herself onto her own horse. Eagle Jack mounted quickly, too, holding Molly's rope in his hand.

"Susanna, meet Molly," he said, as they turned to head out. "Molly, this is Susanna."

Molly was trotting between the two saddled horses. She glanced sideways at Eagle Jack and muttered deep in her throat.

Eagle Jack chuckled. "She's been trying to talk ever since she saw me," he said, "but I couldn't let her make any noise."

He kissed to his mount and all three horses fell into a long trot.

"We have to pace ourselves now in case we have to run later," he said. "The ground's soft from the rain and I don't have time to cover our tracks."

"I can't believe they didn't see you," Susanna said. "That was a legendary exploit. It'll live forever, wherever men sit around the fire and tell stories of horse thievery."

Eagle Jack smiled.

"I really think you're Comanche," she said, "instead of Cherokee."

"The Comanche aren't the only horsemen in the world," he said.

"And the Legend of Molly's Rescue will prove it."

"It may be a legend that doesn't yet have an ending," he said.

"Surely they wouldn't come after you, since you're the rightful owner."

"Ah, but they'd have to be right upon us to know who I am," he said.

It might have been a prophecy. The next minute, from somewhere behind them, the sound of a gunshot tore through the air.

Chapter 15

Eagle Jack looked back over his shoulder. "Folger's still riding that buckskin, I see," he said.

He sounded as calm as if they were sitting on a porch somewhere watching people ride by.

Susanna worked up her courage to look behind them, too. The tall gray horse with the tall man riding was coming after them at a gallop, and the other man was bouncing along, bareback, on a shorter buckskin horse some distance behind the gray. As she watched, the tall man lifted his gun and fired at them again. She saw the flash from the muzzle.

She faced forward, urging her horse to go faster, lifting Fred into his awkward lope as the sound of the shot reached them.

Eagle Jack held his mount at a trot, with Molly right beside him.

"I know we have to pace our horses," she said, glancing at him as she started to draw ahead, "but we might get killed if we don't run."

He grinned at her. "Naw. I've seen Oates shoot before. He's not exactly what you'd call a marksman."

"Anybody can get lucky once in a while."

"We're out of range—he needs a rifle at this distance," Eagle Jack said.

She smooched to Fred again, anyway.

"Come *on*," she said, with a fierce look at Eagle Jack.

"Slow down," he said. He rode up beside her and caught hold of Fred's bridle. "Listen, Susanna, trust me. We need to stay just about this distance in front of them."

She stared at him, then looked back at their pursuers. "Whatever for? What if he *has* a rifle and he just hasn't used it yet?"

"Then I'll have to use mine," he said. "But until then, let's draw them farther away from the track and the farm. If they're camping there, they may be friends with the farmer and I don't want any interference when I deal with them."

Her heart slowed its rapidly accelerating beat. His calmness and confidence took away her fear of getting shot, or most of it, because he was in control of the situation, after all.

However, a new fear, born of the coldly vengeful resolve in his voice, came to life in the pit of her stomach. He wanted no interference.

What was he planning to do to those men?

"Oates was wearing only the one gun," he said, "and no saddlebag for extra ammunition. He'll run out, pretty soon."

"Not if he sees that he's doing no good because we're out of range."

"He's mostly just trying to scare us into dropping this rope," Eagle Jack told her, nodding at Molly.

"He could have all his pockets and both his boots full of ammunition, for all you know."

He gave her an infuriating grin. "Aw, come on, Susanna. Let's not borrow trouble."

"Eagle Jack, what are you doing? You're not going to let them get any closer, are you?"

"Not yet."

Another shot rang out.

Eagle Jack laughed. "What did I tell you? Three more to go, if he started with a full load."

He slowed a little more, and the smile faded from his face as he turned to look at her full-on.

"When they catch up to us, be sure you let me stay between you and them," he said.

"Why would you let them catch up?" Susanna asked.

"I owe them a visit," he said.

Suddenly, his tone had turned flat and hard. He set his jaw and he looked dangerous. She could think of no other word for it. Eagle Jack Sixkiller was a dangerous man.

That thought had come to her before, and it was right.

"I know they beat you up and stole your horse," she said quickly. "But Eagle Jack, don't you think it'd be better to let the law take care of them? There must be some lawmen not too far away."

"I've got a herd to drive," he said. "I don't have time to hunt for the law."

Susanna looked back. The two pursuers were getting closer. They still had as many as three bullets.

"Let's go on," she urged. "We've got Molly. That's all that matters."

"They're horse thieves," he said. "They deserve to hang."

"Too bad you've led them away from the trees," she said, trying to lighten the look in his eyes.

Trying to put a smile on his face.

"You don't have anything to hang them from out here," she added.

He didn't change expression. He slowed their pace even more and looked back to see the men again.

"There's more trees than those," was all he said.

"Eagle Jack . . ."

He ignored that and rode on, for quite a long way.

"Nothing will go wrong," he said, finally. "But

if, by some stroke of bad luck it does, get on Molly and ride for the wagon. Nothing on four legs can catch her."

He glanced at her once, sharply, to see if she'd heard, then he looked back at their pursuers.

"You can ride bareback, surely, since you sit a saddle as well as you do."

"Yes," she said, "but I'm not leaving you, so forget about that."

"Remember what I told you to do," Eagle Jack said. He kicked up the pace. "Let's get this done," he said.

They rode at a short lope, farther out into the open country, back in the direction of the herd, but not exactly the way they had come. While Eagle Jack guided them into a rough patch, rocky and sandy, with less grass and more mesquite, they heard another shot.

They rode another mile or more before he slowed the horses again. The stubborn men began to gain on them.

It wouldn't be long now. Susanna's breath came hard. Surely she wouldn't have to watch him hang them. Surely that wasn't what he intended.

One of them, Oates or Folger, yelled, "Hey, you! Horse thief! We've got you now."

The call came faintly on the wind, but when Susanna looked to see them, Oates was coming closer all the time. Folger, on the buckskin, was still some distance behind him.

"Whoa," Eagle Jack said. "Whoa, now."

Without a word to Susanna, he turned his horse.

Then he said, "Stay behind me, Annie," and started back at a brisk trot to meet the skinny man on the tall gray.

Susanna stayed close behind him. She saw him dally the end of Molly's lead rope around his saddle horn to free his hand for the gun he wore on his hip.

"Drop your weapon and step down, Oates," he yelled. "I'm gonna show you what happens to a real horse thief."

Susanna would have laughed if she hadn't been so scared. Oates had a look of surprise on his face that looked to have been painted there.

"Sixkiller?" he said.

Eagle Jack's gaze flicked to Folger, just for an instant, and Susanna realized he was waiting for the buckskin horse to get within range of his gun.

"Yep," he said, focusing on Oates again, "the same Sixkiller you hit over the head from behind with that two-by-four."

He rode up to within a few yards of the man and stopped.

"That wasn't me," the skinny man protested. "That was Folger snuck up on you like that."

"Drop your weapon, Oates."

Oates's gun appeared frozen in his grip.

"You've got to believe me, Sixkiller."

Eagle Jack drew his gun and shot Oates's gun out of his hand before Susanna could comprehend what was happening. It bounced once, then came to rest against a rock.

"Down," he said.

Oates's hand tightened around his reins for a split second.

"Don't even think about making a run for it," Eagle Jack told him. "I'd much rather shoot you than hang you."

So Oates stood up in his stirrup, wavering a little, and got down from his horse. Behind him, Folger finally realized what was happening and turned his mount around, seeking escape.

Eagle Jack fired again and put a hole in his hat.

Folger pulled up and got off the horse.

"You two partners get together now," Eagle Jack said. "Right over there by that big mesquite tree."

Susanna's heart stopped. Would he actually hang them? He had every right to. No law could fault him for it.

"I can't watch this, Eagle Jack," she said. "Please don't."

He ignored her.

He gestured with his gun from one of the thieves to the other.

"Now."

The one word, spoken low and quiet, was so powerful that both men moved at that same moment, both trying to walk over the rough ground without stumbling and watch Eagle Jack at the same time. Oates hardly dared to look down.

"Don't be shootin' us, now," he said.

"Shooting's too good for you," Eagle Jack said. "Horse thieves hang."

"We was gonna bring her back to you," Folger said. "All we done was borry her a little while."

Eagle Jack fired at his feet.

"Dance," he said. "Entertain the lady."

Then he fired at Oates's feet.

Both men began to shuffle.

"Faster," Eagle Jack said, and thrust his fingers into the pockets of his vest.

He pulled out more bullets, fired once more, then commenced to reload.

Even though these were the men who had beaten him so badly with a two-by-four, and from behind, in a sneak attack, Susanna couldn't help but feel pity. Their legs were shaking so hard they could hardly stand, but they danced anyway. Their boots scraping the ground in that tremulous rhythm made her stomach turn.

It was fear, fear raw and savage as any she had ever felt in her childhood that was emanating from every pore in their bodies. Pure fear, growing by the second to surround them and fill the very air she was trying to breathe.

"Eagle Jack," she said quietly, from behind him. "What are you going to do?"

He didn't answer. She didn't even know if he'd heard.

"Keep dancing," he said, "and then when I say so, Oates, you can go get that rope off your saddle."

"Eagle Jack, please," Susanna said. "I don't want to see this."

But all of Eagle Jack's attention was on his enemies.

"I'll use my rope on you, Folger," he said. "I'll sacrifice it for that, because nobody ever needed hanging like you do."

Their faces paled even more, which didn't seem possible. Susanna felt the blood pounding hard in her head.

He fired at their feet again.

"I cannot stand this, Eagle Jack," she blurted. "Let's go and leave them here."

He was unsnapping his coiled rope from its place on his saddle.

"Please," she said.

Her voice came out loud, although her mouth was almost too dry to speak. "I know how it is to feel such fear," she said.

Eagle Jack looked up.

It must have all been in her eyes, in her voice. He must have seen and heard her memories flashing through her consciousness, memories of her little-girl self whose life was at the mercy of adults who were strangers to her.

He searched her face.

"Tolly died," she said, more softly. "Isn't that enough death for a while?"

He kept on looking at her with his dark, hooded eyes. They told her nothing.

But when he turned away, he left the rope where it was.

"Sit down," he said, to the still-dancing men. "Take off your boots."

Oates made a strangled sound, as if he were trying to say something, but he obeyed without a word. Folger followed suit. When both men were in their sock feet, Eagle Jack looked them over.

"Now your socks," he said.

"Susanna, would you mind?" he said. "Pick up their horses' reins and bring them over here."

He glanced at the horses.

There was a canteen tied to the saddle on the gray horse but the buckskin, of course, had neither.

"I'm doing this for the lady's sake," he said, turning to look at the men again. "You've got no water, no food, and no boots, but you can make it back to the farm. Let's see you hoof it."

He gestured with the gun for them to get up. They obeyed.

"I tell you now that I'll set the Rangers on your trail at the first opportunity," he said. "So y'all might want to consider heading in the direction of the Indian Territories or maybe Louisiana. Your life in Texas will be hell from now on."

The two horse thieves started walking when he pointed the gun at them again.

"Get on out of my sight," he said, "before I change my mind."

When they were a dozen yards away, trying to hurry and pick their way over the rocky terrain at the same time, he got down, gathered up their boots, and tied them together with his rope. They dangled from his saddle.

"Let's go," he said.

"Maybe some of the men can wear those boots," Susanna said. "We lost a lot of clothes and stuff in the river."

He didn't answer.

Wordlessly, they tied the other three horses to their saddle rings—one on each side of Susanna's Fred, and Eagle Jack kept Molly. They rode on, also in silence.

Finally, she tried again.

"Those are nice boots," she said, "probably they could afford them with the money they won with Molly."

He threw her an impatient glance.

"Folger and Oates dressed well," he said. "That was part of their fakery as Kentucky gentlemen."

He didn't look at her again. He didn't say anything else, either. They rode on.

Maybe he was angry with her. If so, she wanted

to know it. She was through with that time in her life when she lived on the edge of relationships, trying to guess how the other person felt about her.

"Are you sorry you let them go?" she said.

"Not too much," he said, staring off into the distance. "A hanging's never pleasant."

"I know it's the code, though. I hate to think maybe you'll feel you didn't do your duty as an honorable man. You let them go because I asked you to."

He looked at her then, fully into her face. He was listening.

"I thank you for making that decision based on my feelings, Eagle Jack. I will always remember what you did."

She saw the humor gradually come back into his eyes.

"If we ever run across them again, you'll have to hang them yourself," he said. "My feelings will require it."

She held his gaze, freely letting her appreciation and affection for him show.

"Fair enough," she said. "We've got a deal."

She leaned from her horse and held out her hand. He took it and shook it, then squeezed it when he let go.

"At least we're going back to the herd with something to show for our scouting trip," he said. "The gray's pretty fast. And he's good-looking.

The boys will be fighting to get him into their mounts."

"And you have to remember, Eagle Jack, that what you did to Oates and Folger is poetic justice," she said.

He smiled.

"It is," he said. "No telling how many other men they've left afoot. I hope they have to walk all the way back to Kentucky, providing they live that long."

"Let's drink to that," she said, reaching for the canteen of water that hung from her saddle. "To a long, long walk for the Kentucky gentlemen."

As the drive moved steadily north through good, grassy country with plentiful water from the recent rains, Susanna decided this was the best time of her whole life. She'd never been around so much laughter and teasing or had feelings of closeness with so many people. She realized that, until now, she'd never truly been a member of any group, never really belonged, and she loved the safe, secure pleasure it gave her.

The whole crew had endless fun with the new horses—racing Molly and the tall gray with horses from the other outfits they encountered and passing both the thieves' horses around to decide how they liked them. There were also the two saddles and other tack to replace some that had been lost, and it took many discussions, bargainings, gambling games, and deals to decide who got them.

It had perked everyone up considerably to have some good news for a change, and as soon as Susanna and Eagle Jack rode in from their lucrative scout that day, the crew had started playing cards and mumblety-peg and betting on their two new running horses. Other questions were who should get the fine boots that had belonged to Oates and Folger, plus the gear that was in their saddle bags. Finally, they were raffled off and then the winners sold them to someone who could wear them and, since none of the crew had any cash money, the deals became so complicated that they entertained everyone on the drive for days and days.

After they'd passed Fort Worth—where she did buy supplies on her own credit and Eagle Jack visited the office of the Texas Rangers—they pushed on to the Red River Crossing. There they swam the cattle and horses and ferried the wagons, all without a tragic or even a disturbing incident.

This went a long way toward restoring the confidence of every man in the outfit as they left Texas. They drove almost straight north, skirting the western edge of the Cross Timbers and the eastern edge of the Great Plains. It was powerful, fascinating country on either side, and the rolling hills seemed to surround her and Eagle Jack as they rode together out ahead of the herd.

"Sometimes I wish we were going to trail them on to Colorado or Wyoming," she said, one day when an overnight rain had washed the sky and the earth and the sun was making everything sparkle.

"By the time we get to Abilene, you'll be so happy to see the end of this trail, you'll jump up and shout," Eagle Jack said.

He was laughing at her a little.

She pretended to be offended. "And just how can you say that?" she demanded, her hands on her hips. "You think you know me so well?"

They were letting their horses amble along as the cool breeze played in their manes and tickled Susanna's and Eagle Jack's bare forearms. It was a day when the sun on naked skin felt like a caress.

"Well, yes, now that you mention it, I do," he said, with that flashing grin she loved. "But even if I didn't, I could say that because you're human."

He was in that happy, teasing mood she loved. Carefree. That was the word for Eagle Jack most of the time and that was what drew her to him the most.

She realized that truth with a start. Carefree was something she had hardly even been, until this trip with Eagle Jack.

Even with the troubles and dangers they'd already endured, even if they encountered many more, when she was ninety years old sitting in a rocking chair on her porch, she would remember this as the most carefree time of her life.

"Oh?" she said. "And I'm just like every other human?"

"No-o," he drawled, looking her up and down in that slow, provocative stare that never failed to thrill her, "I'm not saying that at all."

He let his gaze linger on her mouth while he smiled at her foolishness in jumping to that conclusion.

Then, with a sweep of his heavy lashes, he lifted it to meet her eyes.

"We'll come back to that in a minute," he said. "But right now I want to make the point that any human being gets tired of sleeping on the ground. Any human being gets tired of having no buttermilk biscuits, sand in the stew, and no table to eat at."

She raised her eyebrows in surprise, as if none of those inconveniences had ever come to her notice before.

"No problem for me," she said, with a grin. "So what's your point, Eagle Jack?"

"That you're like everybody else in those ways whether you'll admit it or not," he said, "but . . ."

He looked around at the hillside gently rising in front of them, where the little orange wildflowers called Indian paintbrush waved at the snowy clouds and the green grass spread its blanket to meet the blue of the sky. Then he turned back to Susanna.

"But what?" she said.

"You'll have to get down and let me show you," he said, and stopped his horse.

He dismounted and dropped the reins.

"Come on, Annie," he said, as he came to her. "It's a beautiful day. Let's have a picnic."

He reached up and lifted her off her horse.

His first touch made her go weak. In his arms, she had no strength at all.

The only thing she could manage was to put her arm around his neck.

He carried her to his horse and, holding her in one arm, took down the blanket rolled behind the saddle.

She chuckled.

"I'm not used to a blanket to sit on," she said. "This is a fancy picnic."

"Damn straight it is," he murmured, and when he turned to look at her, his face was so close that she brushed a kiss onto the hard line of his jaw.

"Watch it now," he said, with a grin, "you're gonna make me lose my train of thought."

"Hmm," she said.

"Hang on to this," he said, and held her gaze with his so intensely that neither of them could move for a moment.

Then he laid the blanket across her lap and went to get the leather bag and the canteen hanging from his saddle horn.

"I guess you want me to carry those, too," she said. "And here I am, already all burdened down."

"You don't know nothin' about it," he said. "How do you think I feel, haulin' around a great big girl that weighs more than a side of beef?"

She gasped in mock horror and struggled to get out of his arms. "*What?* Let me down. Let me down, this minute, do you hear me?"

He walked over to the side of the hill, dropped the rolled blanket, and dumped her unceremoniously on top of it. Susanna screamed with laughter and pulled him down on top of her.

"Here . . . here . . . now," he said, as she interrupted him between every word with a hard, quick kiss on the mouth, "this is a *fancy* picnic. We're supposed to spread out the blanket."

She held on around his neck, hard, with both arms and pulled back only far enough to give him her narrow-eyed, dangerous look.

"Are you some kind of a tenderfoot?" she demanded. "Since when is the thick, sweet-smelling grass not good enough for you?"

"Not as sweet as you, Susanna," he said, and started in on the buttons to her shirt.

She pulled the tail of his blue work shirt, an exact match for her own, out of his jeans and ran her palms up under it, caressing his marvelous, muscular back with both her palms.

He shivered, and she marveled at her power.

"You're not sweet, Eagle Jack," she murmured, against his cheek, touching it with her lips and the tip of her tongue.

"No?"

He turned his head and kissed her mouth. Once. Quick and hard.

Then he moved down to kiss the bare skin of the path he was opening between her breasts.

"No," she said, and gasped when he pulled apart the snaps of her camisole and turned the fabric back.

The sunlight and the breeze moved over her breasts but his gaze stayed on them. And then his mouth.

His mouth that was even more magic than his hands. He started in between them and planted a row of slow, slow, wet kisses up the inside of each of her breasts, then raised his head and looked at her through heavy-lidded eyes the color of liquid chocolate, eyes that set a fire burning in her core.

"So," he said, raising up to look at her with his smoldering. dark brown eyes. "If I'm not sweet, what am I?"

"Sexy," she said, and gave him a slow, slow smile.

Then she reached for his head with both hands and pulled it to her. She thrust her fingers into his long, thick black hair and tore away the thong that held it to let it fall, to let it swing around her breast when he took the nipple with his lips and his tongue and brush her skin with the scorching promise of things to come.

He suckled her, he nipped her with his teeth, he licked her skin until she begged him, until she cried out his name and tore at his belt with both her trembling hands.

"No," he murmured. "Not yet, sweet Susanna."

Then he took both her hands and laid them out beside her, her arms flat on the ground and he put them there with a push that meant for them to stay. She lay still, looking at his face through her half-open eyes, trembling at his slightest touch.

It was he who took away her belt, who opened her jeans and slipped all her clothes off, her boots and all the rest down over her feet after them. He was touching her here and there—small, light burning touches like the bite of a flame.

After that his lips and his hands were gone from her but she was holding him with her sure gaze, watching him peeling out of his own clothes and coming back to her. He parted her thighs with his own and knelt between her legs.

He held her gaze with his molten one.

Until the last moment when he bent his head and kissed the flat of her belly. His hair closed around her like a curtain of silk. His lips drew her into himself. For a long, floating moment.

Then he came into her and they moved together in that ancient rhythm that held them to the earth so it could rock them in its arms.

After that picnic day, Susanna knew she could love somebody. Her love for Eagle Jack filled the very air that day and she recognized it for what it was late that afternoon when the sun was going down on the most perfect day of her life.

And, as day after day came to her, one after another, like perfect pearls on a string—they were beautiful days whether it rained or hailed or the sun blazed down, even the two scary days they had to drive the cattle faster with no water, even after they crossed the Kansas line and rode, mile after mile after endless mile, across the flat, empty plains—she actually dared to wonder whether Eagle Jack could, perhaps, love her.

The reason all the days were beautiful was Eagle Jack.

He treated her, all the time, with that same passionate tenderness he'd shown on that picnic blanket or else with the rollicking fun-making attitude that was the backbone of their friendship. Many times, even sometimes with Maynell there and the men all sitting talking around the fire, he looked at her in a way that she imagined was the look of love.

But she had nothing to compare it to and no intention of letting herself lose her good sense, even if she knew for sure that he loved her. There was no way she could ever give over the control of her life to anyone else again.

Until Everett had died, she had never been free. Never even close to being free. She would never give that up.

And besides, she had already promised herself that this drive with him would be a special time separate from the rest of her life. She would hold to that.

She would never forget one moment of it. At least, now she knew what it was like to love someone.

Chapter 16

The first glimpse of Abilene made Susanna wish none of it was true. She wished the town weren't there, she wished they were trailing the cattle all the way to Montana, she wished that she'd never begun to love Eagle Jack, and she wished that he didn't treat her as if he might love her, too, so she could hate him instead.

She wished she could be a different person. Why couldn't she be a normal woman who could love a man and live with him and let him love her in return?

Abilene. The very name of the town, spoken aloud, made her sad. When they'd camped last evening and Eagle Jack had told her they were nearly there, she'd felt a terrible loss. She had hardly slept, and this morning her entire self was as empty as the plains.

The time out of time she had promised herself was past.

The time had come when she must think about her ranch and the cattle sale and how much money she'd be taking home to Texas. The time had come when she must let Eagle Jack stake her so she could bet on Molly.

She hated to get deeper into his debt—in case the mare should lose—but the river stampede had decimated her herd so that the remaining cattle couldn't bring enough to pay off her mortgage for Brushy Creek, much less pay Eagle Jack for the remuda and pay all the men's wages and still give her enough to operate on until time to drive another bunch of cattle north next year. Plus she'd have hotel and food expenses here in Abilene. Thank goodness, so far, Molly had won every race they'd entered her in.

So that's what Susanna had to do. She would try to think of Eagle Jack as her business partner now—only that—and concentrate on the future of Brushy Creek, although, at the moment, her home seemed as far away as the moon. It was the only home she'd ever had, and she could hardly remember what it looked like.

How could any man take over her mind like that? She must take control of it again.

"Do you really think I can win enough with Molly to make up for the cattle I lost in the river?" she asked.

She and Eagle Jack were riding into Abilene from where they'd left Maynell and Jimbo and the rest of the crew camped with the herd out south of town. Everyone else would have his time in town once the buyer took possession of the cattle, but first, to get that done, Eagle Jack and Susanna were moving into the hotel built especially for cattlemen, the Drovers Cottage.

"Yep," he said. "Miss Molly's all rested up and full of herself. She'll bring in the mortgage money for you."

Susanna cast a questioning look at the little mare slow-trotting on Eagle Jack's lead rope. Shaggy head down, ears at rest, legs shuffling along, eyes half-closed, she looked ready to drop off to sleep.

"Will you, Molly? Are you in the mood to run?"

Molly didn't even turn her head at the sound of her name.

"I don't know," Susanna said, "we haven't raced her since we crossed into Kansas. Maybe she's given up the sport and not told us yet."

Eagle Jack grinned. "This is how she's always been," he said. "That loser's look of hers is how we get our best matches and our best bets."

"Eagle Jack, are you sure?"

He chuckled.

"I'm sure. It's happened over and over again."

Susanna looked at Molly one more time, then sat up in the saddle and squared her shoulders.

"Well, then," she said, "let's look Abilene over and pick us out some suckers."

That made him laugh.

"Plain-talking Annie," he said. "She comes right out and says what she means."

"I didn't used to be that way," she said. "Not until after Everett died. Before then, in my whole life, I never said anything straight out of my head or my heart."

He cocked his head and looked at her as if that were one of the most interesting things he'd ever heard.

"That's hard to believe," he said. "Keeping quiet must've been hard for a woman who wants to boss the world."

She pretended to slap at his leg. He pretended to dodge away.

"I decided to set my real self free and I did," she said.

He grinned at her.

"Yes," he said, "and it's a good thing for the rest of us that you did. If your real self was all caged up and fretting, no telling *what* you'd do."

She grinned back at him. "Just be glad you don't have to find out."

A wagon rattled past them and drowned out her words. When it was gone, Eagle Jack gave her a serious look.

"All right, now, Susanna, we're in town," he said. "When we start talking horse race, put your plain talk aside. In fact, let me take the lead and you back me up."

"I can't imagine you taking the lead," she said dryly, "when all you do is rave about what a buggy boss I am."

"That's why I'm telling you now," he said, and they both laughed.

Easily. As they had done a hundred times before. Looking right at each other and saying many, many other things with their eyes.

"Susanna," he said, "I've been saving something for you. Now that we're coming into town, and going to buy new clothes and all, you'll want it."

New clothes. That was another expense she'd forgotten—probably because it was so rare in her life.

"What is it?"

Still holding her gaze, he reached back, unbuckled the flap on his saddle bag, and pulled out a paper-wrapped package.

"Something I bought you the day you got me out of the Salado Jail."

He handed it to her across Molly's back.

She hung her reins around her saddle horn and used both hands. After she picked up the one fold of paper, she cried out.

"Gloves!"

Her heart was beating so fast, out of all proportion to the occasion.

"Oh, Eagle Jack, thank you! No one's ever bought me a gift before."

She stroked the soft leather and looked at its buttery color in the sunlight.

"Never?"

"No. Not store-bought," she said, then she thought about that for a minute, then added, "and not homemade, either."

"Well," he said, in a droll tone, "I'm sure glad you're taking it better than you did the first flower anybody ever gave you."

She felt the heat of embarrassment paint her cheeks as she turned to look at him.

"Look how far you've brought me," she said quietly. "Finally I can accept a kindness graciously."

"Did nobody ever give you *anything*?"

She shrugged and tried to throw off the chill of her childhood.

"Just a hard time," she said, trying for a light tone. "They simply didn't have enough food or clothes or anything else for an extra person in the house. None of my relatives did."

"Well, they didn't have to be mean to you. You couldn't help being an orphan."

"I wish I'd never told you about Uncle Job giving me those whippings," she said. "Or locking me in the smokehouse . . ."

She bit her lip as all the old humiliation came back to haunt her. Whatever had possessed her to tell him all that, anyhow? During the long hours of riding side by side, she had bared her heart to him, mile by mile. She had never meant to do so, she wouldn't have told all that to anybody else—she never had done so before—but Eagle Jack made her feel so safe. Maybe that was the reason.

Now his face was a thundercloud.

"What? What is it?" she asked.

"It's a damn shame, that's what," he snapped. "For you to be treated so . . ."

Something in her expression must have stopped him. She did not want pity. She would not accept it, even though the hurt, confused little girl she had been was alive inside her once more.

"It's about damn time you got a gift, then," he said, with a trace of his old grin. "At least those'll be warmer this winter than the ones with the holes in them."

This winter.

This winter they'd be months and miles apart.

But this was now and they were still together. And Eagle Jack would not take his eyes from hers.

Susanna didn't want to look away. Ever. She was going to be lost forever in this brown-eyed handsome man. If she wasn't already.

And why would he want her forever if nobody else ever had?

She must sell her cattle, win a horse race or two, get the money, and run.

"Eagle Jack," she said, although her tongue

would barely move to obey her, "I think we should take separate rooms at the Drovers Cottage."

Startled, he stared at her. "Why is that?"

"This is a public place and you said it's always full of Texans. There'll be people you know here. And if we continue to pretend to be married, then you'll have to explain why we're not when you get home."

"But the crew . . ." he began to argue.

She stiffened her spine and refused to let herself give in.

"They won't know," she said. "They won't be in town at night until the deal's done. I'm heading home the minute I have my money and get settled up."

He kept on looking at her and she wished he'd look away.

"You only wanted them to think we're married so you'd be safe on the trail," he said speculatively, as if to go over the story one more time.

"And so they'd respect me, since I was on the trail where women aren't supposed to be," she said.

"Right," he agreed.

"Maynell and Jimbo know the truth," she went on explaining. "Marvin and his men aren't with me permanently, and if I ever run across them again I'll just explain that you and I aren't together anymore."

"That takes care of you," Eagle Jack said, "but

I'll be seeing a lot of the men with my beef herd. They'll naturally ask about my wife. What shall I tell them?"

The vision of that happening caught at her throat. The knowledge that she had to separate from him caught at her heart. The word "wife" took her breath away completely. She couldn't stand it.

"Tell them whatever you want, Eagle Jack," she said, "whatever will help you most with all your other women."

He just kept looking at her. Silently.

"We've both known it from the start," she said, "you have to admit that."

"Known what?" he said, in his quietly dangerous voice.

"That we'd have to part."

He didn't say a word. Finally, he looked away and rode out a little bit ahead.

Eagle Jack wanted to slow it all down, somehow. The time seemed to be sliding past him like water through his fingers, and he had a lot he wanted to do with Susanna.

Like escort her to a long, leisurely dinner at the fine restaurant in the Drovers Cottage. If the place had musicians there tonight, they would dance—he'd been wanting to take her into his arms and dance with her.

If he could dance with her, he could go back to

her room with her, he just knew it. He could hold on to her a little bit longer. The very thought of this insanity about not being in her bed anymore—just like that, fast as a snap of her fingers, no more—was killing him. He had to do something about it.

He wanted to see that same look in her eyes that had been there when he gave her the gloves. No woman had ever looked at him like that before.

That look went right through him and it caused him to want to make it all up to her—the terrible childhood she'd survived and the stupid, mean husband who had treated her no better. All of that would have broken a lesser woman. He admired her and he wanted to reward her.

She deserved some easy time with no hard work in it, she deserved some of the pretty things she'd never had. She deserved some fun.

He wanted to sit on the long veranda of the Drovers Cottage with her and see the trains come in and out and watch the endless parade up and down the street of cattle buyers, commission agents, saloonkeepers, gamblers, and all the other kinds of humanity that descended upon Abilene. He wanted to take her to Goldsoll's Texas store and buy her a dress, blue to match her eyes, and then she could wear it to dinner.

He wanted to just walk with her, with her hand on his arm, up and down the main street, called Texas Street, and see her be surprised, as most cowboys were on their first visit, that the establishments on one side of it were more Texan than some Texas towns, with everything named the Lone Star or the Alamo or the Bull's Head and everybody talking about cattle and everybody dressed in a way that showed they were *from* Texas. He could introduce her to some people in the cattle business that she should know.

No, she shouldn't. She was too beautiful and they were all men. A woman who had the looks that Susanna did shouldn't be in business at all. It was dangerous.

But instead of doing anything that he wanted to do, here they were, out on the edge of town riding in to race Miss Molly and win Susanna some money. Rare was the day he didn't care to see a horse race and even rarer was the day he didn't care to run Miss Molly, but this day was one.

She'd been right when she said he'd known from the start that they couldn't stay together forever. He agreed with her on that, one hundred percent. But it was making him crazy just the same.

He didn't know what was wrong with him.

Susanna stood under one of the few trees in Kansas, near the impromptu racetrack, holding the reins of her mount and Eagle Jack's. She was listening to Eagle Jack talking to one of the young boys who were hiring out as jockeys for the series of races that were springing up, and smiling to herself about how closely he was predicting Molly's behavior and her speed. She could only pray that Molly would come through as she usually did, and *win* as she usually did, because she, Susanna, had borrowed a hundred dollars from Eagle Jack—a hundred dollars!—to bet on this race.

But she couldn't afford to fool around with lesser amounts when she must either replace her losses on her cattle or give up on paying off her mortgage. The cattle buyer would meet with her and Eagle Jack tomorrow. As soon as that business was settled and she'd paid everybody off, she had to go home.

The very thought made her heart ache, but she pushed the hurt aside.

The arrangements had already been made. She would go on ahead as soon as possible to take care of paying off the banker's mortgage and to see how Brushy Creek had fared. As soon as the cattle were physically in the hands of the buyer, Maynell, Jimbo, and the men would spend some time in Abilene and then come on the next train or the next, shipping the wagon and the remuda back south with them. The men would do whatever they wanted. Most would come south on the train.

Eagle Jack had made an offhand mention of making a lone, leisurely ride back to Texas, racing

Molly whenever he wanted along the way. Visualizing that made her heart ache, too, because she wanted to be riding beside him.

But Eagle Jack was a big boy who had made this trip before. He could find his way home without her.

Where was his home? All he'd ever said was that he was from up east of Waco, even when she'd hinted to know more.

That was another completely remarkable thing she'd never realized until that moment: she was normally so closemouthed about herself and her past and her present business that she confided nothing. With Eagle Jack, she had been as garrulous as a pathetic, lonely old woman, blurting out things she thought she'd forgotten, things that were much better off unsaid.

What *was* it about him that wreaked such havoc on her?

Maybe his looks. There he was, the muscles of his shoulders and arms rippling beneath the thin fabric of his shirt as he ran his hands over Molly's legs.

"All you have to do is stay on her back," he was saying to his small jockey. "Make sure you've got a good seat and tight legs because when she stretches out, she'll run a hole in the wind."

The boy looked dubious, but he nodded that he understood. Eagle Jack bent over and cupped his hand to give the boy a leg up.

"I'll be right back," he said to Susanna.

Then he led Molly toward the starting line while she got used to the jockey being on her back. Once the short, scruffy mare was standing beside the long-legged Thoroughbred that was her opponent in this match race, several more people began signaling to Eagle Jack that they wanted to make a bet.

Susanna watched him dealing with them all and talking to the two men appointed to hold the money. Her gaze stayed glued to him as he returned to Molly, then, and stroked her shaggy mane. He put his arm around her neck and hugged her while he appeared to whisper something to her.

Molly pricked up her ears and turned her head to nudge him with her nose. It made Susanna smile.

"Eagle Jack knows how to treat a woman, doesn't he, Molly?" she murmured, under her breath.

Then he was walking toward her again, finding his way through the crowd, and her fingers tightened on the two sets of reins she was holding. Her breath caught in her chest.

All she wanted, right now at this minute, was for him to be beside her again. She wasn't even thinking about winning money. She was losing her mind. What was she going to do when they parted for good?

Eagle Jack reached her just before the starting gun fired.

The race went like lightning. The horses were running full out almost before Susanna could transfer her gaze from Eagle Jack to the track. They raced close together for less than halfway down the track, with Molly a neck ahead of the much taller horse, then Molly started pulling ahead. She simply floated—she absolutely looked as if she were moving effortlessly—farther and farther and farther ahead of the other horse, and she kept on going.

"She's just a blur," Susanna said, in wonder. "I've never seen anything like it."

"You've saved your ranch, Susanna," Eagle Jack said, "the odds were ten to one."

Her ranch! Brushy Creek was saved!

"*Molly* saved it, you mean," she cried, and turned to throw her arms around his neck after the mare crossed the finish line four lengths ahead.

But as he hugged her in that one quick moment of victory, she still couldn't feel a thing about the race or her ranch. All she was thinking was soon it would be the last time he'd ever hold her.

Eagle Jack leaned back in his rocking chair, exhaled a cloud of smoke from his new cheroot, and propped his feet up on the railing that ran along the veranda of the Drovers Cottage. With the breeze from the east, it was actually cool enough for life to be enjoyable here in the shade.

It was more than enjoyable to be bathed and shaved and cologned and wearing freshly pressed new clothes. It was a pleasure to get dressed up once in a while.

It was more than a pleasure to be waiting for Susanna to go to dinner with him.

She had refused to let him buy her a dress, or even to help her choose one, but he had achieved the thing he wanted most today, which was her company for a leisurely dinner. There would be some musicians playing there in the restaurant tonight, the desk clerk had assured him. There would be dancing.

"Sixkiller! They told me that I'd find you here."

The sound of his name broke his mood as sharply as a rock thrown through a window glass.

He turned to see Joe Patterson, the cattle buyer he'd sold to for the last three years, coming out of the door of the hotel.

Eagle Jack had no choice but to give up his reverie, stand up, and hold out his hand in welcome.

"Patterson," he said, "I wasn't expecting you to be looking for me today."

"I know our appointment was for tomorrow," Patterson said, "but I've been called back East and I'm leaving on the six o'clock train. We'll have to deal tonight."

Eagle Jack bit back a rude exclamation.

"And the lady with the Slanted S cattle," Patterson said. "I'll need to see her this evening, too."

"She'll be here momentarily," Eagle Jack said. "We're going to dinner."

"Ah! Dinner will be perfect," Patterson said. "If that's agreeable to the two of you. Then I'll have time to see my one other client and I can finish my business and still catch my train."

The screen door opened and both men turned in time to see Susanna step out onto the porch.

Eagle Jack's breath caught.

The dress she wore, of a thin, blue cloth that swirled around her ankles, made her, for a moment, seem a stranger. An elegant, gorgeous lady of a stranger. He had never seen her in a dress before.

He smiled. It did match her eyes—she must've read his mind because he hadn't ever suggested that she should always wear blue. She should, though.

She smiled back at him.

"Susanna," he said, "this is Joe Patterson, the cattle buyer I mentioned to you. Joe, this is Susanna Copeland of the Slanted S."

Joe bowed over her hand.

"I've come to dinner to buy your cattle, my dear lady," he said. "I'm sorry to intrude but I must be on my way at dawn."

"Then, by all means, it's dinner," she said, laughing a little.

Eagle Jack silently marveled at her. She sounded as if she were a pampered lady who never saw the dawn and didn't want to, a soft lady who never rose from her bed until noon, and she looked the part. Yet she had been in the saddle many a morning as the sun came up or even before, on the mornings when she wasn't making sourdough biscuits or slicing bacon from the slab and frying it over an open fire.

Patterson insisted that they both escort Susanna into the restaurant, and Eagle Jack felt a stab of resentment once again. He would get rid of the man as soon as humanly possible.

He needed to dance with Susanna. He needed to hold her in his arms.

He would take control of the conversation, because sometimes Patterson could be as talkative as an old man reminiscing. Eagle Jack would turn the talk to the cattle during the meal and they could settle on the price before dessert. He would remind Patterson of his one last client to see, and then he'd be alone with Susanna.

They would dance. He would go to her room with her. They would make love and talk and he would mention going to see her during the year to come and they would make plans to drive their herds north together next year. It would be an evening both of them would always remember.

* * *

A few minutes later, after Eagle Jack had insisted on the best table by a window and they were seated there, Susanna glanced around at the white-clothed tables, the sparkling china and well-starched waiters. This was the nicest restaurant she'd ever been in.

Yet all she could think of was that if she sold her cattle at this meal, it would be the last one she ever shared with Eagle Jack. After all these weeks, they would have nothing connecting them once the cattle were gone.

But there was nothing connecting them now. Nothing of a permanent nature. She either had to remember that or stop thinking about him.

The clientele of the restaurant was made up of what appeared to be prosperous-looking cattlemen and buyers and agents, most of whom had exchanged pleasantries with her two companions as the three of them were shown to their table. Also, there were a few townspeople and Easterners who were not dressed in boots and big hats like the Texans. She'd been amazed to find that Abilene had several stores that catered to the cattle people by selling everything Texas-style, and their newspaper published articles about how the Texans dressed.

They should print a story about Eagle Jack, because he was the most striking-looking Texan there. He was the handsomest she'd ever seen him, in a starched white shirt and creased khaki pants that looked good with his tooled belt and freshly polished boots. Too bad Maynell was out at the cow camp instead of drooling over him this minute. She would swoon.

The waitress soon came and recited the menu choices, assuring them that there were farm-fresh vegetables and fruits and plenty of cream in the kitchen, for everyone knew that those foods were scarce on the trail. They ordered, and then made pleasant conversation while they waited for their food.

Word of Molly's speed and deceptive appearance had spread all over town since the afternoon race, so Susanna and Eagle Jack recounted the whole story to Mr. Patterson. Then, when the girl brought their dishes of sizzling wilted lettuce with bacon, Eagle Jack turned the talk to the sale of their cattle.

"So am I to understand that you want to make an offer for our herds?"

"Yes," Mr. Patterson said, "I always know that Sixkiller cattle are healthy and they stand the shipping well. People in the North and East can't seem to get enough beef. I'm prepared to take every head you've got, Eagle Jack."

He turned to Susanna with a smile.

"And yours, too, Mrs. Copeland. I rode through them and looked them over this afternoon while you two were out racing the ponies."

Susanna smiled and tried to be happy at the news. It had to be. She had to have the money from the cattle or be homeless and debt-ridden, to boot. She had paid Eagle Jack back from the money she'd made with Molly and she had enough to pay the hands but not enough to pay the whole mortgage. She had no choice. She had to sell the cattle. Saving her ranch was the reason she'd gone through all that hard work and danger.

So why wasn't she feeling a huge rush of relief and excitement about all the money she'd soon have in her hand? Why wasn't she yearning to go home to Brushy Creek?

Because Eagle Jack wouldn't be there.

"Not to be rude," Eagle Jack said, "but I know you have someone else to meet after dinner, so I'll ask this now, Joe. What are you offering us per head?"

"The going rate of twenty dollars," he said. "I'll start out with my top price because I know better than to bargain with a Sixkiller, anyhow."

Susanna listened even more intently. Eagle Jack hadn't mentioned any relatives to her, but this sounded as if he had some who were in the cattle business.

Joe Patterson turned to her.

"Have you ever visited the Sixkiller ranch, Mrs. Copeland? The Sixes and Sevens? I went there and stayed a week one time and it did me no good at all. Eagle Jack and his brothers and his father are some tough customers, I'll tell you. They hammered at my price until they drove it sky-high."

"Nothing but right," Eagle Jack said, with a grin. "You didn't have to chase 'em out of the brush. We'd already done that for you."

His brothers? His father? The Sixes and Sevens? The Sixkiller ranch?

A sick, sharp betrayal shot through Susanna. All of this was news to her, and *she* had spent *many* weeks with Eagle Jack.

Chapter 17

Susanna felt, suddenly, totally left out. Out in the cold of loneliness, the coldest cold there is. She felt not connected to anyone, the way she had felt for most of her life.

And then, when she was old enough to know better, she had let herself become connected to Eagle Jack during those many weeks on the trail. The fierce heartbreak, the physical wrench to her stomach, and the shivering chill she was feeling right now proved that. Yes, they really were connected.

Joe Patterson was looking at her, waiting for an answer to his question.

"No," she said, and she marveled at how calm she sounded, "I've never been to the Sixes and Sevens."

She picked up her cup and took a sip of coffee. She didn't spill a drop.

"Why don't you tell me about it, Mr. Patterson?" she said.

She didn't look at Eagle Jack.

"It's a good distance east of Waco," Joe Patterson began, "a big spread with a beautiful old headquarters built of logs. It's in a partly wooded country on the Sabine River." He turned to Eagle Jack. "That's been Sixkiller land for a long time, hasn't it?"

Eagle Jack leaned back as the waitress appeared and started serving their steaks. "Yes," he said, "ever since a band of Cherokee followed Duwali into Spanish territory. Fifty years ago."

So he had two groups to be part of—the Cherokee and his family. She had misjudged him completely, thinking he was a rootless trail boss who hired out to other people.

And he had never said one word to correct her assumption.

"You mentioned some other Sixkillers, Mr. Patterson," she said. "Are they anything like Eagle Jack?"

"Every one of the Sixkiller brothers is a man who covers the ground he stands on," Patterson said. "They're all men to be reckoned with."

The food looked delicious. Susanna picked up her knife and fork. Tender steak, new potatoes, and fresh green beans with real butter melting on them. Fresh cantaloupe slices. Yeast bread. All wonderful treats after life on the trail. But her appetite had left her.

So Eagle Jack had brothers.

"Are they all as full of fun and pranks as Eagle Jack?" she said.

Then, resolutely, she sliced a bite of steak. She would need her strength. She had business, important business, to conduct.

Are they as reserved and closemouthed about their private lives?

But she would not ask any more questions about Eagle Jack. She would put him out of her mind and get down to this cattle sale.

"Oh, I don't know," Patterson said. "As I'm sure you know, Eagle Jack's hard to keep up with in the fun department."

"Yes, he is," she said, as she passed the bread basket. "I've learned that for myself."

Then she looked at Joe Patterson, holding her breath that he wouldn't call the bluff she was about to make.

"I'm thinking perhaps I should hold out for . . . something above the going rate, Mr. Patterson. We've driven slowly the last couple of weeks and our cattle have quite a lot of flesh on them."

She would've named a dollar amount but she had no idea how much she could say without embarrassing herself as a novice at this game. And she certainly didn't want to make Joe Patterson throw down his napkin and leave in disgust.

Because her cattle had to be sold tonight so she could get away from Eagle Jack.

That feeling did not stem from the fact that she was in love with him, which she already knew she had no choice but to live with for the rest of her life. He had hurt her as a friend.

She'd never had a real friend before, except for Maynell. Evidently, Maynell was her *only* friend.

Joe Patterson just sat there, looking surprised.

"I'm sorry, Mrs. Copeland," he said. "I'd just assumed that Eagle Jack was conducting your sale for you, or that you were acting in tandem."

"I like to take care of my own . . ."

"We do act in tandem," Eagle Jack interrupted. "We both engage in negotiations, whatever they are."

Susanna bit her lip. She didn't care what he said. All she wanted was for this to hurry up and be over. She had to get out of there so she could be alone.

"Mrs. Copeland is right, you know," Eagle Jack said. "I've been thinking, too, that your offer might be less than we could get if we ask for bids from some other buyers."

Patterson put down his fork in dismay (but only temporarily) and made a great show of distress, declaring that twenty dollars was the best he could do. And so the bargaining began. It went on while they finished the meal until they finally settled on twenty-two dollars.

Joe Patterson pushed his empty plate away and reached for his leather briefcase.

"Then if you two would be so kind as to sign the bills of sale, I will, in turn, sign bank drafts for you. That's the way I like to do business. All the details taken care of at the time of the sale, almost like cash on the barrel head."

Once the transaction was completed, he thanked them again and bustled out, on his way to his other client. Susanna waited to give him time to leave the Drovers Cottage because she couldn't bear the thought of having to make small talk with him or anyone else in the lobby.

She lectured herself silently as she put her bank draft into her handbag and accepted one more cup of coffee. This moment had been foreordained from the instant she'd realized what she had in her marriage to Everett. She'd known right then that if she ever found herself free again, she could never trust another man enough to live with him.

And now Eagle Jack had proved that to be a wise decision. He'd not told her everything—in fact, hardly anything—since the day they met, and it was true what she'd said to him back there in Texas. A person could lie by omission just as well as any other way.

But the thing that hurt was that he hadn't trusted her enough to confide in her. Even when she had confided everything in him.

He didn't regard her as an equal. She wasn't important enough for confidences of even the most casual kind.

Eagle Jack touched her hand, and the heat of his touch made her turn to look at him. He was talking about music, something about the piano player. He was saying something about dancing. He was asking her to dance.

"No, thank you."

She took her napkin from her lap and laid it beside her plate while she looked him straight in the eye. That made it almost impossible for her to speak, but she did say it.

"This is the time for us to say good-bye, Eagle Jack."

He looked so shocked and hurt that she could hardly bear it, in spite of the pain he was causing her at that moment.

"Our cattle are sold," she said, "and I've paid you everything I owe you out of my race winnings. We're square, as far as I can tell."

"What is the *matter* with you?"

His voice was low and cold, it didn't carry far, but the tension that had sprung up between them was like a live thing that attracted the attention of the other diners.

Susanna stood up and so did Eagle Jack. He pulled back her chair and she stepped away from the table.

"Let's get out of here and go where we can talk," he said, and threw some money on the table.

"No." She began to walk very fast but he stayed at her side. He took her elbow, although she tried to prevent it. "Leave me," she said fiercely. "I want to be alone."

"Not until you tell me what the hell is going on."

Someone called to Eagle Jack as they left the restaurant for the lobby and when he turned his head, Susanna jerked free and began to run.

As Eagle Jack pounded up the stairs after Susanna, he couldn't remember when he'd been so furious—or so scared. He dodged some more cattlemen he knew on the landing, and then he took the steps two and three at a time.

But when he hit the second floor hallway running, she was halfway down it, almost to her room. She glanced back over her shoulder.

"Go away, Eagle Jack."

"Stop right where you are, Susanna."

She stopped at her door and took the key from her bag. She fumbled with it, but she got it into the lock, turned it, went inside, and closed the door. He lunged for the knob. The key turned on the inside with a definite click.

He banged on the door with his fist.

"Let me in there, damn it! I've never been so mystified in my life. What is it that you're not telling me?"

"Ha! You're a fine one to ask that question."

The door muffled her voice but only a little. Her tone clearly stated that he should know what she meant.

He tried. He had been there through the whole dinner, sitting right there. So why didn't he know what had turned Susanna into a different, completely insane person?

Something that *he* wasn't telling *her*?

She had been all right when she stepped out of the inn and onto the veranda. He would swear it.

It took every bit of control that he had, but he spoke in a more reasonable tone.

"You were at the table with me and Patterson, Susanna. You heard it all. You know everything I know about the sale."

He waited but she didn't respond to that.

"So what is it that I'm not telling you?"

"You're the only one who knows that, aren't you?"

Her sarcastic tone stoked his anger.

"Please, Eagle Jack," she said, "just go away and stop making a scene."

As if he were someone she barely knew. As if what somebody else thought about his behavior was more important than his feelings.

His fury burst into flames. He backed up, almost all the way across the wide hallway, then ran at the door and kicked the knob hard with the heel of his boot.

Susanna screamed as he burst into the room.

"Please, Susanna," he said, in that same sardonic tone she'd used, "you're making a scene."

He turned and closed the door. It swung open again, so he propped it shut with a chair.

Susanna stared at Eagle Jack stalking across the room toward her, his heels clicking purposefully against the wooden floor. She'd forgotten how dangerous he could look.

"I'll call for the marshal," she said, though her mouth had gone dry. "You've just broken into my room."

"I'll go *get* the marshal for you," he said. "But first you're going to tell me what has turned you completely loco."

He didn't stop until he was right in her face, close enough that she could smell the coffee on his breath. His eyes were hard and his jaw was set.

"Talk," he said.

She realized that she was standing huddled over her handbag, which she was holding to her chest with both hands as if she thought he was going to rob her. Pulling herself up straight, she turned and walked to the bed, dropped the bag onto it, and sat down beside it.

Her knees felt weak as water.

"You never told me you had some brothers," she said. "You never told me that your home is a famous old ranch that your family has had for fifty years."

He stared at her. "Glared" would be more like it.

"It never came up."

He was looking at her with a mixture of scorn and disbelief that lit her temper like a fuse.

"Oh, no? What about when I said something about the owner of your beef herd? You didn't say *you* were the owner. Or the Sixes and Sevens, whichever it is."

He did have the grace to look a little chagrined.

"It wasn't important," he said.

"What about all the times I told you about my childhood? All my ugly, awful secrets that I usually can't bear to think about. How come you didn't reciprocate? When I talked about my ranch, why didn't you talk about yours?"

"We were talking about *you*."

"I tried to draw you out, but you wouldn't let me. You *know* that's true."

He shrugged.

"And there's all your men, Nat and the rest, coming to meet us directly from the Sixes and Sevens, right?"

"Yes."

"But in all that time, in all the talk around the campfire, none of them—not even Nat who has such a big mouth—said anything that let me know you're not what you seem to be. Instead, you're a wealthy rancher out adventuring, hiring out to a penniless widow to be her trail boss, playing a part . . ." Her voice almost broke. ". . . including that of her lover."

I took him as a lover and I didn't know him at all.

He looked at her straight.

"I don't talk about myself and my family. My men don't, either," he said.

"Why?"

"It's nobody's business. Lots of people don't think Indians are entitled to have anything. Some might even take it upon themselves to come visit. To cause trouble. There's no sense asking for that." He shrugged. "Lots of reasons."

She thought about that for a moment, holding on to the edge of the bed with both hands. Otherwise, she felt she'd just fall into a heap in the middle of it.

"But you invited Patterson to the Sixes and Sevens and he stayed as a guest for a week."

"We've known him for a long time."

"Well, you knew me long enough to know I wouldn't come raiding your ranch or go around blabbing about it to those who would."

"Yes."

His look was steady.

She returned it. "I know you're a private person, Eagle Jack, but you still aren't being quite straight with me, I'm thinking."

He made a gesture of defeat and gave in.

"Don't you understand, Susanna? I hated to talk about my home and my herds and my horses and my family when you didn't have any of that."

Surprised, she could only look at him.

"It seemed like it would be bragging or something. You were so worried about money and about losing your place."

He waited but she didn't react.

"You didn't even have a decent pair of gloves."

That struck her like a blow.

"Oh? So those were a *pity* purchase? They were. Isn't that right, Eagle Jack?" She leaped off the bed and rushed toward her reticule where it sat in the armoire. "Well, I'll just give them right back to you," she cried. "I don't accept pity from anyone."

To her dismay, her voice broke on the last word.

"Now, hold on," he said, in his authoritative voice that cracked like a whip. "That's not true and you know it."

She whirled to face him.

"I didn't know enough about your situation to pity you, then," he said. "I bought the gloves that very first day, remember? They were nothing but a little thank-you for getting me out of that jail."

That eased her pain a little. A very little.

"You knew I thought you were a man like any other who'd have to hire out as a trail boss. You didn't tell me one thing about yourself but you went ahead and made love with me and I didn't know who you were."

He crossed the space between them in two strides and stood over her.

"What are you *talking* about? Of course you

knew who I was. The Sixes and Sevens isn't *me*. My family isn't *me*."

She stood up to face him.

"You listened to me bare my soul and tell you things about my past and my family that I've never talked about to a living soul," she said.

"I appreciate your trust in me," he said.

Her heart broke in two but she kept her voice steady. "Yes," she said, "I trusted you. But you didn't trust me. You thought if I knew you were a man of substance I'd be after you to marry me. You thought I was a gold-digger, didn't you?"

Genuine shock showed in his eyes but she wouldn't let herself believe it.

"No! That never even occurred to me. I know you, Susanna."

He reached out and brushed her hair back from her face, the way he liked to do.

She pulled away.

"Maybe not as well as you think, Eagle Jack."

This time she was the one who walked to the window, the one who looked down on Texas Street as dusk fell over Abilene.

"Eagle Jack," she said, turning to face him. "You've always said I'm a straight-talking woman. Well, here's what I want to tell you. I will never—I can't, I *cannot*—trust my life over into any man's hands, ever again."

He listened, his head cocked to one side, his

eyes consuming her as he stood there beside the bed.

"So I want you to leave now and never see me again."

"*Why*? I'm not *asking* you to trust your life to me, Susanna." He spoke softly in his low, rich voice. It vibrated in the dimness of the room and reached out to touch her skin. "Remember? I'm not the marryin' kind. I'm scared of settlin' down. So there's no reason in the world we can't be friends . . . and lovers."

"Yes, there is."

"What is it?"

"I love you, Eagle Jack."

She couldn't bear to look at him another instant or she'd run and throw her arms around him, even while she was telling him to get out. She turned her back on him and stared, unseeing, out into the coming night.

For a long while, there was no sound except his breathing, and hers. Faint, faint sounds that could barely be heard.

Then came the click of his heels against the floor. And his voice from the door.

"Don't worry about your lock being broken," he said, his tone gentle as a new rain. "I'll leave my door open and keep watch. I won't sleep tonight."

Eagle Jack lay propped up on all the pillows the Drovers Cottage had furnished him, with one booted heel planted in the coverlet and the other leg crossed over his knee. He was smoking and staring out at the stars over Abilene. He had his shirt off so he could feel the cool breeze from the open window and his jeans and boots on, in case Susanna should need him.

To keep his mind from wandering across the hall into her room, he pondered how a night could be so long and so short at the same time. Staying in here alone, with every nerve in his body wide awake, made every second crawl by and last for an hour. But knowing that this was the last night he'd ever spend anywhere near Susanna—even simply knowing where she was and how she was—made every second of it fly by on wings.

It was true that she could not ever trust another man enough to live with him. Hadn't she told him that a dozen times or more in those very words?

That son of a bitch she'd been married to, that Everett, had soured her on men. And she hadn't trusted any of the several people who had . . . not brought her up . . . he should say who had given her shelter while she raised herself. A rotten bunch if there ever was one.

But why did he care? Because she was his friend and a damn fine woman.

I love you, Eagle Jack.

He still couldn't believe she'd said that. It brought a glow to his heart every time he thought of it.

He would never forget exactly how her voice sounded when she said it, either.

It would be a nice memory. It was an honor.

But he didn't love her back, he truly didn't. He really liked her, he enjoyed being with her, he admired her, and he respected her more than any woman he'd ever known except for his mother.

There was more to her—more interesting facets, more courage, more ingenuity, more stamina—than there'd been to any other woman he'd ever courted or dallied with. Yes, Susanna Copeland was a very, very special woman.

But he didn't love her.

He couldn't afford to love her. He was not going to love any woman because it would cost him his whole way of life—his wanderings at will, his adventures, all the new women who might cross his path.

She deserved a man who would love her and be her husband. A man who would settle down and live with her for the rest of her life.

So he could not let himself love her.

He couldn't settle down, he wasn't that kind of man.

Susanna left her room an hour after dawn because she could not stay within its four walls for one moment longer. Evidently Eagle Jack had been true to his word—which she had never doubted—and left his door open so he could guard hers. It was standing open now but she caught no glimpse of him. Only the sight of his rumpled bed stabbed her in the heart.

She shifted her reticule straps higher onto her shoulder and changed her small traveling bag to the other hand. These were all she would need for the trip home and she could leave them at the station until time for her train.

Downstairs, at the desk, the clerk found a boy to take her bags to the station and another to carry a note out to the herd to Maynell. May and Jimbo were completely capable of bringing the Slanted S equipment back to Texas with no instructions at all. But Susanna wanted to reach out to her only friend, Maynell, this morning because she'd never felt so alone in her life.

She'd love to see May and talk to her for a minute, but there was not time enough to ride out to the herd and back and still catch the ten o'clock train. Besides, the herd might be exactly where Eagle Jack was at this moment.

When she had written the note and dispatched it, she walked to the little café beside Ingersoll's Mercantile for a bite of breakfast. Eagle Jack might be in the Drovers Cottage restaurant, and besides, she had to get away from that entire establishment. If she trailed a herd to Abilene the next year, she would have to take a room someplace else, for the Drovers Cottage would always hold memories of Eagle Jack.

She looked around the little café while she waited for her food. It, too, held memories of Eagle Jack, although she had never been in it before, much less with him.

Resolutely, she reached into her reticule, took out her pencil and paper, and began to list her debts. She would turn her thoughts to home, to returning to and keeping the only home she'd ever known, and she would banish all thoughts of Eagle Jack.

Hadn't she spent her whole lifetime perfecting the art of banishing unwanted thoughts? She made out her list and totaled it, added in her mortgage, subtracted the sum from the amount on Mr. Patterson's bank draft. What was left of her Molly winnings after she'd paid Eagle Jack back for the stake he'd loaned her, his advancing the men their salaries, and his own salary as trail boss had dented it, but she still had money left to live on.

Heaving a great sigh of relief, she put the paper aside and ate her breakfast. She would've predicted that she couldn't eat a bite because the terrible emptiness in her called, not for food, but for Eagle Jack. Just the sight of him.

Or the scent of him. Or the sound or the touch of him.

She did eat, though, because she had spent a lifetime perfecting the art of pushing worries aside so she could eat and sleep to keep up her strength. Well, she intended to keep it up this time, too. She would survive.

At least now she knew what it was like to love someone.

At least now she had many, many good memories to warm her heart through the winter to come.

Once she'd finished eating, she paid for the meal and walked briskly to the bank. She was a business woman, she was a rancher and a cattlewoman, and she intended to build up her ranch.

She kept that her focus as she took care of all her business and walked down the wooden sidewalk, across the dusty street, and underneath the portico of the train station. Just beyond it, on the south side of Texas Street, two cowboys caught her eye. They looked familiar and her mind crazily jumped toward Eagle Jack, even while she knew he wasn't one of them. It was Nat and Marvin, sitting their horses, idly talking as if they were waiting for someone or for something to happen.

She turned away, hoping they hadn't noticed her. She simply didn't have the heart to talk to anyone. She didn't have the heart even to look at them because they made her think so sensually of the weeks just past. The weeks of riding by Eagle Jack's side, laughing at his jokes, smiling at him, and soaking in the sunshine of his smiles that warmed her so.

Susanna sat down on an outside bench facing the tracks and tried to think about going home. About what it would be like when she drove up to Brushy Creek in a rented buggy.

But, instead, she thought about Eagle Jack. He had started on his adventurous, lone trip back to Texas. He was gone. He and Molly would be running races with every fast horse they came across. And Susanna wouldn't be there.

Eagle Jack was gone.

She sat on the bench in a heap of misery until she heard the faraway whistle of her train. A cold thought hit her: she hadn't yet bought a ticket. She could sit around here right at the depot and miss her train. So she forced herself to her feet, went inside for the ticket, collected her other bag, and walked back out to stand beside the tracks.

She wouldn't sit down again. What if she sat down again and couldn't get up? She felt as weak as a newborn kitten that suddenly found itself in a cold new world.

The train pulled in, blowing its whistle and puffing steam. It slowed and slowed some more, and the brakes squealed against the tracks. The car with the conductor on the steps stopped right in front of her.

He must have seen her distress in her face, or she must have been very pale and looking ill, because he insisted on helping her up the steps before the departing passengers could come down them. He came down to the ground and took her arm as if she were a very sick and frail woman, and then, with his loud, mellifluous voice filled with concern, asked everyone to please wait for the lady to board.

The passengers leaving this car were three men—from the East, judging by their dress—probably cattle buyers or agents, and they also must have thought she was ill. All of them looked at her sympathetically and one of them insisted on taking her bags and helping her down the aisle to an empty seat only halfway back in the car.

And then they were gone and her bags were stowed in the rack above her and the seat beside her was empty. She was sitting alone, looking out the window. Looking out at Abilene.

Abilene. The town that had been her goal for months and months, ever since she'd decided to make a trail drive.

Abilene. Where she'd just spent the hardest night she'd ever seen.

Finally, after what seemed an age, the conductor came aboard again and the train began to huff and puff, slowly at first and then faster and faster. Susanna's heart began to beat in the same rhythm.

I will survive. I will survive.

Silently, she chanted the words that had been her litany since childhood. She had survived so many hard blows, she would survive the loss of Eagle Jack.

What was she talking about? She *was* loco. He'd never been hers to begin with.

A person couldn't lose what she'd never had.

The tears she'd been holding back all night and all day rushed her then, spilling from her eyes in a flood. She dropped her face into her hands, fighting them and losing the battle.

A rustle of excitement swept through the car.

"Somebody's trying to catch the train!"

"Conductor! Tell the engineer."

"Yeah, tell him to slow it down. Give the man a chance!"

"Ooooh," a woman screamed, "look at him go!"

Susanna lifted her head and looked out. The sight she saw stopped her tears that instant.

Eagle Jack, riding Molly, was racing alongside the train.

People began to open windows all over the car so they could yell encouragement.

"Go, go, you're gaining ground!"

"You can do it, why that little horse can fly!"

He truly was gaining on the train.

Joy and fear warred in her heart. It was racketing out of her chest and she didn't know what to do.

There was nothing she *could* do.

Eagle Jack was coming to her, but he could yet get killed, right before her eyes.

He passed her window and reached a spot even with the front of the car, then he stood up in the saddle.

Molly kept running. Susanna quit breathing.

She longed, she *ached,* to join in the chorus of voices calling for the train to slow but she'd lost her power of speech.

She leaned forward for a better view out the window ahead of her seat.

Molly held her speed, pacing the train, and the handle for climbing the steps was right at Eagle Jack's hand. He grabbed it but he made no attempt to come in at the door.

Somehow, in the next instant, his big body was hurtling into the car through the window of the first seat. Its occupant, a quite small man, immediately leaped up and into the aisle to get out of his way.

Everybody in the car was screaming or exclaiming, yelling or shouting, except for Susanna. She sat with her hands still clasped to her tear-soaked face, too astounded to make a single sound.

Her heart was in her throat, pounding ninety miles a minute.

In an instant, Eagle Jack was on his feet in the aisle, brushing himself off. He looked up and met Susanna's eyes.

He was grinning, the rascal was grinning at her as if he'd done nothing at all, much less something so dangerous he could have plunged to his death.

That grin filled her with such joy that her heart couldn't contain it.

He started toward her with his light, swaggering walk unchanged by the rocking of the train, which was rapidly picking up speed. A minute more, and Molly could never have caught it.

When he reached Susanna's seat, he sat down beside her as carelessly as if he'd been away for only a moment. He took off his hat, dusted it with one hand, and placed it in his lap.

Then he spoke as if they'd just been interrupted in the middle of a conversation.

"What I was wondering, Susanna," he drawled, "was if I come to live at your place, would you make pie every day and even let me have a slice for breakfast?"

She melted.

"And what would you be doing at my place every morning?"

"Bein' your husband," he said. "I've been thinkin' about it a lot."

"But, Eagle Jack, that's commonly known as settling down. I thought you were afraid of that."

"I am," he said, with his very most charming grin, "but you'd be there all the time to keep me from bein' too scared, wouldn't you?"

Her heart swelled with love.

He reached over and pushed her hair back from her face and used his thumb to trace the trail of the tears rapidly drying on her cheek.

"I don't care if we're at Brushy Creek or where we are," she said, through trembling lips, "all I want is for us to be together, Eagle Jack."

He bent his head and she lifted her mouth to his. The other passengers cheered and cheered while they kissed. They kissed for a long, long time.

Susanna put one of her hands on the back of his neck and held him to her. She was never going to let him go.

They might just kiss all the way to Texas.